Praise for the Mov

MW00416576

"Edgy enough to push a timeworn formula from ~~the base~~ to the balcony. Dumas adds just enough zany to her mix to have readers lining up for more."

— *Kirkus Reviews*

"*Murder at the Palace* has great characters, including Trixie. It's a delightful book, and...the movie summaries just add to the appeal."

— *Library Journal*

"*Murder at the Palace* is a downright hoot. Fans of classic films will love this smart tale of travail starring Nora Paige...Rest assured that although the films involved are old, the story is witty and fresh. Especially enjoyable is watching the thoroughly modern Nora attempt to explain computer passwords to ghostly Trixie, whose idea of modern is a Duesenberg Model X Boattail Roadster."

— *Mystery Scene Magazine*

"This story immediately grabbed my attention...I could not put this book down...And Trixie...oh my goodness, I love her and...had me laughing on the subway...boy I'm excited for the next book in this delightful entertaining debut series."

— *Dru's Book Musings*

"Old movie buffs, fans of San Francisco, and lovers of well-done mystery series debuts will shout huzzah and encore at author Margaret Dumas."

— *Criminal Element*

"Stands with the best modern cozy mysteries and reminded me a lot of the Lily Ivory series by Juliet Blackwell. I'm adding this to my list of must-read series. Recommended."

— *It's All About The Book*

MURDER
ON THE
Silver
Screen

**The Movie Palace Mystery Series
by Margaret Dumas**

MURDER AT THE PALACE (#1)
MURDER IN THE BALCONY (#2)
MURDER ON THE SILVER SCREEN (#3)

MURDER
ON THE
Silver Screen

A
Movie Palace
MYSTERY

MARGARET
DUMAS

HENERY PRESS

Copyright

MURDER ON THE SILVER SCREEN
A Movie Palace Mystery
Part of the Henery Press Mystery Collection

First Edition | June 2020

Henery Press, LLC
www.henerypress.com

Trade Paperback ISBN-13: 978-1-63511-619-9
Digital epub ISBN-13: 978-1-63511-620-5
Kindle ISBN-13: 978-1-63511-621-2
Hardcover ISBN-13: 978-1-63511-622-9

Printed in the United States of America

For the gang I've watched the best movies with:
Dolores, Keith, Richard, and John.

ACKNOWLEDGMENTS

As I write these acknowledgements, I'm under a stay-in-place order due to the Covid-19 pandemic, and I am filled with gratitude. Not just for all the people who helped me write and produce this book - this book seems pretty trivial at this moment. Right now I'm grateful that so far all my loved ones are safe. I'm grateful that, for the most part, this crisis is bringing out the best in people. I'm grateful for every single person who is doing their best to be a light in the darkness. Thank you.

Meanwhile, many thanks to the Henery Press team, especially Maria Edwards, Kendel Lynn, Christina Rogers, and Art Molinares. Massive thanks as always to trusted first readers Denise Lee, Erick Vera, and Anne Dickson, and critique group stalwarts Claire M. Johnson and Michael J. Cooper. And a huge shout-out to the fabulous Martha Francescato for the sharpest eyes ever.

I'm so grateful for the support I've gotten from fellow writers (House of Clues gang, Camille Minichino, and Ann Parker, I'm looking at you) and independent booksellers, particularly Dori Jaroslow at Books Inc. and Anne Saller at Book Carnival.

I don't know what the world will look like after this pandemic. As a writer, what I do is imagine a hundred different outcomes of a given situation and go with the one that's most interesting. But this time I'm really hoping for the boring. I hope, by the time you're reading this, that we're all going to be able to do something as normal, as trivial, as mundane, and as amazingly fabulous as going out to a movie together.

"You're not afraid of ghosts are you? It would be awful if you were."

David Niven as Peter Carter
A Matter of Life and Death (*1946*)

CHAPTER 1

"The world has lost its mind!"

Marty Abrams, the Palace theater's senior (only) projectionist and resident curmudgeon, swept into the lobby riding a wave of irritation. But he also swept in carrying a box of pastries from the café across the street, so I decided to overlook it.

His co-worker Callie didn't seem to notice his mood. "Did you get my cream puff?"

"Technology is ruining everything!" he proclaimed.

"Not cream puffs," she replied. "And I don't know what you're talking about. You love technology. It's literally what you do for a living."

He drew himself up to his considerable height and looked down upon her, the forty-something tower of rumpled flannel addressing the petite powerhouse of bohemian grad student. "How dare you?"

His voice dripped with outrage. She shrugged and took the pink box from him. "Movies wouldn't exist without technology. Projection is technology. Sound on film is technology. Face it." She removed a mocha cream puff and handed the rest back to him. "Every day when you come in here and use your phone to play your overture through the theater's sound system, you're legit embracing technology."

Marty turned a shade of purple that I'd only ever seen once or twice before. As entertaining as his meltdowns could be, I figured I'd better diffuse this one before we lost an entire afternoon's work to it.

I stepped between my two employees. "I take it something

happened?" I said to Marty.

He redirected his glare toward me. "Yes, something happened!"

I waited. I'd spent ten years in the trenches of Hollywood, negotiating and maneuvering on my almost-ex-husband's behalf. Temper tantrums had lost their power to faze me.

"I was at the café," he said. "Minding my own business, just waiting my turn in line, when I saw what this...*person* ahead of me was doing with his phone."

A number of unpleasant possibilities occurred to me in the dramatic pause Marty took. Someone watching porn? Someone tweeting something hateful? Someone using a filter to make his selfie look like Bogart? Anything was possible.

"He was..." Here Marty shuddered and passed me the pastries. "He was watching *Lawrence of Arabia.*"

"Ooohhhh." Callie exhaled in sudden and sympathetic understanding.

"Right?" Marty turned back to her. "Of all films!"

"Of all films," I agreed. *Lawrence of Arabia* (1962, Peter O'Toole, Omar Sharif, and not one woman in a speaking part) is one of the greatest achievements of wide-screen spectacle in the history of film. There is truly a cast of thousands, and that's not counting the camels. Watching it on a phone was completely missing the point of a legitimate screen epic.

"Marty," I asked, fearing the worst, "what did you do?"

"I merely pointed out that he was committing a sacrilege," he sniffed.

I could only imagine at what length and volume he had pointed this out. "And?"

"He *smirked.*"

I steeled myself for another tirade, but suddenly all the fight seemed to go out of him.

"What kind of world are we living in?" he wailed. "With what kind of people? People who *smirk* at the idea of giving a film the respect it deserves?"

"Well—" I began, but he wasn't finished.

"And how complicit are we? What are we even doing here today? What fresh hell are we going to unleash on an unsuspecting world tomorrow?" His distress, once we got past his bluster, was oddly touching.

Callie apparently thought so too. She took the bakery box and offered it back to Marty. "Have a cupcake. It'll make you feel better."

"I don't want a cupcake. I don't even know what's in the box. Lisa just handed it to me and rushed me out of there." He took a deep breath. "She probably didn't want a scene."

She probably already had a scene, and she wanted to end it. Lisa, the owner of Café Madelaine, was a friend. I'd ask her about it later.

Callie raised the lid. "There's, like, a scone..."

"A scone is small consolation for a world gone mad," he sniffed. But he took it.

"I don't really think we're complicit in the end of civilization," I said, in what I hoped was a reassuring tone. "We're still holding on. I consider us a last bastion."

Marty took an enormous bite, scattering crumbs and sighing. He looked up at the vast high ceiling, painted with small gold stars and home to an enormous glittering chandelier. The lobby we stood in was a glorious remnant of a time when movie theaters were modern palaces, with gilt touches on hand-carved wooden paneling, a long glass concessions stand, and an elegant staircase sweeping up to a balcony. Admittedly, if you looked too closely you saw the wear in the deep blue carpet, and perhaps some of the fixtures were less than pristine, but still. This single-screen relic was the kind of theater where a person should see *Lawrence of Arabia*. Or any of the other thousands of classic films we showed.

"We *are* a last bastion," Marty said, squaring his shoulders. "This is the hill we die on."

"Let's not get carried away," I said. "This is the theater we show movies in. At least as long as we can afford to keep the doors open. Speaking of which..." I gestured to the stacked cartons of merchandise that cluttered the lobby. "Shall we get started?"

But that would have been too easy. Instead, we were interrupted by the bang and clatter of the lobby doors announcing the hasty arrival of a third member of my staff.

"Am I too late? Is he here?" Brandon Dunbar, high school senior and part-time popcorn wrangler, glanced around the room with breathless anticipation. Of what, I had no clue.

"Is who here?" I greeted him. "Why are you here? Don't you have school today?"

He waved a hand at this triviality. "Is S Banks here?"

He pronounced the name with a sort of hallowed awe, indicating the lofty position this S Banks person held in the online gaming culture that Brandon had recently become devoted to. "I saw online that he checked in at a coffee shop on Divisadero," he continued. "But he isn't there. Is he here?"

"Who is S Banks?" Callie asked, for which I liked her more than usual, which was quite a lot. "And why are you stalking him?"

"Who's...?" Brandon stood before her flummoxed. Normally he stood before her in a sort of haze of unrequited passion, so her cluelessness must have hit him hard.

"S Banks is the antichrist," Marty told her unhelpfully.

At this Brandon recovered. "He's a genius!" he protested, flushing to the roots of his ginger hair. "He's just the most brilliant game designer on the planet, that's all! What he's doing with AR is just—I mean—he's only the—"

He might have gone on sputtering for a while, but Marty cut him off, nodding. "He's the antichrist." As if they were saying the same thing.

"Okay, enough." I raised my voice before things got even more out of hand. "He may be a genius," I told Brandon, "or he may be the antichrist. He may be both. I don't know or particularly care. What I do know is that the whole point of tomorrow's webcast is to announce his new thing. Whatever that is and whoever he is only matters to us because it matters to Tommy. So how about we start unpacking these cartons?"

Tommy May was a Silicon Valley tech guru and, more importantly, a one-quarter owner of the Palace. He was also a partner in Banks' new offering and the reason we'd be playing host to a gaggle of nerds the next day as they watched a live feed of the webcast announcement.

Setting up for the high-tech unveiling was the whole reason we were working that day. Usually the Palace is closed on Mondays, but since we were one of only eighteen theaters worldwide that would be getting the live stream the next day, we had a little prep work to do.

I'd opened a few of the cartons the night before, when they'd arrived by special courier, shrouded in a veil of secrecy. The tape that sealed them was printed with all sorts of dire warnings about security protocols and strict injunctions against sharing any of the contents with members of the press or general public. I'd taken a peek, expecting marketing pamphlets or brochures or something, which just shows that I have no business living in the epicenter of technology that is the San Francisco Bay Area.

"They're tablets," I told Brandon, who had approached the nearest carton with the same kind of awestruck fascination that Sidney Greenstreet had for the Maltese Falcon.

He stopped in mid-reach and stared at me.

"I got instructions from Tommy last night," I explained. "He sent a text to all the theaters. Apparently the 'old media' way of printing brochures has too many opportunities for information to be leaked, so everything about the game will be delivered online. These tablets will get it all first."

There were fourteen cartons on the counter. "Those are all full of tablets?" Marty said. "How much are they spending on this thing?" He looked slightly queasy.

"I mean, why would they care?" Callie asked. "Whatever they're announcing will be so huge they might as well be printing money."

She had a point. Tommy, who I assumed was already printing

money from a handy little travel app that everybody seemed to use, had partnered with the hottest game developer on the planet: Brandon's hero with the one-letter name. Whatever Tommy and S were going to announce the next day was bound to rake in more money than I could imagine. And I have quite the imagination.

Brandon took a boxed tablet from a carton. He held it in both hands like a grail.

"There's some special app on it," I told him. "Tommy said they'll hit all of them with data, all over the world, tomorrow during the announcement, so everyone attending in the theaters will get the same thing at the same time."

"And I've got one." Brandon hugged the boxed miracle of technology to his chest.

Marty plucked another one out of the carton, holding it between two fingers as if it were toxic. "What are we supposed to do with them?"

"One per seat in the auditorium," I told them. "We need to take them out of their boxes and make sure they're ready to get the bat signal tomorrow. Let's get moving. There are also a couple of banners to hang." I reached into another carton and pulled one out, unfurling a length of heavy crimson fabric more suitable to a medieval castle wall than a theater—even the Palace.

"It's a logo," Brandon breathed.

I looked at the image, embroidered in gold thread. "It's a globe. It probably means there's some sort of travel component to whatever they're announcing, right? Which would explain why S the game guy partnered with Tommy the travel app guy."

Brandon swallowed. "It's going to be *awesome.*"

"Uh huh." I put the banner back in the box. "In any case, we'll find out all about it tomorrow. Meanwhile, the fee for hosting this event is enough to pay our electricity bills for the next six months, so how about we get set up?"

I picked up a box and opened the door to the auditorium, where I found another member of the Palace family hanging out. Beatrix George, more generally known as Trixie, was the longest-serving usherette in the history of the Palace and possibly the only person in the city with less technical know-how than myself. Although she had a better excuse. She died in 1937.

CHAPTER 2

"Hiya, Nora!"

Trixie was perched on the steps up to the stage, waving enthusiastically. I didn't answer her, beyond a quick stealthy nod, because I had some silly desire not to be committed to a quaint little asylum for the completely insane. I was the only one who could see or hear the ghost of the Palace. I knew she was real, but I had no expectation that anybody else would take my word on that.

She scampered up the aisle toward us, the shiny gold buttons and braid of her usherette's uniform gleaming, her little cap at a jaunty angle on her bouncing blonde curls, her wide blue eyes taking in the boxes and the banners with delight.

"What's all this? What are you doing? Gee, are we having a party?" She clapped her hands. "Oh, I love a party! Why, I haven't been to a party in I don't know how long!"

I gave her a warning glance. One that reminded her that I really couldn't chat when there were other people around. She nodded and grinned, then mimed a zipper across her mouth.

Callie, Marty, and Brandon had hauled the cartons into the auditorium and were now doing the math to figure out how many of the theater's seats were going to get a tablet.

"Thirteen boxes, not counting the one with the banners, with twenty-four tablets per box," Callie said. "That means we have 312." She glanced at me.

"There are 311 names on the guest list for tomorrow."

"Ohmygod! Can I have the extra?" Brandon flushed with excitement.

"Sure. If we get to keep it, you can pick it up after the

announcement."

He looked at me like I'd slapped a cookie out of his hand. "What do you mean 'after'? I'm going to be here for the announcement."

"The meeting is at eleven in the morning on a school day," I reminded him.

"What meeting?" Trixie asked me. "What announcement? It isn't a party?" Her lip zipper hadn't lasted long.

"You don't think I'm going to miss this, do you?" Brandon protested. "S Banks! In this theater! Announcing his new—"

"He's not going to be in this theater." I slid a carton of tablets toward the teenager. "He's going to be in some event space in Palo Alto. We're just getting the live feed. You know that. You can watch it later online. After school."

He stared at me, stunned betrayal washing over his face.

"Nora, who's not going to be in the theater? Who are we talking about?" Trixie whispered loudly.

Callie, holding an armful of tablets, gave Brandon a gentle prod with her elbow. "Come on. Let's get started."

But even she wasn't getting through to him. "Nora, you don't understand. I *have* to be here. There's no way to know what S Banks might do. He might be here as a hologram. He might be here as AR and these tablets might be the only ones in the world you can use to see him."

"Um, Nora? What's a hollow gram? Is it like a telegram?" Trixie asked. "I didn't think people used those anymore. Is it something new?"

"This could be the most important announcement in the history of gaming!" Brandon was verging on the hysterical.

"Gaming?" Trixie said. "Like backgammon?"

"Well, I want no part of it," Marty proclaimed. "Whatever this announcement is I predict nothing good will come of it."

I ignored them both, regarding the rapidly disintegrating Brandon. "Listen. I'll make you a deal. I need a call from your mom. Not a text—a call. I have to hear her voice telling me it's okay that you skip school tomorrow morning for this."

It was ridiculous how quickly hope surged back into him. "She'll call! I promise! She will!"

"I'm so confused." Trixie slumped into one of the aisle seats.

I saw a way to end her confusion and put Brandon's nerd knowledge to work. "Let's get cracking," I said. "Brandon, while we're at it, tell us everything we need to know about gaming, S Banks, and whatever the hell AR is."

"Oh!" Trixie sat up and fixed Brandon with her attention. "I just adore hearing about new things."

What we heard, at great length, was that gaming was the most important thing in the world, and that S Banks was the most important guy in gaming. I had a hard time swallowing this, because, duh, movies were the most important thing in the world. But I listened. After all, I'd signed us up for this gig.

"AR stands for Augmented Reality," Brandon eventually explained. By this time Marty had removed himself to the far end of the stage to hang a banner. He'd made quite a production of putting his earphones in to drown Brandon out.

Callie, Brandon, and I had formed a production line of sorts. Callie unboxed each tablet, then passed it to Brandon, who fired it up and checked for the app that would allow it to receive data the next day. He then gave it to me to record the serial number and place it on a seat. Trixie supervised. Brandon talked the whole time.

"Do you guys remember that game that was everywhere about two years ago? The one where you chased virtual alien invaders in the real world?"

I vaguely recalled the craze. I'd been in LA at the time, managing Ted's career and believing I was in a happy marriage.

"I mean, sort of," Callie said. "Was that the thing where you used to see people all over town, walking around in clumps, staring at their phones?"

"Not clumps," Brandon informed her. "Rebel alliances. In the game, Earth had been overrun by alien invaders, and only small bands of rebels were still free. We had to work together to overthrow the alien overlords."

"Through reasoned negotiations and diplomatic outreach?" I guessed.

He stared at me. "By hunting them down and blasting them."

"Right."

Trixie's head had been swiveling to keep up with the conversation. "Gee, that sounds fun!"

Brandon went on. "The app used your GPS to know where you were, and based on your location and sometimes on other things, like time of day or how many other players were around you, you could see the aliens."

"What did they look like?" I asked, prompting Callie to send me a don't-encourage-him look, but I was curious despite myself.

"There were over four hundred unique characters," Brandon told us. "Some were green and slimy, some were purple with tentacles—all kinds of things. Different weapons worked on different ones. They were so cool!"

Trixie made a face. "I don't know, Nora. Slimy and tentacles? Weren't there any nice ones? And how do you see them, anyway? Were there film projectors hidden all over the place?"

I couldn't answer her, but I could give Brandon a prompt. "So you saw them when you looked through your phone?"

"Right, the game used the camera on your phone. That's the reality part. The *augmented* part is that sometimes you'd see a Thupolis in a doorway or a Vlaguard in a crosswalk or something."

Trixie blinked.

"Like a cartoon?" I asked.

"Like CGI," he said. "Way more advanced than cartoons."

That was a shame. Trixie understood cartoons. I'd explain CGI to her later. Possibly with an editorial aside about how it had ruined movies.

"Didn't I hear that a bunch of people died while they were playing that stupid game?" Callie asked. "Like, wandering into traffic and falling off roofs and things?"

"Oh, that's terrible!" Trixie exclaimed.

"A lot of that was urban legend," Brandon said. "I don't think anybody really died."

"I don't know," Trixie said. "Not all urban legends are fake. Look at me, for instance."

I laughed, causing the two non-ghosts I was working with to give me startled looks. Trixie slapped a hand over her mouth.

I cleared my throat and changed the topic. "I wonder what the new thing will be."

Which set Brandon off on a fresh bout of fevered speculation. I gave Trixie a quick grin, but she was listening to the teenager again, eyes wide with wonder at this unimaginable world he was explaining.

Right about that time I got my own little dose of technology, in the form of my phone chiming to remind me that I had an appointment. The four co-owners of the Palace were meeting, and I'd been invited to join them.

"Hey, guys, you'll have to finish up without me. I need to head over to Monica's for the owners' meeting."

Brandon's head snapped up. "Will Tommy May be there?"

"That's why I'm going," I told him. "I finally get to see the great and powerful Oz." So far I'd only exchanged emails and texts with the tech genius. "It'll be good to meet him in person."

A snort from behind me told me that Marty had come down from his ladder. "If he even is a person," he said. "And not some sort of robot."

"Technically, he'd be a cyborg—" Brandon began. I left before he could explain the distinction.

CHAPTER 3

"What's going on?" Robbie asked. "Catch me up. I don't want everyone to think I've been hiding in a cave somewhere."

Robbie was my best friend and the reason I'd fled to San Francisco and the Palace six months ago. She'd offered me safe haven and welcome distraction when my almost-ex-husband Ted— movie star, liar, and world's most charming rat—had left me for his gorgeous co-star and taken all the money with him.

"You *have* been hiding in a cave somewhere," I told her, speaking into my phone as I crossed the street. It was a chilly March afternoon, but I'd decided to walk to the owners' meeting, which Robbie would attend via video call from LA. "You're smack in the middle of pilot season, and nobody works longer hours than you during pilot season. How's it all going?"

Roberta Prowse was one of the most successful showrunners in Hollywood. She already had four hit shows on the air. I knew she was producing pilots for three more this season and I knew she'd written them all. So maybe she hadn't been in a cave, but she'd been buried under a mountain of work. Three mountains.

"I'll tell you later," she assured me. "In excruciating depth and accompanied by much wine."

Robbie was an established hit-maker, but Hollywood is relentless in its search for the new. Add to that the fact that Robbie was a no-longer-young woman of color, and you have a recipe for someone who has to work harder than just about anyone else I knew.

"Suffice it to say, you're so lucky to be out of this game," she said.

I wasn't sure about that. I knew I was incredibly lucky that she'd given me the use of her guesthouse and a job doing something I loved while I figured out my next steps. But a long time ago, before I'd turned into Ted's unpaid manager and agent, I'd wanted the life that Robbie now had.

"I hate my life," she groaned.

"No, you don't," I told her.

"No, I don't. I just hate everyone who isn't us."

"How about your daughter?"

"Everyone who isn't us or Tia."

"I'm sure we could expand that list, but I'm also sure we only have about three more minutes for this conversation." It felt good, for once, to be the one cheering Robbie up. In the last few months she'd talked me off so many ledges that I'd lost count.

"Ugh, you're right. We'll list the people I don't hate later, over even more wine."

"Deal," I told her. "Now, what do you need to know?"

"You tell me," she said. "Are there going to be any surprises at the meeting?"

She and Tommy each owned one quarter of the Palace. The remaining two quarters were owned by Mitchell Black, a sitcom director down in LA, and Monica Chen, who ran a thriving cannabis shop on Divisadero, a few blocks away from the theater. The owners' meeting would be held at her shop.

"No surprises from me," I told Robbie. "I'm not even sure why Tommy invited me." Usually the owners met privately. "He was annoyingly mysterious about it."

"He's like that," she said. "He always acts like he's Steve Jobs the day before the iPhone was announced."

I laughed. "I picture him more like a Vaudeville magician, making sure you're looking at the stage while his partner picks your pocket."

"Is he going to pick my pocket?" Robbie asked.

"You know him better than I do. I've been texting and emailing with him for weeks about his big webcast announcement, but it's been all business. I really don't have a sense of who he is as a person. Everything is shrouded in secrecy."

"Maybe he is Steve Jobs the day before the iPhone," Robbie mused. "Any idea what he's announcing in the webcast?"

"According to Brandon it will be the most amazing game ever," I said.

"That narrows it down. What kind of game?"

"If I knew that I'd design one myself and make a zillion dollars."

"Oh!" she exclaimed. "Do that! Then cut me in and we can both just sit around and watch Cary Grant movies all day."

"I'll get right on it." Like she'd ever just sit around, even for one day.

"And speaking of a zillion dollars..." she said meaningfully.

"I haven't heard a thing." I knew she was asking whether my extensive team of lawyers and accountants had managed to trace any of the money Ted had spirited away from all our joint accounts upon leaving me. "The lawyers just keep telling me to 'sit tight' and 'hang in there.'"

"I hate lawyers," Robbie said supportively.

"I'll hate them less if they get back my life savings."

"True." Then I heard someone in the background on her end, his voice sounding just a few notches past hysterical. "Um, Nora?"

"Go," I told her. "I'll see you at the meeting."

The voice in her office reached screeching pitch as she hung up. I walked the rest of the way to Monica's shop thinking about the gang I'd left squabbling companionably at the theater and the lineup of movies we had on tap for the week.

Maybe I didn't want Robbie's life after all.

The Potent Flower was a chic little boutique decorated in soothing colors and natural wood accents. If it weren't for the affable security guard perched outside you might think it was the kind of place that dealt in overpriced organic home goods. But no, the guard was there because it stocked a bewilderingly extensive array of cannabis products. It was a legal pot shop, and a bustling one.

Before going in I stopped for a moment to check my reflection in the window of the taqueria next door. I'd finally gotten around to finding a hairdresser in my new city, and I'd gotten rid of the last of my Hollywood blonde highlights—as well as a bit more gray than I wanted to admit. I was still a while away from forty, but the past six months had been rough.

As I smoothed my hair and straightened my shoulders it occurred to me that I might have made a bit more of an effort for what amounted to a meeting of all of my bosses, but it was a little late for that now. Since leaving LA I'd gotten into the habit of a quick ponytail and a wardrobe that leaned heavily toward jeans and comfy sweaters. That would have to be good enough.

I showed my ID to the guard and entered the long narrow space of the pot shop, spotting Monica in conversation with two people at a small display table near the back of the store. Monica was a forty-something Chinese American woman who wore yoga clothes every day of her life. I'd never known her to actually do yoga. She'd become one of my closest friends since I'd moved to San Francisco.

She glanced up and waved me over. I maneuvered my way through the crowded store to them. There were more people than I would have expected to be browsing for pot on a Monday afternoon, and a line had formed for the three cashiers along the back wall.

"Nora, so good to see you." She said this while hugging me. Monica was a hugger. "This is Abby Newlyn and of course you know Tommy."

Of course I knew Tommy, but this was the first time we'd actually met. "Tommy, it's so nice to meet you in person."

Nobody passing this guy on the street would have known he was a titan of tech. He was probably in his thirties but he dressed like a middle-schooler. Sneakers, jeans that at some point had been a shade of burgundy but were now faded to an indeterminate noncolor, and a gray t-shirt with a gray zip-front sweatshirt over it. Generic white guy messy hair. Phone in his hand. Did nerds like him look like that because nerds in the movies looked like that, or was it the other way around? I didn't really have time to ponder.

"I'm glad you're here, Nora." He spoke with an intensity that was out of keeping with his slacker appearance. "There's a lot we need to talk about."

"Oh, great." Not great. He'd had every opportunity to talk to me over the past weeks and months. So why had he felt the need for a formal meeting with the partners to do so? If we were back in Hollywood I would have assumed he was one of those insecure guys who needed an audience for everything. Maybe those guys weren't just in Hollywood.

Monica glanced at her watch. "We've still got a few minutes before the call. Tommy and I were just talking to Abby about creating a custom tincture for him. Abby's company makes amazing products. She's a genius at blending cannabinoids."

"Oh, cool." I smiled at the woman they'd been speaking with. I wasn't entirely sure what cannabinoids were, but somehow I had no doubt that Tommy would want them customized.

Abby waved a modest hand. "I don't know about genius," she said. "I just tinker around." She looked to be in her early sixties, with a compact body and the short practical hairstyle of someone who probably swims for fitness. Her product line seemed to consist of tiny green bottles topped with eyedropper lids.

"I'm definitely into it," Tommy told her. "But the guy who'll really want to talk to you isn't—" He glanced toward the door, his face clearing as he found who he was looking for. "Oh, here he is. S!" He raised a hand in greeting.

A ridiculously tall man stood at the front of the shop. He wore a creamy white crewneck sweater and white jeans tucked into black biker boots. His straight white-blond hair fell to his shoulders. He acknowledged Tommy's greeting with a cool nod, pausing to take in the surroundings before starting toward us. He moved like a mid-level deity, with the assumption that people would part to give him way. They did.

I don't know why the deity impression came to mind. Just that morning we'd been discussing whether he was the antichrist. There was only one thing I did know for sure. Brandon was going to die. Because I was about to meet S Banks.

CHAPTER 4

"Brandon will literally die."

This was Callie's reaction to the news that I'd met the famous S Banks. We'd both come to the Palace early the next day to make sure everything was ready for the webcast. At least I'd thought that getting there three hours before the event would be early, but when I'd arrived at eight that morning there had already been a line of eager geeks snaking around the block.

"Are you going to tell him?" she pressed me. "Oh! Can I tell him?"

"You're enjoying this way too much," I said. "And on the subject of enjoying things, do I need to remind you about the 'no photography' rule during the webcast?"

She gave me eyes wide with innocence. "I mean, why would you need to remind me of that?"

"You're telling me you're not planning on filming this thing for a documentary on nerd culture or tech or something?"

"You mean, like, a groundbreaking film that blows open the misogynist underpinnings of online gaming? That kind of thing?" She grinned.

"I mean exactly that kind of thing. And as much as I'd love that kind of thing, you can't film today. It's not just me saying that, it's the team of security guards that Tommy hired to police this thing."

She made a face. "I can't say I'm not, like, *tempted*, but I'm working on something else. So don't stress. I won't do anything."

I decided to believe her. It would be easier that way. I looked out the window, down past the Palace marquee that jutted out over the sidewalk. There were a lot more than 311 people down there.

"Why isn't that security team here yet?"

In addition to making sure nothing was clandestinely recorded at the launch event, the team was supposed check IDs and keep anyone unauthorized from getting in. The invitees were mainly tech press and bloggers, industry influencers who would get the word out about the new offering. But clearly the word was already out to a lot of fans who just wanted to get their hands on it, whatever *it* was.

"It's still early." Callie plonked herself down on the lumpy leather couch. Her wild masses of dark curls were barely contained in a messy bun that made her look even more twenty-first century pre-Raphaelite than usual. "But back to the point. What was S like? And what's the deal with his name?"

I turned away from the window. "Who's the coolest guy you can think of?"

She considered. "Steve McQueen? Bogart? Young Brando?"

"Roll them all together and add a splash of Keith Richards."

"I mean, that's pretty cool."

"He's got that thing that movie stars have. That thing that makes everyone in the room notice them." It wasn't just his appearance, it was that something undefinable that turns an actor into a star. Charisma. Magic. It. I'd seen it before and it almost frightened me. Maybe because I'd been married to it. "And he's really into weed."

Callie nodded. "That tracks."

"He wasn't part of the owners' meeting. He'd just tagged along with Tommy because the meeting was at Monica's." The shop had a lounge in the back. In addition to being a space where her customers could hang out, it sometimes served as Monica's boardroom. Furnished with soothing lighting and low couches, it also had a large table and an enormous video screen that normally showed stoner-appropriate movies, but that we'd used to conference in Robbie and Mitch from LA.

"How did it go, anyway?" Callie asked, bringing me back to the present. "The meeting?"

"Okay. Fine. No big deal." Which was a huge lie, but I saw no reason to ruin her day. It was enough that Tommy had ruined mine.

"Ladies and gentlemen...Tommy May!"

The crowd went crazy as Tommy hit the stage. Both the crowd in the arena where he physically was and the crowd in the Palace, where his image filled the screen and his legend filled the theater. Presumably it was the same in the other theaters that were hosting events all over the world.

"Ugh." Marty snorted in disgust at the spectacle of it all. "This culture rewards all the wrong people."

I'd chosen to watch the webcast from the projection booth with Marty because for once my mood approximated his. I was thinking very dark thoughts about the man on the Palo Alto stage.

"It's an affront to the sanctity of the silver screen," Marty went on. "That screen, where Garbo first talked, where Norma Desmond was ready for her closeup—"

"That screen was replaced three years ago," I reminded him. "Let's not over-romanticize things."

"My point remains valid," he stated.

"I get it." I sat carefully on a stool. "More than you know." Every surface in the tiny room was cluttered with disassembled bits of aged equipment, and I didn't want to commit the mortal sin of knocking something over. "But let's try to think of this as just a short commercial interruption to our regularly scheduled programming. This afternoon we'll be back in glorious black and white."

"Hrumph," he grunted. "Showing technology films. Both of which, by the way, are in color."

I shrugged. "My point remains valid." I'd decided to lean into the tech theme with our programming after the webcast. Our double feature for the next three days would be *Hot Millions* (1968, Peter Ustinov and Maggie Smith) and *Billion Dollar Brain* (1967,

Michael Caine and Françoise Dorléac). In *Millions*, Ustinov uses a computer to embezzle funds from his employer while Maggie Smith hovers around being an absolute delight, and in *Brain*, Michael Caine takes orders from a computer that runs a spy network in some very cold countries. Coincidentally, both films feature Karl Malden, a San Francisco favorite.

"I do like the computers in old movies," I said, a little more wistfully than I'd intended.

"Who doesn't?" Marty asked. "Big gray boxes with lights all over the place, and giant buttons and levers."

"And the spinney tape things," I reminded him. "Don't forget the spinney tape things."

"I love the spinney tape things," he agreed. "I bet this guy wouldn't know a spinney tape thing if it bit him in the ass." He nodded toward Tommy, onscreen in the theater.

We both watched the presentation for a while. Tommy slouched around the stage talking about all the cool things his company had done and hinting at all the cooler things they were about to do. The crowd was with him, but they weren't there for a talk. They were impatient for an unveiling. Tommy teased them until they were practically frothing with anticipation, and then he gave them what they wanted.

"It is with enormous pleasure that I want to bring out our newest collaborator. With his genius for imagining new realities and our deep mapping and geolocation data, I think you'll agree we've come up with something pretty special. Friends, to welcome you to our new reality, I give you S Banks!"

"Give me a break," Marty muttered.

Banks sauntered out from the wings to frenzied cheering, dressed all in creamy white again, looking effortlessly, nonchalantly cool. He held a glass bottle of something murky in his right hand and raised it in a toast. "Who's ready to have some fun? Who's ready to have more fun than you've ever had in your lives?" The crowd roared in response to each question. "Then let's have some fun!" The camera pulled in as he took a swig from the bottle. If he had actually been the rock star he was acting like it probably would have been Jack Daniels. But he was a tech star, so instead it was some sort of green drink that looked both healthy and disgusting. A stage assistant dashed out and took the half-empty bottle from him on cue.

"Is that guy stoned?" Marty asked.

I had the same question. In closeup, Banks' eyes looked glassy and unfocused. The camera pulled back.

"What's the most exciting thing in the world?" he asked the crowd. "What are we all looking for? What would we search to the ends of the earth for?" He paused as people began shouting answers.

"If he says 'true love' I'm going to barf," Marty warned.

"He's only going to say 'true love' if he and Tommy have figured out a way to make money off it."

On the screen, S held up his hands, shaking his head at whatever people called out. He swayed a bit, and again I wondered if he was high. "Nope," he finally said. "I'll tell you what it is. What we all want. What we all dream about at night." He reached into his back pocket and held up what looked like an enormous coin.

"Gold!"

The crowd roared in approval.

"Isn't it what everyone wants?" S continued. "Treasure! Riches! Gold!"

The audience was with him, anticipating what he was about to say.

"There are five of these coins in my new game. Only five in the whole game world." He struggled a bit to get the word "whole" out. He shook his head, looking like he was trying to clear it.

"Does he look...?" Marty asked.

"Terrible." I watched the image of S closely. His eyelids and lips seemed puffy. Had he looked like that a minute ago?

He went on. "There are five gold coins hidden within the augmented world of the game. Five gold coins to be found." Now the word "five" seemed to give him trouble. "Each gold coin has a code on it," he said. "That code, my friends, is worth...one million dollars!"

Tommy stepped forward again while the crowd went insane. "There's only one person on the face of the planet who knows where all five coins are hidden," Tommy yelled. "And I'm sharing the stage with him!" He bowed theatrically to S.

"The game we're announcing is Worldwide Treasure Hunt!" S shouted above the mayhem, his voice sounding rough. "Download the app, follow the clues, and find the gold coins!"

"Hang on!" Tommy yelled. "Let me tell you the rest of it—For every day the treasure isn't found, each coin is worth...*another* million dollars!" By this time the roar of the audience was deafening. "Nobody has a head start, nobody has an edge. Everyone in the world can download at the exact same time." He looked to S again. "All S has to do is hit Launch and the treasure hunt will begin!"

S raised both hands, the giant coin in one, a phone in the other. He looked over at Tommy, opened his mouth to speak, and began to twitch. The crowd was wild with excitement. S threw his head back in what might have been ecstasy or might have been a convulsion. The audience gasped, not knowing what to make of it. Was this part of the show? Then S fell to the floor, thrashing, and it became clear that something was very wrong.

"Get a medic!" Tommy yelled. "Get help!"

At that point, in the midst of a spasm, S must have touched a button on his phone, because every one of the tablets in the Palace lit up and every single person in the audience yelled. The game was live.

S, onstage and onscreen, stilled.

Was the game maker dead?

CHAPTER 5

"What's happening?" Marty yelled. "What just happened?"

Onscreen it was chaos. On the stage in Palo Alto a crowd had surged around the still form of S Banks. Tommy was yelling for help, crew members were rushing around, someone pushed her way through the throng and started performing CPR. The camera only showed the stage, but we could hear the audience roaring in the background over the sounds of pandemonium in our theater. Then someone shouted, "Cut the damn camera!" and the screen went blank, leaving the Palace in darkness and confusion.

"Get the house lights up," I called to Marty as I dashed out of the projection booth. I collided with Callie in the hallway. She must have just run up the stairs.

"Nora, what just happened?"

"We have to calm them down," I told her, moving quickly to the back stairs. "Before they tear the place apart."

I raced down the stairs, Callie right behind me, and entered an auditorium in chaos. Three hundred and eleven tech industry leaders were torn between wild speculation about what they'd just witnessed and frenzied excitement over the game that had just been revealed.

Marty had turned the lights up, and I jostled my way through the heaving crowd to the front of the theater. Brandon met me at the steps to the stage, a stricken look on his face.

"The game is live," he said, dazed.

I took the steps to the stage, standing in front of the screen with my arms raised, trying to make myself heard over all the yelling. "Everybody! Everybody! If you could just take your seats and remain calm we'll try to get some information for—"

Nobody paid any attention.

"Everybody, please—"

There was a piercing whistle, and everyone stopped what they were doing. Some reedy guy wearing an Iron Man t-shirt jumped up on a seat in the back of the auditorium and called for attention.

"Listen! Our tablets have live info about the game. All the rules and stats. And it says..." He glanced down at the screen he held. "It says over two hundred thousand people have already downloaded."

Pandemonium. The theater went mad again until another sharp whistle from the guy up on the seat. "Look! There's a dedicated newsfeed just for us, just on these tablets. That's got to be where we'll get updates on what happened to S, right?"

Murmurs and uncertain glances filled the room.

"He's going to be fine," the guy said. "He's S. He's indestructible!"

More murmurs. I could see everyone wanted to believe their hero was fine, if only because it would mean they could start looking for gold guilt-free.

Then someone else yelled, "Come on! The game has started! Let's do this! It's what S would want!"

Murmurs turned to shouts, and excitement overtook confusion as shouts of "Let's do this!" were taken up. The crowd surged toward the doors, everyone grabbing their tablets and heading out to find whatever treasure fate had in store for them. In a mad five minutes the theater was empty.

I sat heavily on the edge of the stage, all the adrenalin leaving my body. Brandon and Callie both stood staring at me from the bottom of the steps. I glanced up and saw Marty framed in the small window from the projection booth. Trixie, whom I hadn't even noticed, stood in the back of the theater, a stunned look on her face.

"Okay," I said. "What the hell just happened?"

* * *

"S Banks was taken to Stanford Hospital following an onstage collapse while publicly launching his newest game." Brandon read from his tablet in a hollow voice.

It was hours later. We'd gotten the theater put back together and managed to open for the two-thirty matinee, joined after a while by Albert, the oldest (living) employee of the Palace. He'd been far too sensible to want anything to do with the launch event, but he came in to help out with the aftermath. As soon as *Hot Millions* started, Albert sent us all to the upstairs break room, offering to keep an eye on the concessions stand while we waited for word on S.

Speculation had filled every news feed for the past few hours. Now there was finally something real to report.

Brandon swallowed and read on. "Emergency crews performed CPR at the scene and in transit, but doctors were unable to revive the game developer. He was pronounced dead at 12:17."

We were all silent, absorbing the news. I was shocked, even after what I'd seen onscreen. In the hours since the webcast, part of me had decided to believe it had all been part of the show, some sort of publicity stunt.

"Gee, I hope someone came for him." Trixie broke the silence, at least for me. "I hope they were able to find him."

The way Trixie understood the afterlife, someone from your family comes to take you away when you die. Where "away" was had remained a mystery to her, since she'd missed her opportunity to go when she'd fallen from the Palace balcony in 1937. She'd chosen to stay because the man she loved was being accused of her murder, and she'd never gotten another chance. She was stuck here now.

I was the only one who heard her wishes for S. She looked at me, her eyes filling, then turned her head away and vanished. Sometimes she did that, just going *poof* when things got to be too much for her.

I took a breath. "Do they say what the cause was?" I asked Brandon. "Did he have a history of seizures?"

He looked up, still clutching the tablet. "There's going to be a press conference later."

We were all seated at the battered wooden table in the break room. Callie reached over to put her hand on Brandon's arm. He didn't seem to notice.

"Well, my money's on an overdose." Marty stood and opened a cabinet above the sink. He pulled out a bag of potato chips, tore it open, and began munching. "I thought he looked like he was on something even before he started twitching."

"Will Detective Jackson know anything about it?" Brandon asked him.

Detective David Jackson was a San Francisco homicide cop who had investigated several murders in and around the Palace. He was smart, ethical, and incredibly intimidating. He was also, improbably, dating Marty.

"Why would he be involved?" Marty asked. "Unless it was murder."

The word seemed to hang in the air around us.

"I mean, even if it was," Callie said, "it was murder in Palo Alto, right? So our detective wouldn't be involved."

"*Our* detective?" Marty asked around a mouthful of chips.

"The point is—" I interrupted before bickering could break out. "—none of us are involved. Whatever happened, whether it was natural causes, an overdose, or murder, Callie's right. It was natural causes, an overdose, or a murder in Palo Alto. It had nothing to do with us."

"A murder in Palo Alto." Another voice, one I recognized, spoke from behind me. I turned to see Hector Acosta standing in the doorway. "That sounds like one of your B movies from the forties."

"Hi, Hector." Callie instinctively straightened her back and ran her fingers through her hair. Hector had that effect on women. It was something to do with his smoldering dark eyes and the barest hint of a sexy Colombian accent. Plus the fact that he was a retired crime lord. At least, he said he was retired. But apparently you never lose that sort of controlled danger vibe, even if you were retired. Which he said he was. Absolutely.

"Hello." He said it to the room in general, but his eyes had locked on mine.

Marty crumpled the bag of chips loudly. "I think I'd better go change the reel." There was no reel to change—*Hot Millions* was playing from a disc. Nevertheless, Marty made a production out of leaving the break room, eyeing Hector as he passed him. "Hector."

"Marty." Hector kept any inflection whatsoever out of his voice.

Callie sighed. "Come on Brandon, let's go see if Albert needs help."

Brandon, who had been focusing on the newsfeeds coming in on the tablet again, looked startled. He seemed to notice Hector for the first time. "Oh. Right. Hi."

Hector nodded. "I just saw Albert downstairs. He did mention something about the espresso machine..."

A flash of alarm crossed Brandon's face. Albert was a ninety-something-year-old marvel of mental fitness and an irreplaceable member of the Palace family, but he was a little on the frail side to be battling the steaming blasts of the espresso machine on his own. Brandon stood. "Let's go see if he needs help."

Callie gave one last hair flip in Hector's direction as she followed Brandon out, but I could tell her heart wasn't in it.

Hector regarded me from just inside the door. "May I?"

I patted the chair next to me. "Please. Want some coffee? It's terrible." The new machine in the lobby may have been state-of-the-art, but our break room coffee maker was a crime against caffeine.

"I was going to ask if you wanted something stronger."

I glanced at him, taking in his perfectly fitted jeans and the t-shirt that skimmed his flat torso under a lightweight leather jacket that probably cost more than our monthly popcorn budget. "If you've got a bottle of something on you, your tailor deserves a medal."

He laughed, showing even white teeth. "I don't. But I'd be happy to get you away from all of this for a while. There has to be a bar open somewhere around here, and I imagine you've had quite a day."

"That I have," I admitted. "In fact, I've had several."

He raised a well-groomed eyebrow.

"I can't help thinking," I said slowly. "That I'm relieved it was S who died on that stage."

Hector didn't speak. I had his full attention.

"I know it's awful but it's true," I said. "Because if hadn't been S—if it had been Tommy instead—I'd have had a very good motive for murdering him."

CHAPTER 6

"Tommy wants to close the Palace."

Hector and I hadn't gone to a bar. We'd just gone down the hall to my office, where I had a decent bottle of cabernet and some paper cups from the concessions stand tucked away in a file cabinet. It occurred to me that others might have judged me for keeping wine in the office. Hector just reached for a cup.

"Close? You mean for good?" He looked stunned.

I nodded. I didn't trust myself to speak.

"Why? What kind of a—"

I held up a hand to cut off his outraged sputtering, then sat heavily at one end of the couch that sagged under the window. Hector took a breath and sat next to me. "Tell me everything."

I took more than a sip before I started.

"Remember how the Palace used to be involved in some questionable financial practices?" I asked. "And how when I got here and figured it out I decided it would probably be better for everyone if we put a stop to that and didn't all go to jail?"

"I remember." Hector's brother had been murdered at the Palace, in part because of those questionable financial practices.

"Ever since then the owners' profits have plummeted. In fact, if I hadn't started supplementing a little bit here and there, the Palace would be losing money."

"I've always thought it was a bad idea for you to put your own money into the theater," Hector said.

"Funny. I've always thought it was my own decision." I held his gaze until he shrugged slightly in concession to my excellent point.

"But even with that we're still on thin ice," I admitted. "The Tesla money has only gone so far."

When my errant almost-ex Ted had briefly tried to worm his way back into my affections, he'd casually given me a very expensive car. I'd sold it to a high-powered Hollywood producer named Otis Hampton, and unknown to anyone but Hector, I'd used a fair portion of the proceeds to pay for some urgently needed repairs to the Palace. But even with that, and with all the work I'd been doing to find new ways for the theater to earn more, I still had to hold my breath when I balanced the books each month.

"Tommy just can't accept that a classic movie theater in a quiet neighborhood doesn't make the kind of money he was used to. At least, not if it isn't doing something shady on the side." I could still see him, across the table in Monica's back room, getting more and more angry as I tried to make him see the reality of the situation.

"He blames me for everything," I told Hector. "He says it was all good before I came along."

Hectors expression darkened. "Does he have any idea what you've done around here? How hard you work?"

"He doesn't care. I tried to explain, and Robbie and Monica backed me up, but he said the only thing that matters is the bottom line. He said if I can't get the profits back up we should close the theater, stop hemorrhaging money, and 'regroup,' whatever that means."

"It means he's an ass," Hector said. "But if he's an ass who only cares about money he's an ass easily taken care of. I'll buy his share and you won't have to worry about him." He stood.

"Sit down and don't be crazy."

"How is that being crazy?" he demanded. "I can help you. That's not crazy."

"I don't want you to help me. I want—" But what I wanted couldn't happen. At least not yet. "I want to buy his share myself," I finally said. "I just need the lawyers to get their hands on my money in time to do it."

"I'll loan you the money until that happens," Hector said

swiftly. "Done."

"Not done. I can't let you do that since I don't know for sure if I'll ever be able to pay you back. I don't know if I'll ever see the money Ted took again."

The muscle in his jaw flexed as Hector held back what he undoubtedly wanted to say. Then he said it. "You're making this more difficult than it has to be."

I wasn't sure if "this" referred to my current predicament with Tommy, my ongoing predicament with Ted, or the relationship with Hector that we were both trying to figure out.

"I know," I told him. "But I can't do it any other way."

He gave me a long look, then nodded. "All right. Then what will you do about the immediate problem? How much time do you have to act before this character makes good on his threat?"

"Not much." The last thing Tommy had said at the meeting, pointing a finger and staring daggers at me, was "Fix it, and fix it fast."

Just thinking about it made me furious. "How does someone like that even run a company?" I asked. "He should know what it takes to turn a business around. And what kind of a creep spends weeks texting and emailing with me about the stupid launch but waits until he's got me in front of everyone to tell me what he really thinks of me? What kind of a person does that?"

"The kind of person who doesn't deserve you." Hector began pacing, his hands forming fists. Then he stopped. "And why? Why does he need the money? He's supposed to have those Silicon Valley billions, yes?"

"I don't know about billions, but lots and lots of millions."

"In any case, the amount of money he'd been getting from the theater, even at its most, shouldn't have been that significant to him."

I thought about it. "Maybe it isn't about the money. Maybe he just doesn't like me."

"Impossible," Hector said dismissively.

I poured more wine and thought about it. "Maybe it's just the principle of the thing. If the Palace *can* make more money, it *should* make more money." I shrugged. "Or maybe he's got us all snowed. Maybe he isn't rolling in it. Maybe he spent it all. Maybe he's strapped for cash because this new game took a ton of investment. And maybe he's not convinced it's going to be the success everyone thinks it is. Oh!" I sat up. "Or maybe it *will* be a huge success and he killed his partner so he wouldn't have to split all the profits."

"I do so enjoy it when you weave a chain of maybes," Hector said.

"Screenwriter's habit." I fell back into the cushions. "Maybe I should go back to screenwriting. Fictional problems are so much easier to solve."

"How would you solve this one in a movie?" Hector sank onto the couch next to me. "Would Tommy have been the one to collapse on that stage?"

"That would have a certain appeal." I made a face. "But it would just create a new set of problems."

"I agree. The police would undoubtedly come looking for you. You would have had an entirely justifiable motive for killing him." His eyes glittered. "So would I."

"Aw, thanks. That's so chivalrous." I shot him a look. "Also deeply disturbing."

We were prevented from exploring further plotlines by Brandon throwing open the door.

"Nora! Are you watching? S was poisoned!"

"I only know about poison from what I've seen in the movies," I said.

Marty, Callie, and I were slumped on stools at the far end of the concessions stand while the seven-thirty show was underway. Hector had left hours ago, and I'd sent Brandon and Albert home after the five-fifteen. Albert because he was looking tired, and Brandon because he'd been driving us all crazy with his endless stream of updates on the poisoning of S Banks.

"You only know about most things from what you've seen in the movies," Marty pointed out.

"True," I agreed. "Sadly, in this case I don't think *Arsenic and Old Lace* is going to be very helpful." *Arsenic and Old Lace* (1944, Cary Grant, Pricilla Lane and two sweet old ladies whose elderberry wine you should absolutely refuse) was many things, but a useful source of information on present-day poisonings wasn't one of them.

"I mean, I kind of can't believe it was murder," Callie said. "Right there onstage in front of a million people."

"One point eight million people," I corrected her. "At least, that's what Brandon said. If you include everyone in the eighteen theaters and all the fans watching the webcast online."

"Who decides to murder someone in front of 1.8 million people?" she asked. "And why?"

"And how?" Marty asked. "Do you think it was in that smoothie thing he drank? I one hundred percent think there was something in that."

"I thought he looked puffy," I said. "Did you guys think he looked puffy?"

"He looked stoned," Marty said. "Even before he took that drink onstage." Marty had gotten himself a coffee and was systematically adding eight sugar packets to it. "That was weird, wasn't it, that he brought that out onstage during his big announcement?"

"Not if he was paid to," Callie shrugged.

"What do you mean?" I asked.

"Didn't you notice how he turned the label so everyone could see it while he drank? I bet he's got an endorsement deal or something. Like half the people you see on Insta."

I'd stopped looking at Instagram and all the rest of the social media sites right about the time Ted's infidelity had been a trending topic.

"Do you think that's true?" I wondered. The way he'd paused for a drink had seemed weird to me at the time, but what did I know about tech people?

"I'd bet on it," she said. "Which doesn't mean that's how he was, like, poisoned. I mean, would it happen that fast?"

"That depends on what they used," Marty said authoritatively. "In *Arsenic and Old Lace* it worked right away, but they mixed a teaspoon of arsenic, half a teaspoon of strychnine, and—"

"Just a pinch of cyanide." We both finished the quote, exchanging a look.

Callie shrugged. "Okay, but in *D.O.A.* it took days."

"Right," I agreed. In *D.O.A.* (1949, Edmond O'Brien) the victim had lived for several days. "But that was because he had to survive long enough to solve his own murder. And wasn't it some weird sort of radium something?"

"It was movie poison," Marty agreed. "I think it was arsenic in *The Two Mrs. Carrolls*, and that took forever, but Bogey was trying to make it look like natural causes."

A husband killed his wife with poisoned milk in *The Two Mrs. Carrolls* (1947, Humphrey Bogart and Barbara Stanwyck) and a wife suspected her husband of trying to kill her with poisoned milk in *Suspicion* (1941, Cary Grant and Joan Fontaine). "I wonder if guys got away with a lot more poisoning back when doctors thought women could die of 'nervous complaints,'" I mused. "And when drinking milk at bedtime was a thing."

"Probably. And I think arsenic used to be, like, legit easy to get," Callie said. "Can you even get it anymore?" She looked at Marty.

"How would I know?" He shifted his coffee cup away from her.

"I mean, what did Claude Raines use to poison Ingrid Bergman in *Notorious*?" Callie was getting into this now. "Because that wasn't fast, either."

"No," I agreed. In *Notorious* (1946, Ingrid Bergman and Cary Grant) Bergman had lingered long enough to thwart the Nazis. "But is that because Ben Hecht was a screenwriter who knew his poisons or just because he needed Ingrid to hang in there until Cary could rescue her?"

"You're the writer," Marty said. "You tell us."

I stood and held up my index finger. "I'm not a screenwriter anymore." I held up another finger. "We don't know what poison killed S." A third finger. "And we're not going to figure anything out by analyzing the famous poisonings of classic films."

Marty looked at Callie. "Two out of three of those are true."

I didn't ask him which he meant. I didn't want to know.

Arsenic and Old Lace
1944

"Insanity runs in my family," Mortimer Brewster tells his bride, about midway into this movie. "It practically gallops."

And we're off. This is screwball comedy of the highest order, my friends. This is *Arsenic and Old Lace.* You may have seen the play this film was based on as a high school theater production, with some sixteen-year-old girls made up with gray wigs as the sweet old murderous aunts. But if you haven't seen this movie you are in for a treat. Every role is perfectly cast. Just look at them— Raymond Massey, Jack Carson, Edward Everett Horton, Peter Lorre! It's a who's who of classic character actors. And we haven't even mentioned Cary Grant.

Grant plays Mortimer Brewster, and we meet him as he's in line to get a marriage license. This wouldn't be that unusual, except he's the author of a tome known as "The Bachelor's Bible," and was the last guy in New York anyone ever expected to marry. But the lady in question, Elaine Harper, is just too lovely, too sweet, and too charming not to marry. (She's played by Priscilla Lane, and I forgive you if you don't know her. She retired from films only four years later, at the ripe old age of thirty-three.)

But back to that marriage license. However lovely, sweet, etc. Elaine is, Mortimer has some major last-minute cold feet. "How can I marry you? Me—the symbol of bachelorhood...I've written four million words against marriage. Not only hooked, but to a minister's daughter, and not only a minister's daughter but a girl from Brooklyn!"

That's what we in the business call laying out the central conflict. Or, at least, it would be the central conflict if it weren't for what Mortimer was about to discover at his dear old aunties' house...

The aunts in question, Abby and Martha (Josephine Hull and Jean Adair, respectively) live in a quiet, tree-lined neighborhood with a view of the Brooklyn Bridge and a delightful proximity to a leaf-strewn graveyard. One can only wonder what it would be worth in today's real estate market. The Brewster Sisters are, according to the (reassuringly Irish) cops on the beat "two of the dearest, sweetest, kindest old ladies that ever walked the earth." Well yes, but they've got some interesting hobbies.

An eccentric relative is a requirement of any self-respecting screwball comedy, and that role is filled here by Mortimer's brother Teddy (John Alexander) who lives with the aunts and believes himself to be Teddy Roosevelt, charging up the stairs as if they were San Juan Hill, and much occupied by digging the Panama Canal in the cellar.

It's to this delightful home that Mortimer brings Elaine after the wedding. She lives with her father the minister just across the graveyard, and needs to pack a suitcase, because they're bound for Niagara Falls. "Whistle when you're ready," he tells her, and goes to tell the aunts the happy news—quickly, because he's keeping the taxi waiting. They have a train to catch.

But it would be an extremely dull movie if Mortimer and Elaine actually made their train to Niagara. Instead, while looking for the draft of his latest anti-marriage book, Mortimer happens upon a gentleman, hidden in the window seat and very clearly dead. Nobody, *nobody*, has ever been better at reactions to insane situations than Cary Grant, and this has to be his best. He stares, he rears back, he slams the seat shut and sits on it, then has to look again. The body is still there.

Assuming Teddy has finally cracked, he tells the aunts it's time to send his brother to the Happy Dale Sanatorium, and fast. "Teddy's killed a man, darlings!" But they already know about the gentlemen and advise Mortimer to forget all about him. "We never dreamed you'd peek," Abby says reproachfully.

It seems the aunts, not Teddy, have been killing lonely old gentlemen who respond to their ad for a room to rent. It's a kindness, they feel, as the men in question have no families and no place to go. They've been poisoning them with perfectly delicious elderberry wine of their own deadly recipe, and Teddy has been burying them in the cellar, blithely assuming them to be canal workers who died of yellow fever. They're up to an even dozen, they tell Mortimer happily. All given decent Christian burials, so he shouldn't worry about a thing. But he is worried. "Now, I don't know how I can explain this to you, but it's not only against the law...it's *wrong*. It's not a nice thing to do."

So here we are: Aunties happily frosting a wedding cake, a body in the window seat, trick-or-treaters at the back door, Teddy digging in the basement, and bride whistling the wedding march from across the graveyard while the taxi waits outside. It's a lot for Mortimer to take in. Which is right about when his psychopath of a missing brother shows up, accompanied by an alcoholic plastic surgeon, looking for a place to hide out from the law. The brother is played by Raymond Massey (looking an awful lot like a scarred-up Boris Karloff) and the surgeon is a perfect Peter Lorre. Oh, and did I mention they have their own dead body to dispose of? I mean, come on! You've got to watch this movie!

Screwball thoughts:
Let's take a moment to appreciate the screwball—a manic flavor of romantic comedy that veers so far into the absurd that there's a danger of never making it back. (Observe not one but *two* panthers roaming around Connecticut in *Bringing up Baby*.) The action is fast, the dialogue is faster, the cast is overflowing with eccentric characters, and the physical comedy ramps up to a crescendo of slapstick. At the center of all of this lightning-paced insanity is someone who's just trying to do something normal, like leave for his honeymoon with his sweet, clueless bride. (One more thing: I don't care how hard they tried, nobody made a real screwball after 1949.)

Hollywood gossip thoughts:
The gowns here aren't anything spectacular, but they are by Orry-Kelly, who shared an apartment (and, he later claimed, a bed) with Grant before either of them moved to Hollywood and got famous. I'll leave you to imagine what the gossip at the fittings might have been.

Movies My Friends Should Watch
Sally Lee

CHAPTER 7

I did not drink milk at bedtime that night. Not because I had a husband who might poison me with it—Ted had been far more devious than that—but because a glass of red was much more likely to help me get some sleep.

Except it didn't. I finally gave up and opened my laptop a little after two. Something Hector had said was nudging at my brain. Why would Tommy May be worried about money?

A quick search told me what I already knew. Tommy had developed an indispensable travel app about five years ago. It handled all the information a person would need to plan and take a trip, bringing together airlines, hotels, restaurants, public transportation, and even handy little tidbits like where to find a good movie theater in Manila. It tracked your habits and remembered if you liked a high-floor room or were allergic to shellfish, but it went a lot deeper than that. The more you used it, even when you weren't travelling, the more it found out about you, making its recommendations more accurate. And it was totally free.

So how did Tommy make the millions—hundreds of millions— he was allegedly worth? I searched "How do free apps make money?" What I found made me very happy that I'd never bothered to download Tommy's app.

"Am I the last person in the world to know about 'Big Data'?" I asked Monica.

We'd met the following morning for coffee at Café Madelaine, across the street from the Palace. The café was a busy neighborhood hub of caffeine and yumminess that had only recently reopened following a fire a few months ago.

"Probably," she said. "Since it isn't heavily featured in films of the forties. Why do you know about it now?"

I made a face. "Tommy. I'm trying to figure him out."

She was silent until I glanced up to find her regarding me with one of those deeply accepting, fully understanding looks that she was so good at. If she hadn't been a pot entrepreneur she'd have made a great therapist.

I attempted a smile. "Know your enemies, right?"

"It was completely unfair of him to spring that all on us in the meeting Monday," she said. "Closing the Palace? There's no way that's going to happen. Tommy is being completely unreasonable. And don't forget he's only one of four owners."

True, but I hadn't liked the way Mitch, in LA, had nodded along with what Tommy had said in the meeting. If Mitch agreed with Tommy's plan to close the Palace, the board would be evenly split. I didn't know what that might mean.

But at least I knew Monica and Robbie were on my side. On the Palace's side.

"Thanks," I said. "What I'm trying to figure out is why Tommy's being so insistent. Why does he need the money from the Palace? He should be worth a fortune, what with all the personal data from his users that he's been gathering and selling for years. And this game should mean even more money."

"Especially now that his partner's dead," Monica said meaningfully.

I looked at her. "And here I thought I was a terrible person for wondering about that."

"We might both be terrible people." This didn't seem to overly concern Monica. She leaned forward. "What do you think? Did Tommy kill his partner? To get more profits from the game?"

We were interrupted by the arrival of coffee and raspberry muffins, brought to us by Lisa, the owner of the café. "Are you guys talking about the game? Are you playing?" She'd brought coffee for herself as well and pulled up a chair to join us. In her early forties, she was just a few years older than me, with the comfortable figure of a professional baker and hair she was letting gray naturally.

"No, I'm not playing. Are you playing? Why?" Despite all the research I'd done in the wee small hours I'd had no desire to download the treasure hunt game.

"Um, because I could find a million-dollar coin somewhere?"

"Sure, there's that," I allowed. "Except it's two million today. During the webcast Tommy said a million dollars was going to be added to each coin's value every day they weren't found."

"So don't be too hasty," Monica advised. "You might want to give it a few days." She broke off a piece of muffin and popped it in her mouth.

"What's the game like?" I asked Lisa.

"I'm barely into it, but it looks like you solve puzzles that lead you to clues for more puzzles that lead you to…you get the idea. And those AR things are everywhere. They appear as characters in the game to give you the clues, or sometimes to send you off in the wrong direction."

"Sounds kind of cool." Monica took her phone out.

"It is, but I've gotten far enough to figure out that the world of the game is huge," Lisa said. "There are maps upon maps upon maps, and you need to learn the routes and navigate everywhere in this giant virtual space."

"That must be the tie-in with Tommy's travel tech," I guessed.

"Cool," Monica said again.

"I'll still take a movie any day." I popped the lid off my coffee. "But I may be alone in that. Last I checked, there are over twelve million people playing."

"Twelve million and one." Monica was tapping on her phone. "Hey, it's free." She looked up. "How does Tommy make money from this?"

"By watching every move you make and selling your information to the highest bidder," I told her.

"Plus, you can buy things in the game," Lisa said, apparently unphased by the auctioning off of her personal data. "You don't have to, but you can go faster if you buy a key to open a door instead of solving a puzzle to do it. Things like that."

"That's kind of genius," Monica said. "Not the horrifying bit about collecting and selling user data," she nodded to me. "But charging real money for virtual stuff? Genius." She picked up her mug. "Why aren't we all making apps?"

"Profit margins would soar," Lisa agreed. "Think how much I'd save on ingredients if I sold virtual cookies."

"Market them as gluten free," I advised her. "You'll be a zillionaire in no time. Meanwhile, do you have some cookies for me?" Theoretically, the reason I'd come to the café was to pick up our order. We'd started selling Lisa's baked goods in a pop-up stand at the Palace while her shop had been closed for repairs. Her giant cookies had been so popular we'd decided to keep selling them at the concessions stand after the café reopened. "Non-virtual cookies, so we can both make some non-virtual money?"

"That's my favorite kind," Monica said, without looking up from the game.

"Why don't we have an app?"

I'd been thinking about it all day and now asked Callie and Albert. The seven-thirty was in progress and I'd found them with their heads together over some paperwork in the break room.

They both looked up at me, Albert with a slight squint behind his little round glasses, and Callie with a distracted glance. "I mean, because we're movie people?" she suggested.

I took a chair at the table with them. "So why don't we have a movie people app? Why don't we do some of that AR stuff around here? Think about it—what if you could look down the balcony stairs and see Clark Gable looking up at you like Rhett Butler looked at Scarlett?"

Albert's raised his eyebrows.

"Or while you're waiting for the movie to start you could see

Busby Berkeley dancers on the stage, or Fred Astaire in a top hat and tails...we could do whatever we wanted. At least, whatever we could get the rights to."

"Errol Flynn?" Albert suggested. "As Robin Hood, standing on the balcony railing like it was a tree in Sherwood forest?"

"Exactly," I nodded. "That would be cool, right?"

"I'd certainly enjoy it," he said. "I believe you know how I feel about Errol Flynn."

"I believe I do." I knew that *Captain Blood* (1935, Errol Flynn and Olivia de Havilland, wearing very similar wigs) was the first movie he'd ever seen at the Palace.

"I mean, okay," Callie said. "Let's get an app."

"I just have to figure out how we can make money with it," I mused.

Albert nodded. "Yes, perhaps that would be a logical first step. And then you might find someone to make it?"

I waved that detail away. "This is San Francisco. You can't throw a rock in this town without hitting an app developer." Hector's cousin Gabriela was a computer engineer and a regular at the Palace. She could probably point me in the right direction.

I took a closer look at the papers spread out on the table. "What are you two working on? Is that a script?"

They exchanged a glance. "Callie, dear," Albert said, "I think it's time we shared our little project, don't you?"

The last time Albert had told me about a little project, it had been his plan to write a book about the Palace. A memoir about what the theater meant to him, to his family, and to the neighborhood where he'd lived his whole life. He hadn't mentioned it in a while, and I'd wondered if it had gotten to be too much for him. He was over ninety, after all.

"We're making a documentary," Callie announced. "We're using Albert's notes for his book and turning it into a film." She gave me a look that dared me to make fun of her. "I'm submitting it as my master's thesis."

I blinked. "That's brilliant."

"Do you really think so?" Albert asked. "I know we discussed a book."

"A movie is so much better," I said. "It makes so much more sense for the Palace."

"That's what I thought," Callie said. "And, I mean, I think it's going to be good, Nora. I think it's going to be, like, really good."

"I have no doubt," I told them. "How much have you done? Where are you starting? Tell me everything."

"That's what we're trying to figure out," Albert said.

"There are just so many stories." Callie gathered the scattered pages together. "We need to find the thru-line that will take us from the early days of silents up to everything that's happening now."

"Well, not everything," Albert cautioned. "I don't think we should mention that fellow dying onscreen yesterday."

"Agreed," I said. "I'd stick to the murders that actually took place here." Not that there had been that many. Hardly any, really. Just a few. "What happened with S had nothing to do with us."

It wasn't the first time I'd said that, but it would probably be the last. Because right after I said it my phone pinged with an incoming message.

Tommy May had just been arrested for murder.

CHAPTER 8

"Detective Jackson!" I waved at him from across the crowded restaurant, working my way past the crush at the bar. "Imagine meeting you here," I said when I got to the table.

"Yes, imagine." Marty folded his arms and glowered at me.

I hadn't needed Big Data to figure out where Marty would be meeting his boyfriend the detective for a late date after closing down the Palace. I'd overheard him on his phone in the break room.

"Nora." Jackson slid his wineglass over to make room at the table as I pulled up a chair. "This is quite a coincidence."

"I happened to be in the neighborhood." I happened to be there after telling the rideshare driver where to take me, but the detective didn't need that detail. The restaurant, Beretta on Valencia Street, was dark, busy, and—most importantly—open past midnight. "Have you ordered yet?"

"You're not staying." Marty moved his beer glass over to take up the space on the table that Jackson had made.

The detective put a hand on his arm. "I don't think Nora's here for the pizza." He gave me a look that saw right through me. The detective was in his forties, tall and heavyset, with dark brown skin and a goatee so perfect it almost looked painted on. He exuded authority, and he was exuding it in my direction. "I can't tell you anything about the case."

Marty glared at me. "You are *not* ruining pizza night just so you can obsess over a murder that you yourself said doesn't have anything to do with us."

"Maybe it didn't before, but now they've arrested Tommy for

murder," I told him. "That puts it at our doorstep."

Marty's eyes narrowed.

I appealed to the detective. "Jackson, please. You must know something."

"It's not my case," he reminded me. "It's not even in my city, and I don't have a buddy on the Palo Alto PD." He cut me off before I could ask him exactly that question. "I've seen the same news you have. S Banks was poisoned, and they've arrested Thomas May in connection with the death." He shrugged his substantial shoulders.

I opened my mouth with a question, but Marty got there first. "Why?" he asked. "What's May's motive? How do they think he did it?"

Jackson regarded him. "I thought you didn't want to talk about it."

"I didn't want you to talk about it with her." Marty nodded his head in my direction.

"Thanks." I took a sip of his beer. "So did Tommy do it?" I asked Jackson. "Was it about money?"

"Why would you think that?" the detective asked.

"I'm just wondering if Tommy has as much money as we all think he does," I said. "What if he doesn't? What if it's all a front and he's actually drowning in debt or something?"

"Is he?" Marty asked. "That would serve him right. Maybe Banks found out and Tommy had to shut him up before word got out among the rest of the tech billionaires. They might not have invited him to their next oligarch soiree." He sniffed.

The detective ignored him, focusing on me. "Why do you think he's got money troubles?"

Oops. I wasn't planning to let Marty or the rest of the gang know about Tommy's threats in the owners' meeting. I gave him a look. "Don't freak out."

"Great." He grabbed his beer and took a long gulp. "What fresh hell are you bringing to pizza night?"

"Tommy's just bent out of shape because profits at the Palace are down," I told them. "He, um, made quite a point of it the other day. It got me wondering why someone who's supposed to be so rich would care so much about what I assume is an insignificant part of his income."

Marty freaked out. "How bent out of shape?" he demanded. "What, exactly, did he say? What's he planning? I *never* trusted that guy."

"Calm down, he hasn't done anything yet."

"*Done* anything?" This just freaked him out more. "What's he going to do?"

"Nothing," I assured him. "I'm not going to let him do anything. And neither is Robbie and neither is Monica."

Marty looked deeply suspicious. "If you three are circling the wagons it must be a serious threat. Is he talking about closing the Palace?"

Something in my eyes must have told him the truth. He slapped the table. "I *knew* it!"

"He's not going to do anything," I said again. "Especially now that he's been arrested for murder."

"I'd like to murder *him*," Marty said darkly.

"Nice talk in front of the cops," I said, nodding toward Detective Jackson in an attempt to lighten the mood. "I admit I wanted to kill Tommy myself the other day, but there's a time and place..."

"There is indeed," Jackson said. "And here's a tip: The more experienced criminals tend not to shout about their plans in crowded restaurants."

Marty rolled his eyes and finished his beer.

I turned to Jackson. "What do you think? Did Tommy kill S?"

He tapped the rim of his wineglass. "I think...it's not my case."

I shouldn't have been surprised. But I wasn't ready to give up yet. "What evidence is there against Tommy?" I asked. "Do they know what kind of poison it was? Or how he—"

"Are you staying for pizza?" Jackson interrupted. "If so I think we should split an order of calamari first. It's so good here." He gave me a look. "And then, if you like, we might talk about Alec

Guinness poisoning his relatives, or Gene Tierney poisoning herself, but we will not talk about Tommy May, or any other person or persons unknown, poisoning S Banks."

His voice changed from lighthearted to no-nonsense during the course of his invitation. I'd hit his wall of professionalism, and I'd done so often enough in the past to know there was no getting around it. At least not right away, so I might as well have some calamari.

I sat back as the detective motioned to the waiter.

"We are one hundred percent going to talk about this later," Marty muttered.

"I know," I muttered back. "Meanwhile, nice work with Alec Guinness and Gene Tierney." Alec Guinness had played an aristocrat hilariously killing everyone in his family who stood between him and his title in *Kind Hearts and Coronets* (1949, Guinness as every member of the ill-fated D'Ascoyne family) and Gene Tierney had played a narcissist nightmare who'd poisoned herself to frame her sister in *Leave Her to Heaven* (1945, Tierney and a largely clueless Cornel Wilde).

Marty looked slightly mollified. "When I met him he didn't know who Gene Tierney was," he said. "Now look at him."

"All grown up and spewing references," I agreed. "Next thing you know he'll be quoting Bogart."

"What are you two muttering about?" Jackson handed me a menu.

"Not a thing," I told him. "Definitely not murder."

I didn't get home until after one in the morning. "Home" was the minimalist guest cottage behind Robbie's San Francisco vacation house, a few blocks from the Palace.

Before Ted hid all our money I'd planned to buy a place of my own. Because before Ted hid all our money I'd had an expectation of a fairly sizable settlement. I'd not only been his wife for the decade that had seen him rise from obscurity to international stardom, I'd been his unpaid manager and agent along the way.

Any expectations I'd had were shattered when I found out the money was gone. Ted had invested it in a film production that had gone bankrupt. Or so the world believed. I knew different. And I knew different because of Otis Hampton, a man who hated Ted enough to attempt an alliance with me.

I pulled my phone out of my bag as I locked the door and kicked off my shoes, sinking into the couch that took up most of the living room. Otis had sent a flood of texts as I'd shared a pizza with Marty and Detective Jackson. (No matter how often he told me to call him David, he would always be Detective Jackson to me.) I'd ignored them all. If there was one thing I was exceptionally good at, it was ignoring texts.

I got comfortable on the couch. Otis was a Hollywood studio head and media mogul with wild ideas and a bad case of insomnia. Reading all his messages might take a while.

Nora. My sources tell me that Ted and Priya are planning a small, secret wedding in early September in Venice. They'll be there for the film festival and hope the press won't catch on to the wedding until it's over. Meaning he wants the news leaked so every camera in Italy will be there. I can only assume that Ted believes his divorce from you will be final before then. I again urge you strongly not to sign anything until we can recover the money and prove Ted is guilty of financial misconduct. Please confirm this is your intention.

Otis had been dating the breathtaking actress Priya Sharma when she and my husband had fallen truly, madly, and adulterously in love. Otis had found out about their madcap affair the same way I had, by seeing it all over the blogs while Ted and Priya were filming on location. My reaction had been to leave LA and start over again in San Francisco. Otis, a powerful man not used to being denied anything he wanted, had chosen a different path. He'd made it his mission to win Priya back. And the fastest way to do that, he felt, was by getting Ted out of the way.

Otis was convinced that he could prove Ted had hidden our money and lied about the bankrupt film to avoid paying me a settlement. He thought the truth, when he exposed it, would do two things: ruin Ted's shiny likable movie-star reputation, and force Ted to pay me what I'm owed. After that Ted wouldn't be in quite the same tax bracket. Which is when Otis, with his piles of money, would swoop in and woo Priya back. At least that was his plan. It was slightly insane and very convoluted, much like Otis. But the part of it that included finding the money Ted had hidden and paying me my share had a very strong appeal. Which is why I still paid attention to Otis's texts.

I scrolled through five more messages, all along the same lines as the first, and I told myself to focus on the fact that Otis seemed to be spiraling and not on the fact that Ted was planning his wedding to someone else.

A small, secret wedding. Somehow I doubted it would be as small and secret as ours had been. We'd stopped in Vegas on our way out to LA to become famous. Small—yes. Secret—who would have cared? It had been sweet, really. Just the two of us. Because we knew that was all we'd ever need. We were already best friends. Already in love. Becoming husband and wife was inevitable. There was only one way to face the future. Together.

I realized I wasn't paying attention to Otis's texts anymore. I blinked and looked at the last one.

I heard Tommy May has been arrested. If that puts the Palace in any financial difficulties you know you can count on me to help.

Right. But I wouldn't. I was already in Otis's debt from the last time he'd helped, by buying the Tesla that Ted had given me. I'd been grateful for the quick cash at a time when the Palace needed urgent repairs, but now dealing with Otis was feeling more and more like getting trapped in something sticky and web-like.

He was plotting. That much I knew. What I didn't fully know was what role he'd assigned to me.

CHAPTER 9

I was up in my office the next morning, hours before the first show, when I heard someone banging on the lobby doors. In my experience, someone banging on the lobby doors seldom led to anything good, so I made my way down with caution.

A moving van was parked in the loading zone, and a guy wearing shorts and carrying a clipboard stood next to an enormous box at the door.

I unlocked and opened the door. "I think there's been a mistake."

"Is there another Palace theater around here?" He thrust the clipboard at me. "Sign here."

One box, the invoice said. From an address in LA. Ted's address.

"Ooh! What is it?"

I jumped about a foot as I heard Trixie's excited voice behind me. The delivery guy looked at me like I'd lost my marbles. Fair enough. I turned around and gave Trixie a "just a minute" look.

"What is it?" I turned back to ask the guy.

"I just move 'em," he shrugged.

Again, fair enough.

"Can I ask you to bring it downstairs for me?" It looked like a wardrobe box, the kind you hang clothes in for a move. A few months ago Ted had paid someone to pack up all my possessions from the house I'd shared with him in wedded ignorance, and he'd had everything delivered to me here. This box had probably just been forgotten. It belonged with the rest of the them, still unopened, down in the basement prop room.

"Is there an elevator?" the guy asked.

"No, but there's twenty dollars," I offered.

"I'd be happy to."

Fair enough.

"Open it! Open it!" Trixie urged as soon as I'd seen the delivery guy out and returned to her in the prop room.

"I don't even know what it is," I told her.

"That's why you have to open it, you dope."

"I do know what it is," I reversed myself. "It's clothes from my old life, and I don't want them. I don't want any of them."

The prop room was downstairs, below the stage. The room was large, with high ceilings and brick walls, and was a gathering place for junk that had accumulated over the long history of the theater. Bits of sets and racks of costumes from the time when the Palace was on the vaudeville circuit, along with furniture and equipment that nobody had ever gotten around to throwing away. Since the delivery from Ted back in January it had also held twenty-two boxes containing the remnants of my former life. I hadn't known where else to put that much stuff until I felt like I could deal with it. The new box fit right in.

Trixie put her hands on her hips and shook her head in exasperation. "Why, Nora Paige, you've been putting this off and putting it off and I just can't see why. They're your things. Don't you want to go through them? Your clothes. Gee, if I could wear something new I'd jump at the chance." She looked down at the wide-legged trousers of the snappy usherette's uniform that she'd been wearing since 1937. "Not that I don't look cute in this," she dimpled.

"Cuter than anyone has a right to," I assured her. Especially anyone her age. "But I can't get wrapped up in all of this now. I don't have the time. Tommy's been arrested for murder, and—"

"And that has nothing to do with you, does it?" Her hands remained on her hips, determination written on her face.

Well, not really. Although it felt like it did.

"So open it!" She clapped in excitement. "At least open this new one."

I wavered.

"Why, I bet the clothes in here are just grand," Trixie said, passing her hand through the corner of the box. It was taller than she was. "And you know if they stay boxed up down here they're going to start to smell all basement-y." She wrinkled her pert nose.

That was a good point. However much my old wardrobe didn't suit my new life, I didn't like the thought of ruining good things just because I couldn't face the memories they held. If I didn't want them I should donate them. But first I had to steel myself to see exactly what Ted had sent before he'd sold my house.

"Wouldn't it be funny if this is where that stinker husband of yours hid all the money?" Trixie asked.

"Hilarious," I told her. "But let's not get our hopes up."

I started picking at the tape on the large wardrobe box. I assumed the clothes I'd last seen six months ago—designer jackets and chic sleeveless dresses more suited to power lunches at the Ivy than slinging popcorn and sweeping the stage—would be hanging neatly inside.

"Ooh, I can't wait!" Trixie said. "I bet it's something good."

One satisfying tug and the top of the box was open. I folded down the front to see what was inside.

"Gowns," I said. Maybe half a dozen, all carefully packed in tissue and hung on clear acrylic forms that gave them shape.

Trixie squealed. "They're beautiful! Take them out! Take them out right now so I can see them!"

I pushed the tissue aside. One dress was red, with long sleeves and a deep V-neck, sequined to within an inch of its life. Another was sheer and white with elaborate crystal beading and an empire silhouette. The third was a pink satin strapless with a huge bow on the hip.

"Oh, Nora, they're wonderful. I can't believe you ever wore anything this gorgeous."

My mouth had gone dry, so it took a moment for me to answer her.

"I didn't." I finally said. "These aren't my gowns."

Ninety minutes later I'd opened every box Ted had sent back in January. I'd found books, clothes, shoes, and handbags, all of them mine. There was a box with the wineglasses we'd gotten in Venice, and the silver coffeepot we'd picked up at a Paris flea market. One held the contents of my desk, including my lucky fountain pen and scripts I'd been working on a decade ago. There were a hundred things that might have made me break down with emotion, but nothing else that didn't belong to me.

Why had he sent these? Why now? And what did they mean?

I rolled a costume rack over and unceremoniously dumped everything it held onto the floor. Then I carefully, carefully, carefully took each of the gowns out of the wardrobe box and hung them on the rack.

"Nora, you're right." Trixie shimmered with excitement. "These gowns are famous."

"These gowns are iconic," I said. "Every damn one of them."

Both the sequined red and the strapless pink had been worn by Marilyn Monroe in *Gentlemen Prefer Blondes* (1953, Marilyn and Jane Russell), and the white was what Audrey Hepburn had worn to the ball in *My Fair Lady* (1964, Hepburn and Rex Harrison). They were joined on the rack by an ethereal blue chiffon number in which Grace Kelly had wafted around the South of France in *To Catch A Thief* (1955, Kelly and Cary Grant), a short red flapper dress slit to the waist that Cyd Charisse had used to lethal effect in *The Band Wagon* (1953, Charisse and Fred Astaire), and a lavender-gray ballgown in which Judy Garland had left it all on the stage in *A Star is Born* (1954, Garland and James Mason).

Trixie stood behind the rack, her head just visible over the neckline of Judy's ballgown. "How do I look?"

"I'm not sure it works with the hat."

She laughed and cocked her little round cap further to the side, curls bouncing as she did so. "Nora, this is amazing! Why didn't you tell me you had all these dresses?"

"Because I didn't," I said. "I've never seen them before. Except in the movies."

I stared at them, biting my lip and trying to figure out how six of the most stunning costumes in movie history had wound up in my prop room, while Trixie chattered on about how beautiful they were. "Gee, I wish I could wear them," she said, sweeping her arm through them all. She turned to me. "Did they come with gloves and shoes and things?"

I shrugged, still thinking. She gave up on me and went to the large wardrobe box, peeking inside. "No gloves," she announced. "But, say, Nora, there's an envelope down there." She disappeared into the box. I peeked over the top and saw her crouching at the bottom, unable to pick up a thick white envelope.

"Careful, I'm going to tip it over," I said, although it wasn't as if I could hurt her.

As soon as the envelope was in my hands I recognized the stationary. There was a whole box of it with the things from my desk. I tore it open and stared in disbelief at the three words above Ted's signature.

"I need you."

I was still clutching the note from Ted. I'd clutched it all six blocks from the Palace to Monica's shop. I'd clutched it as she'd taken one look at me and ushered me through the back lounge and into her private office. I'd clutched it as I told her about the gowns.

"That's all it says?" She'd settled me into a chair in the soothing saffron-colored meditation nook of her office and was now making me a cup of herbal tea. For once I would have liked her to offer something stronger. "He just sent you six famous dresses and a three-word note?"

I held the evidence out to her. "'I need you.' What's that

supposed to mean?"

Monica opened a jar of honey. "It might mean he needs you."

"He's insane," I said. "First he hides all my money and then he sends me a fortune in costumes?"

"Is it a fortune?" she asked.

I blinked. "Probably. I mean, if they're genuine, which they seem to be, and if I could sell them, auction them off or something, which I could assuming I had a receipt or paperwork that proved—" I stared at her. "He didn't send receipts."

"So he doesn't want you to sell them." She handed me a steaming mug, a thoughtful look on her face. "Why dresses?"

Suddenly I was stabbed with a memory. "We were going to go to an auction," I said, blinking. "Back before I found out about the affair. Ted and I were planning to go to New York for a movie memorabilia auction. But that was going to be in November and everything blew up in October, and I didn't even think...I never even remembered it until just now."

"Drink your tea," she advised. "And maybe breathe."

I couldn't do either. "I had my eye on a Bette Davis broach," I said. "Not on six whole gowns. What in the hell was he thinking?"

She tilted her head. "At a guess, I'd say he was thinking he needs you."

"Of course he does," I fumed. "He hasn't done anything for himself in years. But he doesn't get to leave me *and* take all the money and still expect me to drop everything just because *he* doesn't know how to order a damn pizza!" I might have been yelling by that point.

"He doesn't know how to order a pizza?"

I wafted my hands and slumped, exhausted. "That's what assistants are for." I thought about it. "He must need me for something big. Something specific. He wouldn't have thrown Marilyn Monroe's gowns at a problem he could solve with an assistant. He's too cheap for that."

Monica nodded. "He's also emotionally stunted and weirdly controlling, from the looks of things."

"In other words, an actor," I said darkly.

"Maybe the gowns are an apology," Monica suggested. "Remember back in January when he sent out that tweet? He called you his best friend."

I remembered the tweet. He'd encouraged his millions of followers to come see a movie at the Palace. It had boosted our attendance when we'd needed a boost the most. I stared at Monica.

"Maybe," she suggested, "in some weird way, he thinks you *are* friends."

"Let's add 'delusional' to the long list of things he is."

"Are you going to call him?" Monica asked. "At least find out what he needs your help with?"

"Well, I might," I said. "If he weren't a scheming, lying, cheating liar."

"Sure." She pushed the tea toward me, nodding. "You're better off with a text."

CHAPTER 10

There was a knock on Monica's office door just as I pressed Send on a text that I wasn't sure I should send. Ted had left a three word note for me: "I need you." After much consideration, I sent him a four-word text.

You can't buy me.

When I looked up, Monica was checking the video screen that showed the hallway outside her door. Her security at the shop was tight, which only made sense, considering the amount of cash and cannabis she kept on hand.

"It's Abby," she said, glancing from the screen to me. "She's just bringing a delivery. It won't take long."

"I should get out of here. I've taken enough of your time." I stood. "Thanks for the tea, and for putting up with me."

She got up and moved to the door. "Anytime. And don't do anything with those gowns until I get to see them."

"I won't," I said as she opened the door.

Abby, the vendor that I'd met the other day before the owners' meeting, stood in the hallway wearing a pale blue sweater that complemented her cropped white hair. She held a carton stacked with small brown boxes. "Hi, lovie," she greeted Monica. "I've got all the custom orders from the other day. Kristy told me I should bring them back here so nobody sells them by mistake." She set the carton on Monica's desk before she noticed me. "Oh, hi."

"Hi. It's Nora. We met the other—"

"Of course, Nora." She moved in for a quick hug. "I remember.

You were here with Tommy, and—" She released me and took a step back, biting her lip.

"And S," I finished for her. She'd been deep in conversation with S when the rest of us had gone into the lounge for the meeting. The day before he died.

"I couldn't believe it when I heard." She looked from Monica to me. "Did you know him well?" she asked me.

"Not at all. That was the only time I met him."

She nodded. "So awful."

I remembered that she'd seemed as struck with his rock star aura as everyone else in the shop that day. She'd gaped at him when he approached and had seemed more than a little discombobulated by his presence.

"Did you talk to him long after we went into the meeting?" I asked her, silently wondering *And did he happen to mention anyone wanting to kill him? Tommy, perhaps?*

"I did," she said. "He was interested in everything in the shop, not just my line. I showed him around and answered what I could of his questions. Whatever I didn't know about, Kristy did."

"Kristy's good," Monica said.

"Very knowledgeable," Abby agreed. "I think she made quite an impression on him."

"He definitely made an impression on her," Monica said. "She couldn't talk about anything else the rest of the day."

"I'm not surprised," Abby said. "He certainly bought enough to impress her."

I'd been thinking I should go have a word with this Kristy, but Abby's comment got my attention. "Really?" I asked. "He bought a lot? More than normal?"

"I can't say what's *normal*," Abby replied. "But he bought quite a bit. Three, no four things from me." She frowned in concentration. "Plus a few samples. And he placed a custom order. But he didn't just buy from my line. He filled a basket before he left."

"We'll have a record of what he bought," Monica said.

"Receipts are itemized and tracked by purchaser. Do you think it's important?" She looked at me.

"I have no idea," I said honestly.

"I joked that he must be throwing a party," Abby said. "And he told me the next day was going to be the biggest party of his life." She looked at us. The next day he'd died onstage.

She turned and shuffled through the stack of boxes she'd put on Monica's desk. "I brought his custom tincture. I didn't know what else to do with it. He'd given me his history and I was so pleased to be able to develop this blend for him, before I heard what happened."

She found the box she was looking for. It had S Bank's name on the label, and last Tuesday's date, followed by a handwritten list of ingredients, none of which were legible.

"I'm sorry," I said. "I don't really know much about how you work. What do you mean about him giving you his history? His medical history?"

She nodded. "Things like illnesses and allergies, any prescriptions he was taking, as well as his experiences with cannabinoids. He was excited to see what I could blend for him." She looked down at the box in her hands, her expression unreadable.

"Did he take any prescription drugs?" I asked, wondering if they could have been tampered with. A doctor would never have told me, but I assumed there was no such thing as pot-purveyor-client confidentiality.

I was right. "Just the occasional antibiotic," she answered. "Nothing on a regular basis."

"Right." That let the tampering theory out. But not all drugs were prescription. "I got the impression S was pretty experienced with, um, cannabinoids," I said. "When I saw him on the webcast that day he looked like he'd already taken something."

"I thought so, too," Monica said. "When I watched it online, after."

I turned to Abby. "Do you know of anything that could

intensify the effect of pot?"

She nodded. "Sure, but not enough to kill him. Is that what you're asking?"

"I guess it is. The thing is, I've been wondering about where Tommy would have gotten poison—not that I even know what poison killed S or how hard it would be to get." I grimaced. "On the news this morning they said they probably wouldn't have the results from the autopsy until Friday or so."

"Do you think Tommy did it?" Abby asked.

"I don't know. But the police must have some reason for thinking so."

"We all have some reason for thinking so," Monica reminded me.

"True." Especially if, with S out of the way, Tommy would get more of the profits from the game.

"For what it's worth, I don't think it's that hard to get your hands on poison," Abby said. "Of course, my farm is all organic, but there are still plenty that pour on the toxic weed killer."

"Something tells me Tommy May doesn't take care of killing his own weeds," I said. Would he take care of killing his own business partner?

"Forget about Tommy for a minute. You absolutely have to try on those gowns." Robbie's voice, over the phone, was definite.

I was back in the basement after everyone else had gone home for the night. I'd managed to stay busy throughout the day, mainly putting things together for Friday's midnight movie party, but once the handful of customers cleared out at the end of the nine-fifteen I had the joint to myself. Even Trixie had disappeared. That happened sometimes. She never remembered where she went when she was away, but so far she'd always come back.

"I'd be terrified to even try putting one on," I told Robbie, eyeing the fashion fantasies that were now somehow in my care. "What if I damaged it?"

I'd sent her pictures of the gowns. She was ogling them from her kitchen in Beverly Hills, which didn't give her the perspective I had on how very tiny they were.

"Oh, come on. How can you have Marilyn's gown and not try it on?"

"Have you seen Marilyn?" I asked her. "And have you seen me? I question whether we're even the same species, let alone the same size. Maybe if it was Jane Russell's—she was at least taller—but Marilyn?"

"Okay, then try the Audrey Hepburn," Robbie encouraged. "You can pull off Audrey Hepburn."

"Just because I don't have boobs it doesn't mean I'm Audrey Hepburn," I told her. My figure could most kindly be described as "athletic," which was fine for being the manager of a classic movie theater. It hadn't been quite so fine when I'd been expected to suit up for red carpet events with Ted over the years. I was a normal human woman, not a double-zero sylph or a curvy goddess, which seemed to be the only two shapes Hollywood designers deemed permissible.

"You have boobs," Robbie informed me. "You just don't have the kind that slap you on the chin when you're on the treadmill like mine do. Not that I'm on the treadmill that often."

"Can we stop body shaming ourselves and get back to the dresses?" I asked. "What am I supposed to do with them? They should be in some sort of temperature and humidity-controlled environment or something, shouldn't they?"

"Probably. Do any of the museums up there have textile departments? Maybe they'd be able to rent you some space or something."

"It's just like Ted to give me something that will cost me rent instead of giving me the money that's actually mine." I slumped into a chair, facing my glittering charges. Ted had not responded to my text. "Give him the filthiest of all possible looks the next time you run into him, will you?"

"I can't," she said. "Because that would mean acknowledging

him as someone who exists. He's dead to me. I can't give filthy looks to the dead."

"You should be written up in the encyclopedia of best friends," I told her. "Who else is dead to you?"

"After that meeting on Monday, I would have said Tommy," she said. "But he may not be our problem anymore."

"Oh, so we're allowed to talk about Tommy now?"

"For a minute. Do you think he really killed that guy?"

It was the question of the day.

"I have no idea," I said. "Detective Jackson won't tell me anything, which isn't exactly a surprise. You know Tommy better than I do. Could he do that sort of a thing?"

"I've written several hit shows based on the premise that anyone could do anything, given the right motive," she said. "But the *how* and the *when* of it don't make sense to me. If you're going to knock off you partner, why would you do it so publicly? Why wouldn't you give yourself an alibi?"

I thought about it. "Maybe doing it publicly was the point? The game is front page news everywhere now, not just on geek websites. From a crassly commercial perspective, S's spectacular online death is great publicity." I got up to blow a tiny speck of dust off the white *My Fair Lady* dress. I'd have to drape the tissue around them all before I went home. "And what do you mean about Tommy not being our problem anymore? Can't he own a quarter of the Palace from jail?"

"Maybe, but he won't be in much of a position to call in to board meetings from cell block C."

"No." I saw her point. "That's a cheerful thought."

"Assuming he's actually found guilty," she cautioned. "Let's not forget he's a rich white dude."

"There's that," I agreed.

"And speaking of rich white dudes, I'd better go. I've got a breakfast meeting with one of them in the morning."

"They're *everywhere*," I whispered ominously.

"For now," she said easily. "But there are more of us than there used to be. There will be even more of us when you start writing scripts again."

"And on that note..." I said.

She laughed. "Okay, I won't push. Say goodnight, Gracie."

I grinned. "Goodnight, Gracie."

If I did start writing scripts again, they'd probably be about murders.

CHAPTER 11

"The entire world is losing its mind," Brandon announced, the lobby door clattering shut behind him.

"I feel that way all the time," I told him.

He was there for his regular after-school shift. It was Friday, so the lineup had changed. In keeping with our week-long salute to technology in film—which was seeming like a misbegotten idea at this point—we were showing *The Computer Wore Tennis Shoes* (1969, Kurt Russell and all the usual Disney supporting players) and *The Honeymoon Machine* (1961, Steve McQueen and Jim Hutton). In *Tennis Shoes*, a clean-cut college student gets a computer's data transferred to his brain, resulting in comic hijinks, and in *Honeymoon*, a couple of clean-cut Navy men try to break the bank at a European casino using the government's computer, resulting in comic hijinks. People used to think technology was so funny.

When Brandon appeared the two-thirty was under way and I was ostensibly on duty at the candy counter while mainly scouring the Internet for information on poisons. Just out of idle curiosity.

"Losing its mind about the game," he clarified, slinging his backpack onto a shelf below the counter. "Nobody's found a coin yet and as of today they're each worth four million dollars."

"Shouldn't you be online looking for one?" Maybe I should.

He snorted, reaching for a cup to get himself a soft drink from the machine. "I've been stuck on a puzzle all day. I need to take a break before my head explodes."

"That must be some puzzle."

He nodded, gulping his drink. "That's one of the reasons the

Internet is losing its mind. The puzzles, the world-building—it's way more complex than anything anyone has ever done before. It just doesn't seem like you can win. Or, at least, not without paying a ton for clues."

"What does that mean?"

He took a drink of soda and wiped his mouth with the back of his hand. "Like this puzzle I'm stuck on. It's a maze, and I could solve it in a minute if I paid for a map."

"Real money for a virtual map?" I thought of Lisa and her comment about virtual cookies.

"Two dollars," Brandon nodded. "Real dollars."

"That seems like a reasonable investment for a four-million-dollar coin," I said.

"Sure, but two dollars here and three dollars there and suddenly you're hundreds of dollars into the game and no closer to finding a coin. That's another reason the Internet is going crazy. Some people have spent thousands already. And they are *pissed*."

I wondered if Tommy had realized there would be this kind of hostility toward how the game was played. I wondered if he and S had argued about it.

"Some people are forming alliances, trading charts and maps and codes, but it's hard to trust someone you meet online when there's four million dollars at stake," Brandon said glumly.

"I would imagine so. Do you think the game's making any profits so far?"

My teenaged employee gave me a look that implied I was an idiot. "Only about fifty million dollars."

"What? How do you know that?"

He shrugged. "Everyone knows. Just look at the stats."

There were very few things I wanted to do less than look at the stats. "Still, if all five coins were found today that would be twenty million they'd have to pay out."

"Sure," Brandon agreed.

"And if it goes on much longer, with nobody finding a coin and the payout ticking up by five million dollars a day…"

Suddenly he looked interested. "And if at the same time the payout is adding up, people are getting discouraged and giving up..."

"This could be a disaster," I finished.

Brandon stared at me. "No way." He shook his head. "S is a genius. *Was* a genius. There must be something we're missing."

"Maybe they assumed the coins would be found more quickly?" I guessed. "So the payout would be smaller?"

"But you wouldn't really want that," Brandon countered. "You'd want it to last long enough to build momentum. S's last game was an international phenomenon. That doesn't happen in just a couple of days."

"That was the game with the space monsters?" I asked.

He nodded.

"Did that one have an ending?"

"Sure, you had to find them all and blast them, so the human race could survive."

"But every player found their own monsters, right? I mean, if I downloaded it a month after you'd finished, I could still play."

"Sure," he said. "Or I could play again. The game would be different every time."

"Which isn't the case with this game," I said. "In this game there are only five coins, and everyone's playing the same game, or at least they're all in the same world at the same time, right?"

He nodded.

"What happens when the coins are all found?" I asked. "The game is over, right? Nobody else will play it, or keep playing it, because why would they? There's no more point. The revenue would dry up instantly."

"Unless there's another release or something?" Brandon asked. "I mean, there'd have to be, right? An expansion? A way to level up or something?" For the first time he looked doubtful. "Right?"

"Maybe." Or maybe Tommy had realized that S Banks's game could bankrupt him.

*   *   *

"I was so right!" Callie announced, barging into my office later that day.

"I never doubted you. Right about what?" I hung up the phone. I'd been talking with Lisa from the café across the street about the dessert table she'd be setting up for the midnight movie that night. The movie was *Desk Set* (1957, Katharine Hepburn and Spencer Tracey), one of my favorites, and we expected a big turnout.

"S Banks was totally a paid promoter for Lyquid." Callie flopped into one of the chairs facing the desk.

It took me a minute before I got it. "The smoothie? The thing he drank onstage?"

She nodded. "The Internet is losing its mind."

The Internet was doing that a lot today.

"There's a rumor going around that something in the drink killed him," Callie went on. "People are demanding a recall. They're saying it's tainted."

"Is that true?" I opened my laptop and started typing in a search.

"Who knows? The point is, I *knew* he wouldn't have taken a drink on camera like that if he wasn't paid to. What?"

I'd stopped mid-type. "If he was paid to take a drink onstage," I said, figuring it out as I spoke, "people must have known he'd do it. At least some people."

"I mean, okay..." Callie said.

"And if one of those people wanted to poison him..."

Her eyes flew open. "Omygod! Do you think that's how Tommy did it?"

"That's how I would have," I said. "Not that I would have," I amended.

"I mean, sure," Callie agreed.

"The question is, would Tommy have known S was going to drink from that bottle onstage?"

"How do we find out?"

Which is when I noticed the headline that had popped up on my newsfeed.

"What?" Callie asked, seeing the look on my face.

I turned the computer screen so she could see it.

"Tech entrepreneur Tommy May released on bail as police follow multiple leads," she read. Her eyes widened and she stared at me. "Sooooo...he didn't do it?"

I stared back at her. "That's one question. Here's another: If he didn't do it, who did?"

I didn't have time to think about S, Tommy, motives, or games for the rest of the day. We were going all-out for the *Desk Set* midnight movie party, our grand finale to Technology Week, and there was a lot involved. Most of the movie takes place in the reference department of a media conglomerate on the cusp of computerizing, so our decorations were obvious but detailed. I had to trail a fake philodendron across the balcony landing. I had to haul an old metal desk up from the basement and arrange a rotary phone and a rolodex on it. I had to position a water cooler at the end of the concessions stand, and litter the lobby with reference books and pencils.

We were going to hold a Reference Desk Trivia quiz from the stage before starting the movie, and in addition to the usual popcorn and candy, a food truck parked outside would be selling fried chicken—a nod to the dinner Katherine Hepburn cooks for Spencer Tracy one rainy night. Lisa would be serving her goodies from a stand in the lobby.

One of Callie's film student friends with a passion for set design had used cardboard and aluminum foil to construct a surprisingly realistic replica of the film's EMERAC computer. It even lit up and made a boop-boop-be-do sound that made me happy every time it went off. My only regret was that my budget didn't extend to costumes. I would have worn the hell out of that swing coat Hepburn bought for herself. I made do with a pencil skirt and twin set that I found in Robbie's closet in the big house. At the last minute I twisted my hair up and stuck a pencil in it.

We expected a good crowd. Not only was it a great movie, but our Friday night parties were starting to become a cool local thing. Which is just what I'd hoped and worked for.

I got nonstop texts starting at about five. Monica said she was going to be there, and she was bringing both Abby and her salesperson Kristy. Bringing Kristy had been my idea. I hadn't managed to talk to her earlier in the day, and I hoped I'd have a chance that night. I wanted to know how friendly she'd gotten with S the day before he died.

Another text, from Hector, let me know that he and his cousin Gabriela would be coming, so I put a "reserved" Post-it on the seat next to the open space in the back row where her wheelchair would fit. My phone pinged regularly with incoming updates from friends, customers, and vendors, so when I got a text from a number I didn't recognize I didn't think twice before clicking it.

I'm sure you heard I've been released, but the cops are still coming after me. We need to talk. I've sent a car to pick you up. I need your help.

It was from Tommy.

Tommy needed my help? Why would he ask for *my* help?

I looked up from my screen to the rush of activity all around me, everyone making the last preparations before the doors opened at eleven. Then I looked at the text again and registered something. Tommy hadn't asked for my help. He'd expected it.

That expectation felt horribly familiar. This text from Tommy was insanely similar to the "I need you" note I'd gotten from Ted.

The adult and rational part of my brain knew that Tommy wasn't Ted, but his attitude was identical. He needed something, and his need was the priority. Of course he expected me to drop everything to show up for him. People probably did that every day of his life. And maybe I would have too, once. But I wasn't that person anymore. I blew out a breath and replied.

I'm working. If you need to see me tonight, you can find me at the Palace.

Desk Set
1957

Yes! I've wanted to write about this one for so long. I know I say this a lot, but I LOVE this movie!

You have to understand. For so many years I wanted to work in the Reference department of a massive New York broadcasting company, and I wanted Bunny Watson to be my boss. I wanted to be excellent at something interesting, surrounded by clever, fun colleagues who all like each other. I've grown up a little since then, but not that much. I'd still kill to work for Bunny Watson.

For those of you deprived individuals asking, "Who's Bunny Watson?" I give you Katharine Hepburn at the perfect point in her career. She was forty-nine when she made this film. No longer the effervescent young thing of her early screwballs, not yet the arch dowager she'd become. She's the Katharine Hepburn who knows who she is and likes it. She trusts herself. And in this movie, as Bunny Watson, she's simply a joy. She's a rare tropical fish, and you'll know what that means when you see the movie.

Okay, so what's it about? It's about the modern American workplace (circa 1957) and how people like the girls in Reference were worried about being put out of their jobs by a computer. Ah, technology! It's always been a love/hate relationship. We love the flashing lights and beeping noises, we hate the idea of it being better than us.

Let me start with some history. Before there was the

Internet, there was the Reference department—a room full of books and smart women. When anyone wanted to know anything, they called the girls in Reference to find out.

The Reference department we're concerned with here is part of the Federal Broadcasting Company, a fictional TV network. We meet the three women who work there as they answer the near-constantly ringing phones. "Reference Department, Miss Costello, Miss Blaire, Miss Saylor..." This is where all the single ladies work. Played by Joan Blondell, Dina Merrill, and Sue Randall, they also talk about clothes, give unsolicited dating advice, and loan each other money. Have I mentioned how much I wanted to work there?

Overseeing this bookish paradise is Bunny Watson (Hepburn) the best boss ever. She sweeps into the office with a breezy "Morning kids, wait till you see what I snagged at Bonwit's." (That's a now-defunct department store.) She's been shopping, yes, but she also worked until ten the night before and was over at IBM for an early meeting to look at their new computing machine. Work/life balance? Bunny Watson invented it.

She's also dating her boss. I know, I know, but it wasn't considered squicky then. The only negative about it seems to be that they've been seeing each other for seven years and she still isn't sure if he's going to ask her to the big dance. Bunny! You can do better!

The boss in question, Mike Cutler (Gig Young, being exactly what you want Gig Young to be), drops in to see Bunny in her office and when he goes in for a kiss she slips out of his grasp and reminds him that everyone can see therm. "Who do you think you're kidding? Everyone knows you haven't got a brain in your head," he says. "The only way you keep your job is by being nice to me." He's kidding, and she laughs, but still. Ouch. She needs someone who's going to admire her intelligence, not undercut it. Cue Richard Sumner.

Sumner (Spencer Tracey. Did I not mention this is a Hepburn and Tracey movie? In Cinemascope? And color? It totally is! Why aren't you watching it right now?!) is a "methods engineer" which is sort of an "efficiency expert." These days we'd call him a consultant and we'd be just as nervous about him showing up as the girls in Reference are.

When the big wig's secretary calls to warn the girls that Sumner is on his way, she describes him as "Some kind of a nut, I think, or somebody very important. Probably both." She's right. He's just installed a machine down in payroll, and now he's brought his tape measure to Reference. This can't be good.

The scene where Sumner interviews Bunny is often trotted out to illustrate the magic that happened between Tracy and Hepburn. With good reason. He's gruff and businesslike as he presents her with a series of brain teasers. She's engaged, intelligent, and completely self-possessed as she answers them. She's used to being evaluated by men. When she gets the first question right he stares at her in surprise. "That's correct." She doesn't blink an eye. "Yes, I know."

That "Yes, I know" was a radical statement. She didn't dumb herself down to make the man feel good. She didn't apologize for surprising him with her intelligence. Have I made it clear yet that Bunny Watson was and is a role model? And, thank heaven, Sumner agrees. By the time they're finished he's looking at her with a sort of delighted appreciation. Yes! Remember that the next time your boss/boyfriend asks you to proofread his presentation, Bunny.

But Sumner is also there to ruin everything. One of the girls, Peg (Joan Blondell, in what may be my favorite Joan Blondell role ever) has found out that he's there to install one of his EMERAC machines in Reference. (EMERAC stands for Electro-Magnetic Memory and Research Arithmetical Calculator. Weren't computers fun?) "He's trying to replace us all with a mechanical brain!" Peg wails. "That means the end of us all!"

Events unfold. Cutler goes out of town instead of taking Bunny to the dance one rainy night, and Bunny ends up caught in the rain with Sumner. She invites him up to her place to have dinner and get dry. What follows is an innocent evening of fried chicken in bathrobes. But when both Cutler and Peg show up it turns into something else. It turns into comedy perfection. If you don't laugh out loud by the end of this scene, when both Bunny and Peg are collapsed with laughter, I really have to give up all hope for you.

There's also a company Christmas party that makes me wish I could teleport back to 1957 just for the holidays. There's something completely magical about Bunny and Peg getting squiffy on champagne together before the gang from Legal shows up with hooch and a piano. (BTW, I've worked a lot of different places, and the gang from Legal has yet to show up with hooch and a piano. Sigh.)

How will it all work out? Will Sumner's computer be the death of Reference? Will Bunny wise up and give Cutler his marching papers? Will it all work out for these crazy kids? Watch the movie and find out!

Screenwriting DNA:
Phoebe and Henry Ephron wrote the script here. If their last name sounds familiar it's because they're Norah's parents. And I swear you can tell. The back-and-forth between Hepburn and Tracy contains DNA for some of Norah's best scenes. When Tracy looks at a tipsy Hepburn and says "There's something about the way you wear that pencil in your hair that spells money" you can almost hear how Tom Hanks would say it to Meg Ryan.

And the award for most Katharine Hepburn line goes to...
In the scene where Cutler discovers Bunny and Sumner hanging out at her place in bathrobes, he simmers for a while before finally saying, "You know, being this civilized is ridiculous. I mean this looks fairly primitive to me. Unless of course there's some other explanation." Whereupon Bunny, with perfect patrician pronunciation, asks, "Other than what?" Only Katharine Hepburn could have given those three words the kind of emphasis that crystalized Bunny's entire personality. So. Damn. Good.

The Clothes!
OMG the clothes in this movie. Would it be worth it to go back to a time when the "girls" were in Reference and Legal was "all men" just for the opportunity to wear the sweater sets, circle skirts, and swing coats these ladies have on? It would not. Of course not. Still, if costume designer Charles LeMaire had set out to make a case for women getting careers in Manhattan, he could not have

made a more compelling argument. And I still want that red swing coat with the green lining that Hepburn wears in the Christmas party scene. Do you hear me, Charles LeMaire? I want that swing coat!

Movies My Friends Should Watch
Sally Lee

CHAPTER 12

There's an old Hollywood truth about how you succeed in show business: give the people what they want. It was clear by the line stretching down the block from the Palace doors that the people wanted Tracy and Hepburn.

"I didn't realize there were this many pencil skirts in the city," Callie said when I went to check on the ticket booth. She was wearing a severe gray suit with cat-eye glasses, her hair pulled ruthlessly into a low chignon. "Or fedoras."

"Everyone's here tonight," I said, mentally running the numbers on how much all those lovely ticket sales would amount to.

"So, like, about that..." She shot me a glance while outside a customer fumbled for his credit card. "My parents said they're coming, and you're literally forbidden from talking to them." She gave me her strictest look, which the glasses helped.

I grinned at her. "It's hilarious when you tell me what to do." Then I caught sight of Hector and Gabriela about ten people back in the line. "I'll see you later." I backed out of the little booth, saying one more thing just before I closed the door. "And I'll see your parents, too."

I ushered Hector and Gabriela into the lobby, bypassing the ticket booth. "People who fix the theater's Wi-Fi get in for free," I told Gabriela when she protested. I was a little guilty that she'd become our unpaid computer troubleshooter in the last few months, but I'd get over it. I knew it would have cost a fortune to pay someone for the sort of thing she was happy to do while chatting about Ginger Rogers between the seven-thirty and the nine-fifteen.

Gabriela was wearing a skirt and soft sweater in shades of gray-blue. She never let her chair get in the way of her fashion sense. Her long dark hair was pinned under to look like a classic fifties wave, and her lipstick was Technicolor red. "Okay, but what about him?" She nodded toward Hector.

"He fixes other things," I told her, looking at her cousin.

Hector hadn't attempted a retro costume, which wasn't a surprise, but it was a shame. I'd spent a few moments in the shower that morning imagining him in a gray flannel suit with his hair combed back away from his face. But tonight he wore his usual impeccable jeans with buttery soft leather jacket. His hair, as always, was perfect. "Anything you need," he said quietly.

It took a moment for me to realize Gabriela had spoken again.

"Nora, I think that guy is trying to get your attention." She waved at someone a few paces away to my left.

Hector and I both looked. "Detective Jackson," Hector said, in a tone that fell short of welcoming.

The detective was looking in my direction and nodded when we made eye contact.

"Why don't we go get some cookies or something," Hector said to Gabriela, gesturing toward Lisa's station. "Nora has work to do."

"I'll see you in there," I said as they moved away.

"I'm counting on it," Hector replied.

I worked my way through the crowd to the detective. "Tommy May has been released?" I greeted him.

"Hello to you, too." His deep voice was easy to hear above the increasing din in the lobby.

"Hello," I said. "What happened? What have you heard?"

Of course he didn't answer. Instead he turned my question back on me. "What have you heard?"

I opened my mouth to say "nothing" before realizing that

wasn't exactly true. "He sent me a text."

The detective's eyebrows raised at the same moment the EMERAC machine made its boop-boop-be-do sound. A cheer went up.

I answered over the noise. "He said he wants my help."

Judging from the look on his face, it took considerable self-restraint for Jackson to withhold his opinion on that.

"I know, I know," I said. "I have no idea why. It wouldn't break my heart to see him in jail for the rest of his life, but he said he was sending a car for me to go down to Palo Alto tonight."

Jackson gave me a sharp look. "Are you going?"

"Of course not." Then, "Should I?"

I expected him to come back with something standard about staying out of it and letting the police do their jobs, but he hesitated.

I looked at him more closely. "Do you want me to?"

The detective looked distinctly uncomfortable.

"You do!" I stared at him. "Why...?" And then I got it. "You want me to tell you what he says."

Jackson cleared his throat. "I would never ask you to do that."

"Right." I nodded. "You never would." But that didn't mean he wouldn't listen if I found something out.

"Are you going?" Jackson asked.

"How can I with all this?" I made a gesture that took in the increasing madness in the lobby. People were lined up to take selfies at the old-fashioned desk. Brandon and our other two high-school staffers, Claire and Mike, were selling popcorn, candy, and drinks as fast as they could. Albert was greeting everyone who came through the lobby doors like they were lifelong friends, while subtly keeping everyone moving in the direction of the concessions stand or Lisa's dessert table. And Trixie was scampering around waving and...wait. *Trixie?* What was she doing?

"What about going to see him in the morning?" Jackson asked.

I gave him a blank look. "Tommy May," he reminded me.

"Right. Tommy. I told him if it was urgent he should come

here tonight."

"*Here?*"

I grinned, moving away from the detective, heading toward Trixie. "Fasten your seatbelt," I said over my shoulder. "It's going to be a bumpy night." Which was not a line from *Desk Set*, but it seemed to fit the occasion.

"Trixie." I kept my voice low. "How are you? What are you doing?"

Trixie usually didn't hang around for the midnight movie parties. There was too much commotion. Mainly she just flitted into view now and then, here and there, like something you see out of the corner of your eye. Like a ghost.

And since she was a ghost I motioned for her to follow me out of the busy lobby. I could mutter one or two things in the mix of the crowd, but for a conversation of any length we'd need some privacy. Because I'd hate to be hauled away by those nice gentlemen in the white coats before Reference Desk Trivia even started.

She followed me into the stairwell of the employee stairs. "Are you okay?" I asked her when I'd closed the door. "You don't usually like crowds."

"I don't," she agreed. "Everybody's always walking through me and yelling in my face without knowing it, and not seeing me no matter how hard I try. It's—" She shivered. "It makes me feel even more like a ghost than I normally do, if you know what I mean."

"I hadn't thought of it like that." I forgot, sometimes, that however much Trixie bubbled with excitements and interests, she had a very lonely existence.

She must have seen a look on my face because she waved her hands. "Oh, I don't really mind. It's just that tonight I thought I'd give it a try—being seen, or felt anyway." She straightened her shoulders. "The way I figure, the more people I try with, the more chances I have that someone might notice me—like Callie's mother did that one time, remember? Maybe there are other people like her, who can just sort of tell when I'm around. Don't you think?"

She bit her ruby red lip, her eyes wide with hope.

"Of course I think. There's no way to know without trying. But listen, I've got good news. Callie's mom is going to be here tonight."

Lillian Gee had visited the theater not too long ago. She considered herself sensitive to the spiritual world, which would have caused massive eye rolling if I'd met her before Trixie. Now I knew better. The fact was that Lillian had felt cold when Trixie hugged her. It wasn't much, but it was something.

"Really?" Trixie clasped her hands together. "Oh, Nora, do you think she'll sense me again?"

"There's only one way to know." I opened the door.

"Gee, I can't wait. I'm going up to the balcony landing where I can keep an eye out for her." She shimmered back into the crowd. "I just have a feeling that good things are going to happen tonight."

She couldn't knock wood, but as I closed the door, I did.

I spotted Detective Jackson, head and shoulders above most of the customers, moving toward the balcony stairs. I assumed he planned to watch the movie with Marty from the projection booth. I was just wondering how comfortable the large detective would be in the small crowded room when I realized Hector had come over to join me.

"Where's Marty tonight?" he asked.

"Upstairs. I've banned him from human contact at these things ever since the lollipop incident with *Some Like It Hot*." I gave him a significant look. *Some Like It Hot* (1959, Tony Curtis, Jack Lemmon, and Marilyn Monroe, who always got the fuzzy end of the lollipop) had been our Valentine's Day midnight movie a few weeks ago.

Hector winced at the memory of the lollipop incident.

"Where's Gabriela?" I asked him. At some point I wanted to ask her opinion about an app for the Palace.

"She invited some friends from work," he said. "They're already in the theater, strategizing for your trivia game."

"Did someone say 'trivia'?" Monica had arrived without me noticing. She was wearing her usual workout clothes and was accompanied by a young woman in shorts over tights and a sweatshirt bearing the logo of the Potent Flower, Monica's shop. "Because I'm the worst at trivia," Monica said. "But I'm really good at eating popcorn while other people play."

I hugged her in greeting and Hector leaned down to give her a peck on the cheek.

"You must be Kristy," I said to the young woman, assuming she was the sales assistant who had spent so much time with S the day before he died. "Welcome to the Palace."

"This is so cool," she said, looking around. "Is it like this every night?" She was probably in her early twenties, tall and willowy, with shoulder-length lavender hair and striking green eyes. It was no surprise S had been taken with her. She seemed like a geek's dream girl.

"Not exactly," I admitted. There were more people in the lobby at that moment than had been in the theater for the past week. Unfortunately, that meant there were really too many people around for me to have the kind of conversation with Kristy about S that I wanted to.

I was just trying to figure out how I could whisk her away somewhere quiet for a moment when we were joined by Monica's custom-blend supplier, Abby.

"Here you are." She was wearing jeans and an olive green jacket with dozens of pockets. She hugged Monica, then Kristy, then me in quick succession. "This place is amazing! And I just love *Desk Set*, but you can keep Tracy and Hepburn. For me it's all about Joan Blondell."

"You're a woman after my own heart," Hector said.

I couldn't help noticing that Abby gave him the same sort of look most women give him upon first meeting. Something like the look Audrey Hepburn gives Cary Grant at that ski resort in *Charade* (1963, Cary, Audrey, and Paris). It's a look that says "Yes, please," and it seems to be largely involuntary. I blame his hair.

He smiled and Monica introduced them as I checked my watch. I was supposed to be onstage in ten minutes to start the trivia.

I scanned the crowd. There was no sign of Tommy. Of course there wasn't. Aside from the fact that he probably wouldn't dream of going to see someone at their convenience rather than having them come to him, he was out on bail facing a murder charge. He might not even be allowed to leave his house.

I was just taking a moment to enjoy the thought of him wearing an ankle monitor when I glanced up at the balcony landing and saw Trixie waving furiously at me. She pointed to of the bottom of the stairs, yelling "Callie's mother!" Then she fizzled out of sight.

Reference Desk Trivia might have to wait.

CHAPTER 13

"Nora! How wonderful!" I was swept into the embrace of a middle-aged Latina whirlwind as soon as I was within her range.

"Mrs. Gee, it's so good to see you." The crowd at the bottom of the stairs broke around us, everyone heading in to find seats.

"Call me Lillian, please." She beamed at me, and I realized she was wearing a perfect replica of the Katharine Hepburn coat I'd lusted over. Of course she was.

"Lillian, you look amazing." She was the source of Callie's wild curls, but tonight she'd tamed her own with a chic chignon. She did a little twirl and struck a pose just as Trixie popped into view behind her.

"Do you think she'll feel me again?"

"Nora, dear, I'd like to introduce you to my husband." Lillian reached for the arm of a compact Chinese man in a timeless gray suit who stood on the first step of the stairs.

"Here goes." Trixie wrapped her arms around Callie's mom in a full-body hug.

Lillian stilled. She'd been looking up at her husband, but now she turned wide eyes to me. "She's here!" she announced in a thrilled voice. "I can feel her!"

"It's working!" Trixie squealed.

"Now, dear..." Lillian's husband had come down the stairs and was giving her the kind of look that usually accompanies a husband saying "Now, dear..."

Trixie nestled her head on Lillian's shoulder in contentment.

"Dr. Gee." I extended my hand. "I'm so pleased to finally meet you. Callie's told me so much about you." Callie had told me exactly two things: that he was a doctor and that I would never meet him.

"Er, hello." He nodded perfunctorily in my direction, his attention on his wife.

Lillian had a faraway look in her eye, as if she were communing with the spirit world. Which she was, in the form of the blonde bombshell currently draping herself around her like a boneless cat.

Then she focused on me. "Nora, we absolutely must hold a séance," she said. "I insist."

Her timing was terrible, because Monica, Abby, and Kristy had just caught up with me. They heard what Lillian said and they were all immediately on board with the notion of trying to raise the ghosts of the Palace.

The ghost of the Palace was equally taken with idea.

"Nora, please," Trixie pleaded, her arms around Lillian. "I've never been to a séance."

"Um..." I said, brilliantly.

"I don't think—" Dr. Gee began.

"Come on," Monica encouraged. "It'll be fun."

I wasn't so sure of that. On the other hand, it would drive Callie out of her mind when she found out, and that was always entertaining.

"Nora?" Trixie's blue eyes were huge and pleading.

I couldn't say no.

"Sure," I agreed. It might be crazy, but it also might help Trixie. "If you really want to. Let's do it Monday, when the theater's closed."

I left Dr. Gee rubbing his forehead like a man resigned while the rest of them all started planning the séance. I had to get to the stage. Reference Desk Trivia could wait no longer.

It was close to three in the morning by the time I locked up the Palace. The moviegoers were gone, the cleanup was over, we'd all basked in the glory of a successful event, and I'd declined Hector's offer to come back and give me a lift after he took Gabriela home. I'd wanted to be alone. I usually do after a big social thing. Walking the few blocks back to Robbie's guest house in the quiet of the wee small hours sounded like just what I needed.

What I did not need was to open my office door, intending only to grab a jacket and my bag, and instead find a man snoring on the couch.

I yelped in surprise and he stirred but didn't wake. He was splayed face-up, wearing jeans, a t-shirt, and a hoodie, with a baseball cap lowered to cover most of his face.

Most, but not all. Once I got over being startled, I recognized him. About fifteen options flitted through my mind, from turning around and leaving him to calling the cops to whacking him with the nearest blunt object. I settled on going to my desk, sitting in my chair, and yelling at him.

"Tommy!"

He shot up to a standing position before he was fully awake, his hands held out, his whole body tensed. Then he registered where he was, saw me at the desk, and slumped.

"Nora. What the hell?"

"I could ask you the same thing. You may own a quarter of this place, but I wasn't aware that gave you napping privileges."

He sank back onto the couch, wiping a hand over his eyes. "You're the one who told me to come here."

"I didn't mean at three in the morning."

His eyes widened as he checked his watch. "I must have fallen asleep. God, I'm exhausted. This has been a nightmare." He passed a hand over his face. He did look exhausted, his complexion tinged with gray beneath his out-of-season tan. "Where have you been?" he asked accusingly. "Didn't they tell you I was here?"

"Didn't who tell me? When did you get here?"

"Right before the movie started. You were onstage doing something, but Monica saw me. She was with those two women from her shop. And Callie absolutely saw me—she made me pay for a ticket!"

I bet she did. I really did love that girl.

"Well, I know you're here now." I wafted my hands. "I'm less sure of why. How do you think I can help you?"

He blinked. "I need coffee."

I might have taken him down to the excellent espresso machine in the lobby. But he didn't deserve excellent espresso. Maybe if he'd said, "Could I have a cup of coffee? or "Is there any coffee left?" But he hadn't.

"Let's go to the break room," I said. The coffee would be terrible.

Ten minutes later we were seated across the much-scarred table in the break room. This was not the first time I'd had a conversation with a rich, powerful, entitled man who assumed I existed to do his bidding. I'd been married to one. And I'd done a lot of negotiating with others of the breed in the years I'd spent in Hollywood. I'd found myself unconsciously slipping back into negotiation mode as we'd gone down the hall to the break room. My method was simple—I mentally put myself in charge. I gave myself all the power in the room. Lord knows they never would.

"Where's the agave nectar?" Tommy glanced around the kitchen. It had come as a shock to him that I hadn't made his coffee for him. Now he couldn't find an acceptable sweetener.

I passed him a box of sugar packets. "Our budget doesn't stretch to agave," I informed him.

He passed on the refined white sugar. He probably had a nutritionist who sampled his blood weekly for such toxins.

"Now," I said as Tommy winced at his first sip, "what do you think I can do for you?"

He took the baseball cap off and ran a hand through his already messy hair. "I need help," he said. "I've got the best lawyers and private detectives money can buy, but I'm not impressed with their results. I haven't had the bandwidth to pay much attention to what you do up here, but I know you've been involved in a couple murder investigations. I want you on my team. Maybe you can see something that the professionals don't. I can't afford to leave any options on the table." He looked at me. "My life is at stake."

I swallowed. As much as I hated that this man had threatened to close the Palace, it was hard to look him in the eye and hate a person who was asking for help. Even though he hadn't said anything like "Please help."

I looked at him, considering.

"Please," he said.

Ugh. Fine.

At least I'd satisfy my own curiosity.

"Did you kill S?" I asked.

"No!" Tommy seemed affronted at this most basic of questions. The best lawyers money could buy probably took a less direct approach.

"Why do the police think you did?"

He pushed the coffee cup aside. "I had opportunity—I was with him all morning before we went onstage. And they think I had a motive."

"Which was...?"

"Two things," he said. "One, everyone knew I'd had it with all of S's secrets. He really was the only person on the planet who knew how to find the coins. That wasn't a gimmick. But it went beyond that. S was the only one who fully knew how the game would evolve." He grimaced. "I had concerns about the game's profitability over the long term. He kept telling me to chill and trust him. And I couldn't argue with how much money his last game made, so I did trust him—up to a point. I mean, he said he had a plan, but we're talking about real money, and..."

"And you were already in financial trouble," I finished for him.

He looked startled.

"Why else would you care about the income from the Palace?" I reasoned. "It isn't hard to figure out that you're not swimming in millions anymore. What was the other thing?"

He opened and closed his mouth, struggling with what I'd put so bluntly. "Does everyone know I'm broke?" he asked.

"Apparently the police know," I said. "Which is enough.

What's the second motive?"

He blinked, still stuck on the fact that his secret was out.

"Tommy," I said sharply, "why else do the police think you killed him?"

"We argued," he said. "That morning, before the webcast. I found out he had this endorsement deal with some energy drink—"

"Lyquid," I said. "The thing he drank onstage."

Tommy banged the table in anger, and it occurred to me, probably a little late, that I was alone with an accused murderer in an empty theater in the middle of the night.

"We were launching a product." He stood so suddenly he knocked over his chair. "And the man was incapable of being professional for one goddamn morning!"

I put both hands flat on the table and leveled a look at him. "Calm down," I told him. "Or leave."

He hesitated, seeming surprised, then he swallowed, took a breath, and put the chair to rights. He sat, crossing his arms, his face clouded with anger. "The guy showed up high," he said. "I mean, everyone in the business knew about him, but I guess I was stupid enough to believe he'd show up just once—for arguably the most important event in his life—not completely stoned out of his mind. And then he tells me he's going to drink that stupid smoothie on camera."

"How much were they paying him?" I asked.

He glared at me. "A quarter of a million dollars."

Wow. I'd have to tell Callie. And maybe figure out how to get an endorsement deal.

I refocused. "So you argued about that," I said.

He scowled. "You might say we argued. Or you might say that I yelled at him and he smirked at me. The guy took nothing seriously."

I thought about the enraging power of a smirk. "I might have wanted to kill him, too."

"I didn't kill him," Tommy reminded me.

"Right," I agreed. "How do the police think you did it?"

He looked at me warily. "With poison, I guess. Isn't that what everyone says? Everyone thinks the poison was in that drink."

"Who's everyone?" I asked.

He looked surprised. "The Internet?"

Of course. "The Internet didn't arrest you," I informed him. "The police did. Have they tested the drink?" I remembered seeing a stagehand take it from S after he'd taken his lucrative sip on camera.

"My lawyers tell me tests take time." The tone of his voice communicated quite clearly that Tommy was not accustomed to waiting for anything. I felt an unexpected flair of solidarity with his lawyers.

I wondered if Detective Jackson would have access to the crime lab results when they came in. Probably. But that didn't mean he'd tell me. Particularly since all I'd be able to tell him in exchange was that Tommy was insisting on his innocence. Which wasn't exactly ground-breaking news.

Tommy leaned forward, cradling his head in his hands, his anger seemingly spent. His voice when he spoke was muffled. "Does everybody really know about the money?"

Naturally that's what he'd focus on. Never mind that he was facing a murder charge. "Not everyone," I said. "Probably not most of the people downloading the game."

He groaned. "I'm going to have to pull it." He looked up, reeking of self-pity. "That bastard completely screwed me."

I stared at him. "By getting murdered?"

He shrugged that detail off. "He's gone and I'm left holding the bag. I have no idea how long it will take to find those coins."

"And the payout goes up every day," I said.

"Don't remind me."

"Do you really think S had a plan?" I asked. "Was there another level or something?" Brandon had been speculating about it, but I hadn't really paid attention. "If there was, wouldn't S have written it all down somewhere? Aren't there technical documents or something? Especially since S smoked so much pot—wouldn't he have been afraid of forgetting his own brilliant idea?"

"We've been looking everywhere," Tommy said. "Nobody can find any plans. No specs, no schemas, no code. Whatever his plans were, they died with him."

Tommy's stupidity left me breathless. What kind of a person would jump into a business that seemed guaranteed to bankrupt him? How could he have had such total and blind faith in S? Was it arrogance? Had so many people told him he was a genius for so long that he actually didn't think he was capable of doing something so enormously stupid? Which is when it hit me.

"That's it," I said softly.

He gave me a bleary look. "That's what?"

"I think you might be protected by the enormity of your stupidity."

He flushed a lurid shade of purple. "What the hell—"

"Listen," I cut him off. "That's why you didn't do it. S had you hostage and you knew it. As long as he was the only one who knew how the game would play out, you needed him."

Tommy blinked, his mouth hanging open.

"You would never have killed him." I sat back. "Not with that much at stake."

His eyes widened. "Oh. My. *God!*" He leapt to his feet, sending the chair flying again. "That's it! That's my defense! Do you think the cops will buy it?"

"I don't see why not. I hate you and I buy it."

He stopped, staring at me. "You hate me?"

Whoops. I hadn't intended to say it, but now that I had... "You threatened to close the Palace. How do you expect me *not* to hate you?"

His jaw actually dropped. "I don't want to *close the Palace!*"

Like hell he didn't. "You said you did." Before I knew it I was on my feet, furious, facing him across the table. "You said it quite clearly at the owners' meeting."

He shook his head and waved his hands. "I didn't mean *close* close," he said. "I just said we should close it while we regroup."

"That's closing it!" I yelled. "What else does 'regroup' mean?"

"It means regroup!" he yelled back. "Explore strategic alternatives, pivot, something like—I don't know—filing for non-profit status."

I'd been on the point of calling him a very unoriginal name, but that stopped me cold.

"*What?*"

He took a breath. "If we can't make it profitable, we could re-incorporate as a non-profit so the owners can at least get write-offs," he said. "Nora. How could you think I wanted to close the Palace?"

I sank back into my chair. Was he telling the truth?

"Look," Tommy said, calming down, "I may not get up here much but trust me. I love the Palace."

"You—"

"Well, naturally he does," said a bright voice. "Everyone loves the Palace." Trixie winked into view and perched on the table. She looked from Tommy to me, smiling expectantly. "What did I miss?"

CHAPTER 14

I wrapped things up with Tommy soon after Trixie appeared. Not because he could see her, but because I was too tired and too frayed to continue a conversation with him while Trixie was around. Especially when I could tell she was bursting to talk to me.

I walked Tommy down to the lobby and sent him home with instructions to let me know what his lawyers thought of his new defense.

"I will, and..." He struggled with the next bit. "Thanks, Nora."

A thank you? From him? I was too shocked to respond.

The minute the doors closed behind him Trixie launched into an excited report of the plans she'd overheard for the séance.

Oh, right. I'd agreed to hold a séance.

"Lillian will be there and Monica and those two other gals who were with her—I didn't catch their names—"

"Probably Abby and Kristy," I said.

"Sure," she nodded, curls bouncing. "And Albert, and Hector and his cousin—"

"Gabriela," I supplied. I wondered how they'd even heard this thing was happening. Had Callie heard about it yet? Because I really wanted to see the look on her face when she did.

"Don't you think it's awfully nice of them to go to so much trouble to meet me when they don't even know me?" Trixie asked. "I mean—oh, you know what I mean. They know *about* me 'cause of the way I died and all, but they don't *know* me."

"It's awfully nice," I agreed.

"They don't even know I'm the only one. They think there are other ghosts hanging around, too. Like that showgirl everyone's always talking about from the old Vaudeville days, and even that fella who died right when you got here, remember him?"

"Vividly." I'd found the body of Hector's brother on my first day at the Palace. It wasn't something I was likely to forget.

Did Hector really think he'd be able to contact his brother from the misty beyond? Did Hector believe in ghosts? Because if he did...

"I hope they're not disappointed that it's just me," Trixie said, looking doubtful. Then she brightened. "Gee, I can't wait!"

"Trixie," I said. "I know you're excited, but maybe you shouldn't get your hopes up too much."

She waved her hands. "I know. Nobody else might be able to see me, no matter what kind of hocus pocus they do."

That raised some alarming questions in my mind. "What kind of hocus pocus are they planning?"

She shrugged, grinning. "Oh, candles and things. Between Lillian and Monica they had all sorts of ideas."

"I bet they did. Still..."

"I know, Nora." She sobered. "They probably won't be able to see me, and that's all right. It would be wonderful if they could, but just the fact that they want to is pretty darn great."

"It is," I agreed, wishing, not for the first time, that I could hug my friend.

As I finally walked home I gave thanks that Trixie hadn't shown up in the break room a few seconds earlier and heard me arguing with Tommy about closing the Palace for good. I couldn't imagine what the thought of that might do to Trixie, who seemed destined to spend the rest of eternity in the theater where she'd died.

I considered myself Trixie's caretaker. As long as I was able, I'd keep the Palace safe for her. But how long would I be able? The thing about eternity is that it's longer than one lifetime.

I didn't believe in séances, but I hadn't believed in ghosts before I'd met one. I wondered if Lillian, in all her metaphysical explorations, had ever come across a way to help a stranded ghost move on. It was something I hadn't really considered before. Trixie assumed she'd missed her one chance to go when she'd chosen to stay behind after her death. But what if there was another way?

I looked up at the sky, the stars dim in the dear-dawn light, and I did what I do best. I worried.

After a solid three hours sleep I woke to worry about something else. A text from Tommy.

The lawyers think the thing about S holding me hostage over the game is a good start for a defense. But what they really want is a plausible alternate theory. That means I need to point the finger at someone else. Meet me for breakfast. I got a suite at the Four Seasons. Let's brainstorm.

Typical. I'd handed him a nice little get-out-of-jail-free theory and now he wanted more. No, he *expected* more.

I did not reply. Instead I threw the covers off and fumed. Once again he expected me to drop whatever I was doing and come to him. At the Four Seasons, no less. Tommy and I had very different definitions of what it meant to be broke.

But as I showered and dressed, fuming gave way to thinking. And I thought the lawyers were right. The police were unlikely to give up on Tommy as a suspect unless they had a more promising line of enquiry. So I was back to the question I'd asked Callie the day before—if Tommy hadn't killed S, who had?

This was the kind of question best mulled over coffee. I was halfway to the kitchen before I remembered I was out. I cursed cruel fate and sent a text to Tommy.

I'll be at Café Madeline in ten minutes.

He could come to me.

*   *   *

"Coffee," I said pleadingly to Lisa when I got to the Café's counter. "Much, much coffee."

"Sit," she ordered, assessing me with a professional's eye. "I know how tired I am after last night, and you were still at it after I left. I can't imagine how you must be feeling. Why are you up so early?"

I didn't mind her question, since it was accompanied by her filling a giant cup and grabbing a chocolate croissant before steering me toward a window table.

I sat and took a restorative sip. "You are a goddess and I worship you," I informed Lisa.

"Sure. You and everyone else." She joined me at the table. "What's up?"

I took a deep drink before answering her. "I'm meeting Tommy for breakfast and brainstorming."

Her eyebrows went up. "Tommy who? Tommy May?" She lowered her voice, darting a look at the customers around us. "The guy who murdered his business partner?"

I took a bite of croissant and started to feel the tiniest bit awake. "He didn't do it," I said. "At least I'm pretty sure he didn't."

"Why are you even talking to him?" she asked. "I seem to recall you and Monica wanting to kill him a few days ago over something he said in a meeting."

Oh. Right. We'd talked about that at the very table where I now sat. "That may have been a misunderstanding," I told Lisa. "Either that or he's realized he has to change his mind about the Palace if he wants me to help him." I'm not an idiot—this thought had occurred to me. Was Tommy just manipulating me—telling me what I wanted to hear—to get my help now that he needed it? And if that were true, would I be able to count on him not changing his mind again once he was cleared?

I downed the rest of the coffee. "There's a lot I need to figure out," I told Lisa. "Thus, a breakfast meeting."

She nodded, then glanced at something out the window. "That has to be him now."

I looked out and saw a low-slung sportscar in the process of parking across the street. The car looked like the one James Bond drives, and it was parking illegally in the loading zone in front of the Palace, so I agreed with Lisa. That had to be Tommy.

I saw his silhouette in the driver's seat as he unbuckled his seatbelt. He took a long drink of something before opening the door. Probably an energy drink, but I'd bet anything it wasn't the brand S had endorsed.

"Why do people drink those energy drinks when there's coffee in the world?" I asked Lisa.

"Branding," she said. "I'll get you a refill and some menus." She left with a grin.

Tommy extracted himself from the car, and I noticed he didn't look for oncoming traffic before stepping into the street. I was mentally calling him an idiot when he staggered. He stopped in the middle of the street and shook his head, as if to clear it. Then he looked toward the café window, and our eyes met as he put a hand to his throat. An expression of panic flooded his face. He opened his mouth and said something, but I couldn't make out what it was. Then he fell to the street in a heap.

CHAPTER 15

Marty and Callie showed up for work to find me watching as the last of the police cars left, escorting the tow truck that took Tommy's car.

The police had come after I'd seen Tommy fall. After I'd run out into the street as Lisa called 911. After some other café customers had come to help. After we'd carried Tommy from the street to the sidewalk. After we'd realized that whatever help would come would be too late. Tommy was already dead.

Then the police, and a promise of more police to follow up later. I'd told no fewer than five officers exactly what I'd seen: Tommy had parked, taken a drink, left his car, died.

Callie and Marty ushered me into the theater and up to the break room. We were on our second pot of terrible coffee and about our hundredth possible theory of the crime by the time Albert arrived, accompanied by Hector.

"Look who I found outside," Albert said.

"I came as soon as I heard." Hector knelt by my chair. "Are you all right? Is it true? Is Tommy dead?"

"I'm fine," I told him. "I just can't believe it."

He gave me a searching look, then rose and turned to Marty. "What does Detective Jackson say?"

"Usually something about staying out of active investigations," Marty replied.

"They told Nora he'd be here later," Callie volunteered. She didn't look up from her phone. She'd been glued to her screen, following the news. "Meanwhile," she informed us, "the gamer blogs are on it."

"Oh, dear." Albert sat in the chair next to me. "I don't imagine that will be helpful."

"Actually, it might be," I said. "The reason Tommy was meeting me this morning was so we could come up with a plausible alternate theory of who killed S. Last night we figured out that Tommy had a good defense story, but his lawyers wanted to be able to point to someone else. Maybe the blogs will come up with someone."

"Space aliens, no doubt," Marty muttered. "Or women who don't want to sleep with them."

Hector was staring at me. "What do you mean you figured out Tommy's defense last night? And what do you mean you were meeting with him this morning? I assumed he'd just come to the theater looking for you this morning."

I shook my head. "We talked last night. He was waiting for me in my office after everyone left. Napping, actually. Callie, he said you sold him a ticket?"

"Damn right I did," she nodded. "No freebies for billionaires, isn't that our policy?"

"It is," I agreed. Even billionaires who might be down to their last couple million.

"Wait." Hector held up his hands. "You entertained a murder suspect here? Alone? In the middle of the night?"

Oh. That's what he was upset about. "Well..." Hector was looking at me with a mixture of fury and incomprehension. I blinked. "It's pretty clear now that he wasn't the murderer."

Hector let forth with a volley of Spanish that it's probably just as well I didn't understand. Callie, who spoke Spanish fluently, regarded him with raised brows. "I mean, wow," she muttered when he was done.

"Perhaps we could all calm down and agree that what's in the past is in the past?" Albert suggested mildly.

"Do we have to?" Marty asked. He was grinning, apparently enjoying someone else yelling at me for a change.

Hector glared at me in a way that clearly communicated we

weren't finished discussing this, as Albert gave Marty the kind of reproving look only available to ninety-something-year-old grandfathers.

I decided to ignore them all and turned to Callie. "What's everyone saying online?" I asked. "Isn't there some sort of theory about the wisdom of the crowd? What's the prevailing wisdom of the Internet?"

"I'm on it." She consulted her screen.

I drank some more terrible coffee, avoiding everyone's eyes.

"Here's one. This guy thinks a rogue game developer did it," Callie told us, scrolling. "Some mythical guy who's the 'real inventor' of all of S's games, who'd finally had enough." She made a face. "Or this one says that the whole golden coin thing was a hoax, there was never any money, and the players are now turning on S and Tommy."

"They turned on S before they ever saw the game," Marty reminded us. "How would they have known it was a hoax before it even launched?"

"Never let a fact get in the way of a good conspiracy theory," I replied.

Hector had poured himself a coffee and now joined us at the table, still not happy with me. There was something simmering behind his eyes, and it wasn't the good simmer that occasionally made me think dangerous thoughts. I re-focused on Callie.

"Here's one that says it's revenge for someone who died playing S's last game," Callie went on. "The thing where you chased the monsters. It says the father of someone who fell off a building while playing has gone all vigilante."

"Did that even happen?" I asked. "Someone falling off a building?"

"What did you just say about truth and conspiracy theories?" Marty asked.

"Good point. And anyway, the vigilante dad theory only explains why someone would have killed S. Tommy's partnership was after that monster game. He didn't have anything to do with it."

"Guilt by association?" Albert suggested.

"Or maybe the killer didn't plan to kill Tommy at first," Callie said. "But maybe Tommy saw something when S was killed. That would have made him, like, a loose end that the killer had to clean up."

"Are you sure you only want to make documentaries?" I asked her. "Because that's a nice little plot idea."

She shrugged.

"I suppose it's possible Tommy saw something," Albert said doubtfully.

"If he did, he'd have already told the police," I said. "At least, he'd have told them if he realized what he'd seen was important. If he realized it could clear him of suspicion." I shook my head. "Meanwhile, what I saw with my own eyes was Tommy drinking something in his car and dropping like a stone just a few seconds later. It was faster than the way S died. There were no spasms, or..." I shuddered, and Albert put his sinewy hand over mine. "But it sure looked like poison again."

"Perhaps a different kind?" Albert suggested.

"Or a different dosage," Marty guessed. "If it's a serial killer they may be refining their process. What?"

We'd all turned to stare at him. All except Callie, who was back on her phone.

"A serial killer?" I asked. "Are you really going there?"

He sniffed. "Ask me when the next tech guru is killed."

"Serial killer or not, the two deaths must be linked, don't you think?" Hector asked, finally deciding to get over himself and join the conversation.

"How could they not be?" I agreed.

"Here's another theory," Callie read. "Tommy killed S because he wanted control of the game, but then he couldn't control it, so he was going to pull it?" Her brow wrinkled. "I mean, I think that's what this is saying." She glanced up. "Online conspiracy theorists don't seem very concerned with, like, proper punctuation."

"Nutjobs, the lot of them," Marty muttered.

"Hang on—they're saying that Tommy was planning to end the game?" I asked Callie.

She nodded, focusing on the screen. "They think one of the gamers killed Tommy because he was close to finding a coin and didn't want the game shut down before he could claim the money." She blinked. "Does that make any sense?"

"Not to me," Hector said. "It assumes first that Tommy was going to shut the game down, second that this person knew about Tommy's plan, and third that this gamer decided to take the time to kill Tommy instead of just finding the coin and getting the money."

"That is a lot of assuming," Albert mused.

"It's right about one thing," I said. "Tommy told me yesterday that he was planning to shut it down."

"Seriously?" Marty asked.

"He felt like he had to. This is...what? Day five? So each coin is worth five million dollars? That's twenty-five million in payouts and it's still going up. I don't know the latest on how much the game has brought in so far, but I bet the gap between revenue and payout is getting narrower every day."

It was silent for a moment as we all mulled that over.

"I wonder what happens to all the money now," Albert said.

Hector put his cup down. "Surely Tommy's company is still responsible for paying the prizes, assuming the coins are ever found."

"Probably," I agreed. "I can't imagine his death would change that. The question is, will his company have enough money to pay the winners by the time there are any winners? And if they take the game down, will they be obligated to refund the money that people spent in it while they were playing?"

"Those are the kinds of question that makes me very happy I didn't go to law school," Hector said. "But it does seem that with Tommy's death the company now has an excellent excuse for calling a halt to the game."

"True," I said. "If Tommy had pulled it, I'm pretty sure the gaming world would have turned on him. But if the company does it now, saying it's out of respect for S and Tommy or something...or if they just come clean and say the details of the game died with its creators and they can't continue without them..."

"Except who at the company has the power to make a decision like that?" Marty asked. "Who's in charge of this thing?"

"Probably the person who killed Tommy," Callie said. When she realized we were all staring at her she put the phone down. "That isn't my theory, it's just swirling around online with the rest of them."

"It raises a good point, though," I said. "Who's in charge?" Then I was jolted with something that hadn't occurred to me before. "Ohmygod," I yelped. "Who owns Tommy's share of the Palace?"

"That's a very interesting question." An unexpected deep voice made us all jump. Detective Jackson was standing in the doorway. "And it's one my Lieutenant is asking as well."

Something in the way he looked at me, the seriousness, the purposefulness, made me very nervous.

Hector stood, facing him. "What are you saying?"

Jackson ignored him. "Nora, I need to speak to you privately."

CHAPTER 16

"Wait—what?" Marty looked from the detective to me and back again. "David! You don't think *Nora* had anything to do with anything?"

Jackson gave him an even look. "What I *think* is that Nora and I need to speak privately."

"Now, wait just one minute." Hector started for the detective.

I put a hand on his arm. "Stop. It's fine. I'm sure Detective Jackson just wants my opinion on everything. You know how he always wants my opinion." I grinned, but nobody was buying it, so I tried something else. "Everybody needs to get to work, anyway. We haven't even opened up yet."

Albert stood. "Come, everyone, let's get set up. The twelve-fifteen show must go on."

"I mean, that popcorn won't pop itself." Callie said lightly. But she looked worried. She knew what it was like to be questioned by the police.

"Right," I said. "Get to work."

They filed out, all except Hector. "I'll call you later," I told him.

He crossed his arms. "I'm staying."

This tendency to assume I couldn't take care of myself was one of Hector's few faults. "Fine," I told him. "Stay right here." I turned to the detective. "Let's go to my office."

"Tell me about last week's owners' meeting," Detective Jackson began.

My eyes widened. We'd gone to my office and I was seated at

my desk, Jackson in one of the guest chairs. This arrangement should have given me some sense of control, but it just made me self-conscious.

"What do you want to know?" I asked. "I told you all about it the other night." I'd shared a pizza with Jackson and Marty two nights ago, and I'd been pretty clear about my feelings toward Tommy. But Jackson had to know I'd just been blowing off steam. Didn't he?

"You told me a lot of things the other night," he said. "Among them was that you wanted to kill Tommy May." He looked at me expectantly.

I stared at him. "Well, I mean…you don't really think…" I couldn't even finish the thought. "Marty said the same thing!"

"Yes, but Marty was with me all last night and this morning when Tommy was killed. Was anybody with you?"

"No, I—" I couldn't believe he was seriously asking me if I had an alibi. This was crazy, and it was starting to get truly frightening, probably because of the little notebook Jackson had pulled out of his pocket. That little notebook told me this wasn't just a simple chat. That little notebook was for writing things down that a suspect said under questioning.

At least he hadn't read me my rights. Yet.

"You told me Tommy threatened to close the Palace," Jackson reminded me.

"That was a misunderstanding," I said. "Tommy and I talked about it last night. He said he hadn't made himself clear—that he wasn't arguing to close the theater for good, just for some financial restructuring, so we could become a non-profit or something."

The detective looked at me. "That's quite a misunderstanding."

I blew out a breath. "I know what you're thinking. Was that just something Tommy said to get me on his side because he wanted my help?"

"Was it?"

I blinked. "I suppose we'll never know."

Jackson wrote something. "You say Tommy wanted your help.

Did you help him?" The pencil remained poised over the notebook.

"I think so," I said. "I realized that he was the last person who would have wanted S dead because S was the only one who knew where the coins were and how the rest of the game was planned out. Tommy's whole business was in massive trouble without S. That seemed like a logical argument for his defense."

"So you parted on good terms last night?"

I'd said goodbye to Tommy at the lobby doors. "He thanked me," I said. "And then he texted me this morning asking for more help." Expecting more help.

"Which is why you were waiting for him at the café."

I nodded. Then I thought of something. "Who else knew he was coming to meet me?"

Jackson raised an eyebrow. "This is the part of the conversation where I ask the questions."

"Right." I nodded again. I felt like I was losing my mind. "What was your question?"

"Let's skip straight to the big one, for the record." He looked me in the eye. "Did you kill Tommy May?"

My jaw dropped. "Of course not!"

He wrote something.

"Are you kidding?" I sputtered. "You can't actually think—you know me!"

Jackson held up a hand, finished writing, and closed the notebook. When he looked back up something had shifted. "It's not about what I think or who I know. It's about being thorough and being able to honestly tell my lieutenant that I questioned you."

I blinked. "Then you don't think—"

"Nora." His deep voice rumbled. "You are just about the last person in the world that I can see doing violence to anyone. Anyone except that ex-husband of yours, anyway. Now if *he* ever shows up poisoned..."

I slumped back into my chair. "Thanks for scaring me half to death." Then I sat up. "Are you saying Tommy was poisoned?"

Jackson's mouth twitched. "And she's back." He tucked the

notebook into his pocket. "You know it's too soon to know definitively how Tommy May died."

"But S was poisoned," I reasoned. "And the deaths have to be related."

"The deaths don't have to be anything," Jackson said. "And I might as well tell you, since it will be announced at a press conference in twenty minutes, S might not have been poisoned. At least not intentionally."

"*What?*"

"He was killed by a reaction to bee pollen. Probably from that smoothie he drank on camera."

"Bee pollen? Are you serious? It wasn't murder?"

"I'm told people take it all the time. They say it increases energy, reduces inflammation—you know, all the usual claims the health nuts make with no actual proof."

Jackson wasn't exactly noted for his healthy lifestyle. It was one of the reasons he was perfect for Marty. Their preferred food pyramid had French fries at its base.

"Have you tested the smoothie?" I asked. "The energy drink? Did it have a massive dose or something? How much would it take to kill someone? Would you have to be allergic to bees, or would too much pollen kill anyone?"

Jackson just looked at me. I assumed we were getting beyond the scope of the announcement that would be made at noon. "We're in contact with the drink maker for their exact components," was all he said.

"Does that mean you didn't test the bottle S drank from?" I asked. My mind raced. "Does that mean the bottle is missing?"

Jackson's face was completely blank.

"You do still think it was murder, don't you? I mean, the police are still investigating it, right? They don't just think it was some sort of accident?"

"We might have, but now?"

I nodded. "Now that Tommy's been killed."

"Might have been killed," Jackson cautioned. "For all we know,

Tommy May might have died of an aneurism or some other perfectly normal—"

"Highly coincidental—"

"Tragedy," he concluded.

"Sure," I said. "But I bet he didn't."

After Jackson left I watched the press conference on my laptop, but didn't learn anything beyond what he'd already told me. I was gratified that a few of the reporters asked the same questions about bee pollen that I had. Also perversely gratified that the police didn't tell them anything more than Jackson had said. I could only assume that every bee expert in the country would be getting calls from reporters before the hour was out.

Once the twelve-fifteen was underway I made the rounds of the theater, reassuring everyone that Jackson and I had just had a nice quiet conversation, and that I wasn't in any imminent danger of being hauled off in cuffs in the back of a paddy wagon.

I sent a text to Hector, letting him know, then sent texts to Monica and Robbie, asking if they had any idea who would own Tommy's share of the theater now. They didn't.

This could get messy. How do we find out if Tommy had a will?

That was Robbie's question. I replied.

I know he had a team of lawyers working on the murder charge. I'll see if I can find out who they are and if they know anything about it.

Great. Just what I needed. More lawyers.

I locked up around midnight, setting the alarm before leaving through the lobby doors. Outside, a tiled walkway lined with movie posters led to the ticket booth at the sidewalk. Because I'd turned the lights off, the walkway was dim, the only illumination coming from the streetlights. But that was enough for me to make out a figure near the ticket booth when I turned around, a figure with something in their hand.

I'd just locked the door behind me. I made a fist around my keys. "Who's there?" I called, at the same moment the figure said, "It's just me."

Hector stepped out of the shadow of the booth. "Don't be frightened."

I sagged against the door. I hadn't realized how much adrenalin had flooded my system until I didn't need it anymore. "Why didn't you just come inside like a normal person?"

"I was going to come inside like a normal person, but I had to finish a call." He moved toward me, his phone in his hand. "I just hung up when I saw the lights go out and I thought I might frighten you if I was waiting right outside the door."

"Sure. This was much better." My heart was still racing. But it did that a lot around Hector these days, even without him lurking in dark walkways.

"I apologize," Hector said when he reached me. He cleared his throat. "And I also apologize for behaving like a testosterone-soaked caveman earlier today."

I looked up at him. "Where did you pick up that very apt phrase?"

He shrugged, and it may have been the shadows, but I swear he blushed. "Gabriela might have used it when I told her how we left off this morning, with you shutting the door in my face to talk to Detective Jackson on your own."

"Have I mentioned how much I like Gabriela?"

"You have. She likes you too. More than she likes me, at the moment."

"Don't worry. You have a way of redeeming yourself."

Our eyes met. It was dim and suddenly very warm in the

walkway.

"Um..." I said softly. "What are you doing here, anyway?"

"Um...What?" He'd gotten very close to me somehow. I could feel the heat of his body. "Oh." He took a step back, his face clearing. "I thought I might take you home." He held out his arm as if he were some rakish gentleman and I was a dowager duchess. "Unless you have any objections."

"Not a one."

When we got to the sidewalk I looked around. "Where's your car?"

"I know you prefer to walk."

So he walked me home to the little guest house, under streetlights that seemed just a bit more sparkly than usual.

We chatted about nothing for a few blocks. It wasn't until we were in sight of Robbie's house that Hector broached the subject of my talk with Detective Jackson. I filled him in.

"After he left, I realized how incredibly lucky I am," I told Hector. "I'd been researching poison online the morning before Tommy was killed. Suppose someone else had been on the case and had looked at my browser history or something?"

"Someone still might," Hector warned. "I won't feel you're safe until they've caught the real murderer."

"Thanks, that'll help me sleep," I said, wondering if I would look more or less guilty if I cleared my browser history. Probably more. "In any case, there might not be a murderer," I told him. "You heard about S and the bee pollen?"

"I did. What do you make of that?"

"I don't know what to think. But apparently the Internet has decided that S got a bad batch of that energy drink he endorsed," I told him. "Brandon brought me up to speed on the latest cyber gossip this afternoon. They're saying Tommy might have had a bottle from the same batch. Everyone's saying they should dump their drinks down the drain and sue the company."

"Is that what the police think?" Hector asked. "That it was just some sort of industrial accident?"

"The police aren't on social media," I told him. "At least I don't think they are. Personally, I think Tommy would have died of thirst before he'd ever take a sip of something that S endorsed. He was beyond furious that S drank the thing during the webcast."

"Tommy's death was different from the first one, as well," Hector said. "From what you saw I doubt he ingested the same thing as S."

Tommy's death. Had it only been that morning? I shivered.

"Are you cold? Take my jacket," Hector said, beginning to shrug out of his soft leather coat.

"I'm fine. And we're here." We'd just turned down the path alongside Robbie's house. Past the gate was the small yard and guest house.

"I still can't believe you met with that man alone last night," Hector said as I unlatched the gate. I'd been wondering how long it would be before we'd return to that touchy subject. "I know, you're a sensible adult woman who can take care of herself," he said, sounding like he'd memorized the phrase, "but it still makes my blood burn to think of you taking that risk. For all you knew he was a murderer."

"I honestly didn't even think about that," I said, choosing to omit the moment when Tommy had lost his temper in the break room and I'd very much thought about that.

"That doesn't make me feel any better," Hector grumbled. "You being oblivious to a risk doesn't make the situation any less risky."

"*Oblivious*?" I flared. "If that's what you think—"

"I think you take too many chances," he cut my protest off, his voice raised. Dim safety lights blinked on when we entered the yard. They provided just enough light to see that Hector was simmering again, and not in a good way. "How many more close calls do you have to have with potential murderers? How many more times do you think—"

"He wasn't a murderer!" I protested loudly.

"You didn't know that!" he shouted.

"Neither did you!" I yelled. "And who says you get to be the one who gets to say what's dangerous and what isn't? What—"

"I get to say what's dangerous because I understand danger! Because I've lived a dangerous life! I've seen things and done—" He cut himself off and looked at the ground, his jaw working. When he looked up and spoke again his voice was low and controlled. "I get to say because I know what danger is, and it isn't fun. It isn't adventurous, and it isn't exciting. It's just something that can get you killed." He gave me a look that shot straight through me. "I get to say because I care about you, and if you can't see that you're not very good at this detective thing."

I didn't think. I moved on pure instinct, wrapping my hand around the back of his neck and pulling him to me in a kiss that had been a long time coming. A kiss that sent hot sparks along every vein in my body.

Then I pulled away and looked up at him. "I care about you, too," I told him.

He hesitated less than a second before pulling me to him, melting me into another kiss, this one long and deep and insistent. I felt my feet leave the ground, and I didn't know if it was because he lifted me or because I was floating.

When he released me we looked at each other for a long moment. I was sure Hector could hear my pulse pounding. The neighbors could probably hear my pulse pounding.

Then something like coherent thought seemed to return to Hector's eyes. He blinked, and he swallowed, and without a word he turned and walked away.

CHAPTER 17

"That did *not* just happen."

I said it out loud as soon as I was inside the house.

"That could not have just happened."

But it had. After six months of simmering looks and undeniable attraction, Hector and I had shared a kiss. An epic kiss. A phenomenal kiss. The kind of kiss they make whole movies about. Good movies.

And then he'd walked away.

"Does every man on this planet exist just to drive me crazy?" I asked the empty room.

There was no answer.

There was, however, wine.

"Did you hear? Can you believe it?" Lisa greeted me when I staggered into a busy Café Madeline the next morning somewhat the worse for wear. Or, at least, somewhat the worse for having been passionately embraced and wordlessly abandoned, and having fruitlessly searched for an explanation in a bottle of merlot.

"Heard what?" I asked, not taking my sunglasses off. "And I can't believe anything, anymore."

She slid a hot mug of salvation across the counter toward me. "They just announced what killed Tommy," she said. "I heard it on the radio."

I drank deeply, afraid to ask. "Bee pollen?"

"Arsenic."

I took my sunglasses off and blinked at her in the bright

morning light. "*Arsenic?*"

"As in old-school, classic, straight-from-an-Agatha-Christie poison," she nodded.

"How?"

Our conversation so far had been at the counter, crowded with Sunday morning brunchers. Now she gestured toward our usual window table, where a young couple was just leaving. Once we sat she leaned forward. "It was in his orange juice."

"Orange—? Is that what he drank in his car?"

"Room Service at the Four Seasons confirmed that he'd ordered a large orange juice in a travel mug that morning," she nodded. "He must have taken it with him and not had any until he parked."

"The police tested it?"

"They must have, because the news said it was highly concentrated," she confirmed. "The arsenic, not the juice."

"No, I'm sure the juice at the Four Seasons is freshly squeezed," I said, a little dazed. Then I focused. "How did the poison get in the juice? Was the room service guy an assassin?"

"They didn't get into that on the radio." Lisa shrugged. "But can you believe it? Where do you even get arsenic these days?"

"I don't know." I had my phone in my hand before I thought the better of it. I put it on the table. "If I wasn't afraid my search history would be used against me, I'd look it up," I said.

"What do you mean, used against you? Nobody thinks *you*...?"

I gave her a look. "Yesterday was quite a day."

She regarded me for a moment, then flagged down a passing server. "Chip," she said, pointing to me, "the lady's going to need a caramel chocolate baby cake." She turned back to me. "Because I'm going to need to hear everything."

"Oh, Nora, you don't look so hot."

Trixie was waiting for me as I let myself into the lobby and turned off the alarm. I looked at my reflection in the glass doors and had to admit she wasn't wrong. I hadn't even bothered to pull my hair into a ponytail, and there were dark purplish craters under my eyes.

"If anybody ever offers you caramel chocolate baby cake for breakfast after you had wine for dinner," I advised her, "say no." I put the box with our daily order of cookies from Lisa's shop on the glass top of the concessions stand.

"Gee," she blinked. "Can I do anything for you?"

"Unless you've got a working time machine, probably not. But how about if you keep me company?" I said. "We can read all about Tommy's murder."

"Ooh! Are we going to investigate?" She scampered up the stairs beside me.

"Let's start with reading and take it from there."

"Why, anybody can get arsenic," Trixie said breezily. "Ask at the pharmacy. They don't keep it out on the shelves, but they have it behind the counter. Or you could just go to the five and dime and buy rat poison. That has arsenic in it."

We'd just spent an hour or so on the computer in my office, pouring over all the online reports about Tommy's death. The facts seemed clear: There were high levels of arsenic in the orange juice that Tommy drank in his car. At such a concentrated dose it would have taken effect almost immediately, resulting in the quick and dramatic death I'd witnessed. Where the arsenic came from, and how it had gotten into the juice, were unknown.

Which is why we were discussing where to get arsenic. Apparently in Trixie's day it had been easy as pie to pick up a little deadly toxin while running errands. I didn't have the heart to tell her there hadn't been a five and dime in the neighborhood for fifty years.

"Rules have gotten tighter about that sort of thing," I said instead. "But I've seen people get it in old movies. Didn't you have to sign a poison book or something, so there would be a record?"

"Sure," she nodded. "Just in case you were planning on taking care of your husband instead of the rats."

"Right," I said, thinking of my husband the rat. "It isn't that easy to get anymore."

She blinked. "Then how do you kill rats?"

"Um...traps?" I really didn't know. Maybe there just weren't as many these days. Maybe all the other poisons of modern life kept the population down.

"Talking of arsenic reminds me of my sister Betty," Trixie said, perching on the arm of the couch. "Isn't that funny?"

"You're not about to tell me your sister was a poisoner?"

"No, silly, she was a seamstress. And she never liked to work with green fabric because it was supposed to be bad luck. But *that's* because in the olden days—the Victorian times, you know—they used to use arsenic to color the fabric this really pretty green. Girls who worked in the mills used to die all the time from it, and it poisoned the ladies who wore green dresses and gloves, but they didn't even know why. Isn't that sad?"

"It's awful." I forgot, sometimes, how far removed Trixie's living years had been from mine. She was closer to the Victorians in their poisoned dresses than she was to the millennials who made popcorn at the Palace.

"Gee, I haven't thought about Betty in ages," Trixie said wistfully. Then, right about when my heart was aching for her, she shook herself and smiled brightly. "Anyway, I'm sure there's some arsenic around here somewhere. Why, we used to use it all the time for rats and mice."

"I sincerely hope it's long gone," I told her. Particularly if the police still suspected me of having anything to do with the murders. I'd hate to be caught with a cupboardful of vintage poison just lying around. Did arsenic go bad? That was probably another question I shouldn't have in my browser history.

We were just about to take a look at what wild stories the gamer blogs were spinning about Tommy's death when my phone pinged with an incoming message. It was from Callie.

Hey, Nora. I'm down in the prop room. Anything you want to tell me about this rack of fabulous gowns?

I looked up at Trixie. "Um, I'm going to need a minute."

"What do you mean you forgot all about them?"

I'd just told Callie how six famous gowns had found their way into our prop room last Thursday. And how that had slipped my mind.

"How could you forget you had Marilyn Monroe's 'Diamonds are a Girl's Best Friend' gown hanging in the prop room?" she demanded.

"Oh, I'm sorry," I bristled. "Little things like witnessing murders and being questioned by the police tend to be somewhat distracting."

"Sure," she said. "Except *Marilyn Monroe's gowns*!"

I saw her point.

"What about all the rest of it?" she asked, looking at the mess I'd made of unpacking all my other possessions the other day. "It looks like a tornado hit Saks Fifth Avenue."

Again, I saw her point. "I need to figure that out."

"You think?"

I perched on a table and took it all in. "I can't believe it's come to this."

Callie sat next to me. "Look. Your husband is shady AF, and it literally sucks that he took all your money, but...damn. Those are some gorgeous gowns."

"Gorgeous gowns I can't do a thing with," I told her. "I can't sell them, I can't even exhibit them, without proof of authenticity."

"And Ted didn't send that?" she asked.

"He just sent a note, saying he needs me," I said darkly.

"Oh," she said, then "Oooooh," as if she suddenly understood.

"Oh, what?"

"Oh, he's holding you hostage," she explained. "Or he's holding the gowns hostage." She waved her hands. "Either way. He said he needs you, right? I bet what he means is he needs you to do something for him. And I bet the receipts or whatever he has for the dresses are his leverage. You do him the favor and he gives you the stuff you need to be able to sell them, if that's what you want."

I stared at her. "You're right." How had I not seen it? "That rat! Why hasn't he told me what he wants?"

She shrugged. "Why wouldn't he just give you the money he owes you? Your man is shady."

"He's not my man." I reminded her as I pulled out my phone to send him a text. Then I changed my mind. Ted needed something from me. Something worth a substantial investment in Hollywood couture. Let him stew.

"Meanwhile..." Callie said.

I looked at the glittering rack. "Right. Meanwhile, I have no idea what to do with the gowns."

"The gorgeous, historically important, incredible gowns?" Callie said.

"Right, those." I'd swathed them in a clean sheet the other day before abandoning them, but Callie had removed it when she'd discovered them. They shimmered and glinted, winking at me. "Robbie told me I should call a museum."

"Never mind a museum." Callie typed something into her phone. "I'll ask my mom."

"Your mom? Is she a collector?" Nothing about Lillian Gee would surprise me.

"She's more of, like, a wearer, but I know she gets her furs stored somewhere in the summertime." Realizing how that sounded, Callie shot me a look. "Yes, I said her furs. She lives in California and has furs. Do you have something to say about that?"

I gave her wide eyes. "Not a thing."

"That's right you don't." Callie nodded and went back to her phone. "I make her donate to PETA every year when she gets them out, but I can't stand it when other people, like, judge her."

"Mothers are complicated," I said, hoping to sound supportive.

"Don't let mine see these gowns," she warned. "She would literally insist on trying them on." She tapped something on her phone. "Done." My phone chimed with an incoming text. It was the address and phone number of a professional garment storage facility located South of Market.

"I should come to you with all my problems," I said. "Oh, can you ask your father if he knows an allergist, or where to get arsenic?"

She stared at me. "I'm going to need you to, like, explain a little."

I nodded. "S Banks died from bee pollen. I was thinking an allergist might be able to say how common that is, and how allergic a person would have to be to actually die from it, or how much pollen they'd have to be exposed to."

"Uh huh," Callie said, her face blank. "And the, um, arsenic thing?"

"Haven't you heard? Tommy was poisoned with arsenic in his orange juice."

She nodded, but her phone pinged with a text before she could answer. She read it, swore, then stood and faced me. "Don't freak out."

I'd have to remember how counterproductive those words were the next time I used them. "What's going on?"

"I mean, it's no big deal, but you might want to, like, take a step back from the murders for a while."

I had a very bad feeling about this. "What was in that text, Callie?"

"I mean, it's just Brandon. He's upstairs looking for you."

My eyes narrowed. "Why?"

"Um...because people are, like, saying you killed Tommy?"

"Oh, that." I waved my hand, relieved. "I told you Detective Jackson just had to ask me a few questions. He doesn't seriously think—"

"I don't mean Detective Jackson," Callie interrupted. "I mean, like, people."

I looked at her. "What people?"

She held up her phone. "*People,* people."

She meant the Internet. The Internet thought I was a murderer.

Notorious
1946

Why am I telling you to watch *Notorious*, out of all the Alfred Hitchcock movies out there? Ingrid Bergman, people. The glory that is Ingrid Bergman.

Bergman plays disgraced socialite Alicia Huberman, whom we meet outside the courtroom where her unrepentant father has just been convicted of treason. It's 1946 and he still thinks the Nazis were great guys. So, yeah, he's totally guilty. Alicia is as well, by association. At least that's what the world thinks.

And if the world is going to cast her as bad, she's going to live up to every bad thing it says about her. For example, on the night of her father's trial she throws a party, wearing an amazing midriff-bearing striped top and drinking to forget. She's sailing tomorrow, heading to Havana where with enough rum and the right parties she can forget it all.

But...there's a mysterious man. We see him only from behind. He stays late, drinking, and by the time the other guests have left we realize two things: She's hopelessly broken and he's Cary Grant.

Cary is a government man by the name of Devlin. Just Devlin. And when Alicia wakes up hungover the next morning, he tells her why he's there. "I've got a job for you."

It seems there are Nazis in post-war Rio. Since they

worked with her father they'll assume she shares his sympathies and welcome her (because it would never dawn on them that a woman could form her own opinions).

Faced with a choice between a yacht to Havana and a spy gig in Rio, she chooses Rio. She chooses America. Honestly, she chooses Cary Grant. And I ask you, who wouldn't? If a guy like that believes in you when nobody else does, you're going to do things for him. Dangerous things.

Once in Rio, Alicia gets an apartment and cuts back on her drinking. Eight days have passed and she's clearly trying to prove herself to Devlin. But she knows what he's thinking: "Once a tramp, always a tramp."

And she's right, because here's the thing—he believes she's a patriot, but he also believes she's a tramp. And this is going to play out for the rest of the movie. He admires her. He may even love her. But mostly, he judges her.

It kills Alicia that Devlin can't see how much she's trying to change. Finally, on a windswept hilltop, she confronts him. "You're sore because you've fallen for a little drunk you tailed in Miami, and you don't like it. It makes you sick all over, doesn't it?" He does the only thing he can think of to stop her (accurate) accusations. He takes her in his arms and kisses her. I get the feeling we missed a lot in those eight days.

But while these two crazy kids are trying to work things out, a room full of old white men back at Spy Headquarters are making plans to pimp her out. They don't just want Alicia to join the fun Nazi social whirl, they want her to seduce one guy in particular. And since she's already damaged goods, she shouldn't have a problem with that, right? Ugh.

Enter Alex Sebastian (Claude Raines, being his deliciously oily self). He's a German, working to build the Nazi war machine up again. Also, he has the hots for Alicia from the old days (In *Casablanca*, maybe...? Sorry! Sometimes I can't help myself.)

Anyhoo, being a Nazi has its perks, as Alicia finds when Sebastian invites her to a dinner party with the gang. He lives in a mansion with a sweeping staircase and a Teutonic mother. Played by Leopoldine Konstantin, she has a light accent, a Heidi braided crown, and distinct aura of evil. She'll be trouble, mark my words.

Each tuxedoed Nazi at the party is more odious than the last. Central casting must have had a field day ("Send in the Arians!"). Alicia observes all. Sebastian is putty in her hands.

It goes on from there, but I've already said too much. Let me just tease you with the prospects of a wedding, Devlin crashing a Nazi cocktail party, some truly cold-blooded shit from Sebastian's Wagnerian mother, and poison! You've got classic Hitchcock camerawork on that mansion's marble staircase, Cary Grant in a tux, and hot and cold running Nazis—something for everyone.

What you don't have is the Cary Grant you know from every other movie he's ever been in. There's no amused glint in his eye, no barely suppressed glee. Instead, aside from one or two moments, he's cold, hard, and detached. He may love Alicia, but he's also jealous, frustrated, and cruel. And why? Because Alicia did *exactly what he asked her to do.* That doesn't sound like Cary, does it? You know who it sounds like? Hitchcock. I'm just saying.

Killer line

When Sebastian finds out Alicia is a spy, he has to keep it from his fellow Nazis. He knows they'll kill him if they find out. His terrifying mother tells him not to worry. "You are protected by the enormity of your stupidity." I've spent half my life waiting to use that line on someone.

More!

If you want to see Cary Grant lying to Ingrid Bergman in a completely different context, I can't recommend their later film, *Indiscreet*, enough. It's a frothy comedy with perfect timing and absolutely sparkling dialog. Plus, many occasions for Ingrid to wear amazing gowns and for Cary to do what Cary does best in a tux. Watch it!

Movies My Friends Should Watch
Sally Lee

CHAPTER 18

"You're notorious," Callie said.

"How could people think that? Why do people even know me?"

We were taking the back stairs up to my office. When we got to the top we were met by Brandon, flushed and worried looking.

"Have you heard?" he asked. "They think you killed S and Tommy."

"*Both* of them?" I moved down the hall. "That's ridiculous. Why would I kill either of them? And how does anyone even know who I am?"

"Someone put it together that Tommy owned the Palace and that you work here and that you were questioned by the police," Brandon said.

"One quarter of the Palace," I said. "He only owned a quarter."

"Not really the point," Callie said, following us into the office.

I shook my head. "What, exactly, are they saying?" I sat at the desk and opened the laptop.

Brandon closed it. "I don't think you want to see it."

I stared at him.

"Um, the guys on the forums, they can be a little..."

"Crazy? Misogynistic? Disgusting?" Callie offered.

"I was going to say 'hotheaded,'" Brandon said. "They get a little carried away. You know, with, um, speculating."

"Okay." I kept the laptop closed. "So how carried away are they? And why on earth do they think I would have killed anyone?"

Brandon began. "They think you wanted to kill Tommy all along because you're some sort of disgruntled employee. The most popular theory is that you poisoned something you thought Tommy would drink at the launch announcement, but that S drank it by mistake—"

"I wasn't even there!" I protested.

Brandon swallowed and looked to Callie. "They're just making things up," she said. "I wouldn't worry about it."

Brandon made a strangled sound. I turned to him.

"Um, I'd worry a little," he said.

I took a deep breath. "Okay," I said. "How do they think I killed Tommy? Did I magically teleport myself into his car and pour arsenic in his juice?"

"They think you were in the car with him," Brandon said, flushing a deep crimson. "They think you, um..."

I gaped at him. "That I spent the night with him?"

Brandon looked up at the ceiling, turning bright pink. "Um, yeah."

"So let me get this straight—I'm a disgruntled employee who was in Palo Alto poisoning the wrong person even though over a hundred people saw me right here in this theater moments after S was killed, and I was also sleeping with my boss, whom I then poisoned after a night of passion at the Four Seasons even though twenty people saw me in the café and rushed out with me to help him when Tommy collapsed? Is that about it?"

"I told you they were crazy," Callie said, scrolling furiously on her phone.

"Why should I be worried?" I asked Brandon. "You said I should be worried, but I can't believe anyone would take this seriously."

"Well, not if they stop to think about it," he agreed. "The thing is—"

"They're *crazy*," Callie said again, not looking up from her screen.

Brandon pointed at her. "That," he gulped. "What she said."

I looked at Callie. "Has it gone mainstream?"

She glanced up and shook her head. "It's all just on the gamer blogs. It hasn't migrated to social media yet."

"I suppose that's something." I hadn't gone viral. Yet.

"You should lay low," she advised. "Don't go to any of the gamer forums—they'll track your identity in a hot minute. And don't try to defend yourself."

Brandon nodded vehemently. "Anything you say will just be twisted around. You'll just fan the flames."

"I'm supposed to just let them say whatever they want about me?"

"Let it burn itself out," Callie urged. "By this afternoon they'll be on to someone else."

I sat back, feeling queasy. "Remember what I said the other day about the wisdom of the crowd?" I asked them.

They looked at me.

"The crowd is crazy."

By mid-afternoon I couldn't take it anymore. I felt like every single person who came into the theater was looking at me like I was a murderer. Never mind that the senior citizens who brought their grandchildren in for classic films didn't exactly fit the profile of rabid gamer fanboys. I still felt notorious.

Ultimately I pulled my hair into a ponytail, put on a baseball cap, and stopped off at the ticket booth to tell Callie I needed a walk.

"Nice disguise," she said. "What about sunglasses?"

I took them from my bag and put them on.

"Perfect."

I walked toward downtown, wanting to tire myself out with as many hills as possible. Walking was my therapy. It was how I got my head straight, and I had a lot to get straight. I turned left at Filmore and went uphill and down until I found myself at the marina, looking out over the bay.

I wasn't the only one walking the city. The first few times I saw them, I didn't really pay attention to the clumps of young people wandering around together, intent on their phones. But by about the third time I'd been bumped into, I figured it out.

They were playing the game.

Once I realized what was happening, I looked at the groups more closely. Mostly clusters of four or five players, some as large as a dozen, each concentrating on their screen, looking at the world around them through their cameras, seeing who knows what kind of AR everywhere.

I sat on a bench at the Marina Green, my back to the sparkling bay. I was more interested in the gamers drifting around on the jogging paths and open grassy field. There were at least three groups of players meandering within eyesight. I watched them, fascinated.

They formed loose circles, each one facing out in a different direction, so among them they had a three-sixty view of the world. Occasionally someone would shout, and they'd all point their phones in the same direction, oohing and ahhing and arguing about what they were seeing and what it might mean. They wandered into the paths of oncoming joggers and cyclists, and didn't seem to notice. I thought about the rumors of people stumbling into traffic, oblivious, when playing S's last game. Watching these players, it seemed entirely plausible. Inevitable. I wondered how many of them might get hurt. I wondered how many of them frequented the gamer forums.

Eventually they all wandered off, presumably following more clues, and other groups came. It was pretty clear by then, at least to me, that no virtual gold coin worth millions lurked on the Green.

Watching them, I thought things over. The Internet—or at least some weird offramps of it—thought I was a killer. Meanwhile, there was an actual killer running around poisoning people. If I figured out who that was, would the Internet leave me alone? I had no idea. But I took out my phone and jotted down notes of what I did know, hoping some obvious clue would leap out at me.

- S was poisoned with bee pollen.

- Tommy was poisoned with arsenic.
- They were together the day before the webcast, at least for part of the day at Monica's shop.
- S bought a lot of weed that day and was a regular user. He seemed high onstage even before he got sick.
- Tommy and S argued the morning of the webcast.
- The bee pollen may have been in the energy drink S drank onstage.
- The arsenic was in the orange juice Tommy drank in his car.

Nothing leapt out at me, probably because I didn't know enough about either victim to know who would have wanted them both dead.

I found myself wondering who else had been with Tommy and S the morning of the webcast in Palo Alto. Did either of them have an entourage? Assistants? Someone close enough to S to know if he was allergic to bees? Someone close enough to Tommy to know he'd been staying at the Four Seasons? Someone with access to both bee pollen and arsenic? Did either of them have a girlfriend who might have been with them? No, that wouldn't fit. Why would one girlfriend want both men dead?

Then I remembered Kristy. Abby had told Monica and me that S had spent a lot of time with her in the shop that day. I had no idea if he might have told her anything meaningful, but I couldn't think of anything better to do, so I got off the bench and headed for the Potent Flower.

"Ohmygod he was amazing," Kristy said.

We were talking in the lounge in Monica's shop, Monica having given permission for her sales assistant to take a break. There were a few other patrons in the room, talking among themselves on the low benches that lined the walls, or working on their laptops at the central table. We kept our voices down.

"He was a genius," Kristy said, the dim light of the lounge giving her long lavender hair a hazy sort of glow. "If you told me he was an enlightened being from another world, or another dimension, I would totally believe you. I mean, just look!"

She pointed at the giant video screen on the wall. It took me a minute to realize what I was looking at. "Is that the game?" I asked.

She nodded. "Thirty-second live streams from player's phones all over the world."

One half of the screen showed wobbly hand-held videos while the other half had scrolling text that looked like comments players were making. The videos were of streets, buildings, parks, and anywhere else on the planet people were playing the game, occasionally including one of the AR effects. I got a glimpse of what looked like a CGI chimney sweep on someone's roof, and then a fortune teller sitting on a building's front steps.

"It's a whole world," Kristy said, transfixed. "He built a whole beautiful world, and they killed him."

It looked like the same old world to me, with the random addition of the AR characters, which I had to admit did look pretty cool.

"What do you mean, 'they' killed him?" I asked her.

She didn't take her eyes off the screen. "His enemies," she shrugged.

"He told you about his enemies?" That sounded promising.

"He didn't have to. I saw what he was going through. You should have heard the way that other guy yelled at him, and right before he went onstage. So disrespectful! Like he could have done anything without S."

"Wait—are you talking about Tommy? Are you saying you were there in Palo Alto? The day of the launch?"

"Sure." She looked surprised that this wasn't common knowledge. "S and I really connected, you know? He hung out here in the lounge after we met that day. And then we went out, and then back to his place, and when the car came to take him to the

venue in the morning, he just assumed I'd come along, so I did."
She glanced at me. "We were soulmates. We both knew it."

"Right," I said, my mind racing with questions. "Did you notice
when S started feeling sick? Was it before he went onstage, or just
after he took that drink? Did you see who took the bottle from him?
Or if anyone had it before he took it onstage?"

She finally turned her attention away from the screen, fixing
me with a look. "Isn't it obvious what happened?" she asked. "That
guy Tommy poisoned S, and then when he realized that he couldn't
run the game without him, he killed himself." She shrugged.
"Simple."

I blinked, not quite knowing how to respond. I was spared the
need to when there was suddenly a blinding flash of light from the
screen. Music blared, and the image of a giant gold coin appeared,
rotating and sending off sparks. Everyone in the lounge started
murmuring, then yelling in excitement.

Kristy leapt up, clapping and whooping. "They found one!" she
yelled joyfully. "They found the first coin!"

CHAPTER 19

A few moments later the lounge was swarming with people, all of them shouting with excitement, drawn in from the shop to see what was going on. The giant video screen blared the news that the game's first virtual coin, worth six million dollars, had been found in a small town in Germany. I saw Monica making her way to me.

"I guess this means Tommy's company won't be pulling the game," she said.

I looked at the fevered crowd around us. "There would be rioting in the streets."

I realized Kristy had disappeared in all the excitement. "Did you know Kristy was at the event in Palo Alto the day S died?" I asked Monica, raising my voice above all the noise.

She stared at me. "No! *What*?"

"She and S were soulmates," I said, managing not to roll my eyes. I scanned the room for her. "Where'd she go?"

"There," Monica said with some relief, pointing to the far end of the room. Kristy and the other employees were moving through the crowd, gently but insistently getting the patrons out of the lounge and back into the shop. Monica's employees reminded me of sheepdogs, if all the sheep were high.

"Listen, I should get back to—" Monica began.

"Go," I told her. "This is crazy."

"Call me later if you want to play the game after all," she said with a smile as she headed out of the lounge. "It looks like it might be worth it."

"Kristy," I approached the sales associate once order had been somewhat restored. She was still radiant with excitement. "We need to talk."

"Sure," she said. "But not right now. I've got to go. My shift is over in five, and my squad is gathering to play. There are more coins out there."

"Wait." I put my hand on her arm as she turned to go. "What about S?"

A flash of impatience crossed her face. "I told you what happened," she said. "Tommy killed him. I saw him throw that bottle at S when they were fighting. He's the only one who could have poisoned it. It had to have been Tommy."

"I really didn't think Tommy did it," I said to Trixie. "But maybe I'm wrong. Maybe he just played me."

We were in the break room. I was making a pot of terrible coffee and telling her everything Kristy had said.

"Do you think that girl told the police what she saw?" Trixie asked. "Is that why they arrested Tommy in the first place?"

"He didn't say anything about there being a witness," I said doubtfully. "But, then, he wouldn't."

She perched on the table, her petite shoes on a chair, biting her lip in concentration.

"Well, let's just think it through," she said. "Why...?" She scrunched her face. "No, but how..." she tapped her forehead. "No, who!" She beamed. "That's the question—if Tommy killed that other fella, then who killed Tommy?"

"And why?" I asked. "Who and why?"

"At least we know how," Trixie offered helpfully.

"There's that," I agreed. "I have to talk to Kristy again. She said she saw Tommy throw the bottle at S. Did she see him open it? Did she actually see him tamper with it?" I shook my head. "Never mind why he'd just happen to have a lethal dose of bee pollen on him."

"Don't worry," Trixie said. "You can talk to her again tomorrow, can't you?"

I gave her a blank look.

"At the séance, silly!"

Oh, dear lord. I'd forgotten about the séance. Again.

I spent most of the day Monday in my office on the laptop, playing what felt like several rounds of whack-a-mole with lawyers.

First I set out to find Tommy's personal lawyer. The latest news was full of information about his criminal defense team, but I assumed they were not the same bunch who would have handled his will. I kept sleuthing until, in an online profile from a few years back, I saw the name Marc Picco mentioned as Tommy's longtime attorney. I found Picco's website and sent him an email asking who the ownership of Tommy's one quarter of the Palace would pass to now that he was dead. The lawyer might not tell me, but least I'd find out if he was the right guy to ask, and I'd be able to tell the other owners who they should get in touch with.

After that I searched through the small print of Tommy's company website, looking for the name of his corporate law firm. I hoped they could answer the big question about Tommy's presumed motive for killing S: With S out of the way, would Tommy make more money? I had no expectation that these lawyers would tell me anything about anything—why would they? So instead of asking them, I wrote to *my* very expensive team of lawyers down in LA and told them to find out whatever they could, hoping that a little attorney-on-attorney action might yield some information. You never knew.

And as long as I was writing to my lawyers, I took the opportunity to inform them that my supposedly bankrupt, almost-ex-husband Ted had enough money to buy a fortune in Hollywood memorabilia, in the form of famous movie gowns. Where had he come up with that money? And when, *when*, would I be free of him for good?

I did not send a text to Ted, asking what he needed me to do so much that he'd attempted to bribe me into doing it.

I did not send a text to Otis Hampton, asking whether his team of private investigators had come up with any leads on where Ted had stashed our life's savings.

I did not send a text to Hector.

Lillian Gee, noted fashionista and amateur spiritual medium, showed up for Monday night's séance fully looking the part. She wore a flowing black lace dress, ropes upon ropes of black jet beads, and tiny black silk roses in her thick wavy hair.

"If you say one word to mock her," Callie greeted me in the lobby. She and her mother, as well as Albert, were already at the Palace when I got back from the walk I'd taken in an attempt to get into a séance-y mood.

"Never in a million years," I promised. "What's all this?" I looked at the half-dozen high-tech bags and crates surrounding her on the floor. "Spectrographs? Ectoplasm detectors? Ghostly voice recorders? And, by the way, I'm not mocking your mother. I'm mocking you. I didn't even think you were coming."

Lillian was out of earshot, talking animatedly with Albert on the far side of the lobby. I could tell the aged devotee of the Palace was almost as enthusiastic as Callie's mom was.

Callie gave me a dark look. "It's my camera equipment. I'm filming it. Didn't she tell you?"

"Nobody told me anything." Aside from Trixie, that is. But it was probably a little early in the proceedings for me to bring up my conversations with the Palace's famous ghost.

Oddly enough, I hadn't seen Trixie all day. I'd been in and out of the theater setting things up and banging out emails with not a peep from her. I hoped that her excitement over the séance hadn't been too much for her. When things got to be too much for her, she had a habit of going *poof*—simply disappearing for some indeterminate length of time.

"Nora!" Lillian opened her arms and floated across the lobby when she spotted me talking to Callie. "I'm so excited! I can just feel the energy—can't you?"

"I feel something," I said, returning her hug. "Hi, Albert."

"Nora," he said with a smile. "I have a feeling this will be a night to remember."

"We can only hope." I knew Albert had seen Trixie. He'd known her in life, when he was just a ten-year-old kid and she was a bombshell usherette he and his friends had all crushed on. But he'd once told me that he'd also seen her since then, just glimpses over the years. I had a feeling the aged Albert was still half in love with her. And I had a feeling he suspected I knew more about her than I was saying.

"I put a table and chairs on the stage," I told them. "How many are coming?"

"Well," Lillian clasped her hands together. "The four of us, and your friend Monica is bringing friends."

"Abby and Kristy," I nodded.

"So that's seven." She turned to her daughter. "Calandria, dear, what about your colleagues?"

"Brandon's off playing that game," she said. "And I banned Marty from the building. I figured you wouldn't want his negativity."

"Exactly right," she said, nodding sagely. "The spirits can sense an unbeliever."

I knew one spirit who made it a habit to watch a movie from the projection booth with her favorite unbeliever at least once a week, but I wasn't the expert here.

"Gabriela said she was coming," I said. "With Hector." I felt self-conscious saying his name, as if everyone would be able to sense something had happened just by the way the word "Hector" left my lips.

Would Hector show up? Would he act like no epic moonlit kiss had happened between us? And if he did, would I be able to refrain from bludgeoning him to death in frustration?

"I think that's them," Callie said, looking out the lobby doors to the sidewalk.

She was right. Hector's car had pulled up. I watched as he got out and took Gabriela's wheelchair from the trunk. It felt so weird to watch him opening her door and assisting her into the chair. So weird because it was so normal, when it felt like everything had changed.

Then Hector straightened and looked up the walkway to the lobby. Looked directly into my eyes, as if he knew I'd been watching. My heart stopped. He raised a hand, the expression on his face completely neutral. Then he got back into his car and drove away, and I miraculously managed to neither collapse on the lobby floor nor go running after him.

Albert held the door for Gabriela. "Good evening, my dear."

"Hi Albert, hi everyone." She looked at me. "Hector sends his apologies. He had something he couldn't get out of."

Which is right about the time I stopped feeling weird and self-conscious about Hector. I started feeling something different. I started feeling furious.

CHAPTER 20

My follow-up interview with Kristy would have to wait. She was a no-show for the séance.

"She's off playing the game," Monica told me when she arrived with Abby. "Along with half the city, from the looks of it out there."

"Half the world," Abby said. She was wearing the same green multi-pocketed jacket that she'd worn to the midnight movie. "At least, the under-thirty half. Running around in the dark without looking where they're going. They're liable to get themselves killed."

"Well I'm glad you guys could make it," I told them. "Everybody else is already inside."

We entered the auditorium, and I had to admit, the place looked suitably atmospheric. The house lights were down, with only a few freestanding lamps on the stage providing light. There's nothing like a near-empty, near-dark theater with almost a hundred years of history to get a person's imagination going. The few remaining flecks of gold leaf glinted on the detailed art deco woodwork surrounding the stage. The balcony was shrouded in mysterious darkness. The back recesses of the stage were dim and shadowy.

Never mind that the ghost we were trying to conjure was one of the brightest, bubbliest people I'd ever met. The stage was set for old-school spiritualism.

Earlier that day I'd raised the movie screen and hauled the battered round table down from the break room to the big empty stage. I'd gone to a neighborhood fabric store for a length of dark blue velvet that I'd draped over the table before surrounding it with mismatched chairs.

I'd been nervous at the thought of how many candles Lillian might bring, given the fact that there had been a fire on the stage a few months ago. But it turned out she only had three large white pillars that she placed in the center of the table. She hadn't lit them yet.

"What's she doing?" Monica whispered as we walked down the center aisle to the stage.

"Purifying the space," I whispered back, feeling ridiculous.

Earlier Lillian had produced something that looked like a rough cigar, which she'd informed us was a sage wand. She'd lit one end until it smoldered, and was currently waving the aromatic smoke all over the stage. When Abby, Monica, and I walked up the ramp to join everyone, she waved it over us as well. Which was fine. A little purification couldn't hurt. Although, in my experience, Trixie was more drawn by the scent of fresh popcorn.

Monica coughed discretely, but Abby closed her eyes and raised her arms as the smoke circled her, seeming to get into the spirit of the thing.

"Are we all here?" Lillian asked. "Let's begin."

Callie joined us at the table, her expression guarded. Her cameras, three of them, were set up on tripods around the table and were already filming.

I was increasingly nervous as we all took our seats. Albert was on my left. Next to him was Lillian, then Abby, Gabriela, Callie, and Monica, who was on my right. I was nervous not because of what might happen, but because of what might not.

There was no sign of Trixie.

I knew that even if she showed up, the others still probably wouldn't see her. Trixie had tried to show herself to Albert, Callie, and just about everyone else who'd hung around the Palace in the last eighty-plus years. So far, I was the only one who had ever really seen her, and that was after I'd been conked on the head by a broken light the first day I met her. I truly wanted her to be able to make contact tonight, but I wasn't counting on it. I didn't think Lillian planned to conk anyone on the head.

"We are seven," Lillian began, her voice suitably dramatic, "which is a very auspicious number for contacting the spirits. In Chinese, the number seven—*chi*—sounds like the word for 'vital energy,' and the seventh month is the 'ghost month,' when spirits are known to visit earth." She looked around at us. "There are seven days in the week, seven stars in the Pleiades, seven wonders of the ancient world. In Christianity there are seven gifts of the holy spirit, and seven deadly sins."

I couldn't help but wonder if she'd have had similar facts if all nine of us had shown up.

"I believe we are seven for a reason tonight," she continued. "There is power in seven."

I thought I heard the tiniest sigh coming from Callie's direction.

"Now, some guidelines to remember," Lillian said. "We need to be very clear in our intention. We gather here to contact the ghosts of the Palace. But once we enter the spiritual plane, there's no saying who might try to contact *us*." She looked meaningfully around the table. "We need to enter into this circle with only love in our hearts."

Across from me, Abby compressed her lips into a firm line and nodded.

"I'm sure everyone at this table has experienced loss," Lillian continued. "We all have someone on the other side. Some more than others." She placed her hand over Albert's briefly. "We must remain open to all possibilities."

Because I just happened to be looking across the table, I caught a flash of something in Abby's expression. Pain? Longing? Was there someone she was hoping to contact? Someone she'd lost? Someone who wasn't a chatty usherette?

"When we light the candles, our journey will begin," Lillian said. "Please do not attempt to speak to me once I begin initiating contact. The thread between the worlds is very fragile."

We all nodded, and I was reminded, suddenly, of Madame Arcati, the batty medium who holds a séance in *Blithe Spirit* (1945, Rex Harrison, and Margaret Rutherford as the medium.) I realized with a start something I'd never put together before. When I'd gotten conked on the head in the balcony that day, *Blithe Spirit* had been playing onscreen. Specifically, the séance scene. Had that had something to do with why I could see Trixie afterward?

More importantly, where *was* Trixie?

Lillian stood, and produced a silver filigreed matchbox from a pocket in the folds of her lacy dress. She lit the three thick candles, intoning "Light in the darkness" each time a wick took the flame.

She sat and held her hands out to Albert and Abby, indicating that we should all hold hands. We did, forming a circle around the table and waiting for what would happen next.

What happened next was humming. Lillian closed her eyes and began making a tuneless droning sound. The rest of us glanced around uncomfortably, not sure if we should close our eyes as well. While we were still figuring it out, Lillian's humming found a melody. It took me a minute, but then I thought I recognized it, improbably, as the old folk song "Mockingbird." I had no idea why she'd chosen that song, but the tune, beginning with "Hush little baby, don't say a word..." was definitely what she was humming. I looked around to see if anyone else had picked up on it, but everybody's eyes were closed except Abby's. She was staring wide-eyed at Lillian.

Then, suddenly, the humming stopped and Lillian's eyes flew open.

"I sense a spirit!"

She wasn't wrong. Out in the auditorium, Trixie had appeared at the far end of the center aisle, and was walking slowly toward the stage, her hands held out in front of her like she was a hypnotized bride in a Boris Karloff movie. My initial surge of relief faded when she got closer and I saw that her eyes were closed. It looked like she was being drawn to us. Had Lillian actually summoned her?

I swallowed, worried that the séance had done something to

Trixie. I'd assumed it couldn't do any harm, but what did I know? Trixie looked like she'd been possessed as she walked slowly up the ramp to the stage. The gold braid of her uniform winked in the flickering light, her cap was at its usual jaunty angle on her curls, but there was no, for lack of a better word, *life* to her.

I could tell by the way they were all glancing around nervously that nobody else saw her, but Lillian shivered. "You are welcome here, Spirit," she said.

Trixie stood still. Then one eye squinted open as she took a peek at her surroundings. When it was clear I was the only one who could see her, she opened both eyes, putting her hands on her hips and tossing an errant blond curl out of her eyes. "Why, I should hope to say I'm welcome here!"

I sagged in relief.

"Come on, now, no fooling!" Trixie stamped a petite foot. "Can't anybody else see me at all? I made that whole entrance and everything. I looked just like Elsa Lanchester. I know I did!"

Everyone else was still looking around for an apparition, oblivious to the outburst of the exasperated ghost in their midst.

The ghost looked at me and sighed. "Hi, Nora. Isn't this something? All that fuss and nothing works."

"Spirit, have no fear!" Lillian commanded. I realized I was the only one at the table not looking toward her expectantly.

"'Course I don't have any fear," Trixie said. She approached the table, pausing between Abby and Gabriela. "Hello!" she yelled, waving. "Olly-olly-oxen-free!"

She put her hands on the shoulders of the women on either side of her. Abby didn't seem to notice, but Gabriela reacted immediately. She looked in Trixie's direction. "I think I feel something."

"That's good," I said, encouraging Trixie.

She jumped with excitement. "She feels me, Nora!" She turned all her attention on Gabriela, bending to wrap her in the same sort of hug she'd used on Lillian the other day in the lobby.

"It's cold," Gabriela said. "It's really cold. Is that—"

"The spirit is manifesting!" Lillian said joyfully.

"Nora! It's working!" Trixie exclaimed. She'd moved from Gabriela and was now hugging Callie, to no visible effect. Then she went around the table, trying Monica, Albert, and finally Lillian.

"I sense you, Spirit!" Lillian said. "Show yourself!"

"Well, gee!" Trixie said. "What the heck do you think I've been doing? I'm right here."

I muffled a laugh, which got me reproving looks from Albert and Abby. Trixie waved her hand in front of Lillian's face. "Right here!" she bellowed. "It's me! Trixie! Nice to meet you!" She moved around the table again. "Albert! Even you can't see me? Callie! I'm right here!" She walked through Callie's cameras, turning once to wave at the lens. "Hello! Anybody?"

She was getting more and more worked up, her frustration painfully evident. I couldn't take it anymore.

"Trixie!" I called.

Everyone, including Trixie, turned to stare at me.

I swallowed. "Is the ghost of Beatrix George among us?" I asked solemnly.

"Oh! Nora! That's brilliant!" Trixie came back to the table.

"She's here!" Lillian proclaimed. "I feel her energy."

Trixie pointed at her. "She feels me."

"Trixie," I deepened my voice. "Can you give us a sign?"

Her mouth formed an "O." "That'll show them. What should I do? Should I move something?" Her eyes darted around. "The matches?"

I knew that, with great effort, Trixie was sometimes capable of moving physical objects. I owed my life to that ability. Now she went over to Lillian and put both hands around the silver matchbox on the table. She concentrated, her penciled brows coming together, biting her bottom lip. Then, with a mighty grunt, she moved her hands.

The matchbox stayed in place.

"Darn it all!" Trixie fell halfway through the table with her effort. "What's the matter with me? Why can't—"

"Trixie," I said urgently, "if it's you, and if you're here, put out the candles."

She straightened, staring at me, her look of frustration slowly replaced by a determination I'd only seen once before.

"I know you can do it, Trixie," I told her. "I believe in you. We believe in you."

We were all still holding hands around the table, and everyone began murmuring "we believe in you" together, turning it into a chant.

"I can do it," Trixie told me. "I know I can."

I nodded.

She moved to stand between Lillian and Albert, then she leaned forward, raising her hands over the candle flames. As she lowered her hands, the three candles, one by one, winked out.

"Holy shit! Mom!" Callie jumped to her feet, breaking the circle, as pandemonium broke out on the stage.

"I did it!" Trixie yelled, jumping in excitement.

"What just happened?" Monica shouted.

"Beatrix!" Lillian bellowed. "Beatrix George, show yourself!"

Albert stood, a searching look on his face. "Trixie? Is it really you?"

"It is!" Trixie shouted. "It's me! And I'm here!" She turned to me, pulsating with joy. "I'm here!" she said again, triumphant.

And then—*poof*—she vanished.

CHAPTER 21

"Who else could use a drink?" I asked.

The séance had effectively ended as soon as the candles went out. Trixie had disappeared, and Lillian could sense it.

"The fragile thread has been broken," she announced, speaking above everyone's excited chatter. "The spirit has left us."

Trixie had gone *poof*. But she'd gone *poof* happier than I'd ever seen her. I hoped she'd be back soon. I couldn't wait to talk to her about it.

Monica, Gabriela, and Abby surrounded Lillian, exchanging notes on what they'd just experienced. Callie turned her back on us and started doing something with her cameras. I looked to Albert, worried that it might all have been too much for him, and found him regarding me with a thoughtful expression on his face.

Before I could go over to him, Monica broke away from the cluster around Lillian. "Did you say something about a drink?" she asked me.

"At least one," I said.

A while later we found ourselves in the lobby, seated at various levels on the balcony stairs. We could have gotten the chairs from the stage, but it didn't feel like anyone wanted to go back into the auditorium. So to the stairs it was, where we talked ourselves out, drank wine from paper cups, and devoured a shocking amount of candy from the concessions stand. Something about our brush with the supernatural had made everyone crave chocolate.

Lillian was still on a high, although she was quick to share her triumph with me.

"It's clear you have a gift," she told me earnestly. "You must work to develop it. Who knows what kind of contact you might be able to make with the proper training?"

"Who knows?" I agreed.

At one point Abby went to the concessions stand, saying she needed a cup of tea. I followed.

"Are you okay?" I asked her, remembering the look of rapt attention she'd had on her face during the séance. We were far enough from the others that I didn't think we'd be overheard. "I know this was all pretty intense."

She nodded, dropping a tea bag into a paper cup. "Very. I wasn't sure what to expect."

"Can I ask you, when Lillian was humming that song it seemed like..."

She looked at me, tears suddenly filling her eyes. "My son loved that song when he was a baby. I used to sing it to him all the time."

Oh. She had a son. And she referred to him in the past tense.

"When did you lose him?" I asked quietly.

"Three years ago. It was a hit-and-run. I still can't quite..." She turned away, fussing with the hot water valve on the coffee maker.

"Abby, I'm so sorry," I said.

"They never caught the driver," she told me. "Nobody was ever punished. Nobody paid for what they did to my boy."

"That's awful." I had no idea how else to respond.

Abby exhaled. "I've learned that you have to do whatever you can to go on," she said. "Tonight that meant attending a séance." She glanced at me. "Usually, it means focusing on my work. The relief I can provide people is a great comfort to me."

"I'm sure it is," I said.

"And I think my boy approves," she said. "I think that's why Lillian hummed that song. I think he was..." She looked up. "Here. With me."

Who was I to say she was wrong? "I think he's probably always with you," I told her. I also thought Lillian's humming was the sort of maybe-coincidence-maybe-not thing that kept mediums in business, but what did I know? I'd only ever met one ghost.

Abby wiped her eyes. "You're very sweet." She reached into one of the many pockets of her jacket. "Please, I'd like you to have this." She handed me a green bottle about the size of my pinkie finger, topped with an eyedropper cap. I recognized it as one of her blended cannabinoid tinctures. "It's a simple mixture of my own, and I've found it does wonders to help me sleep. Something tells me you could use a little help getting to sleep."

Something like the gigantic circles under my eyes, probably. And the fact that I'd been yawning for the past half hour.

"Thank you." I took the tiny bottle. "I don't usually—"

She waved her hand. "Don't worry, you won't start craving Cheetos or want to listen to the White Album backwards," she smiled. "Just put a few drops in a cup of herbal tea at night. I guarantee you'll sleep better."

I put the bottle in my pocket. I couldn't sleep any worse.

Albert was the first to call it a night. He rose from his position on the bottom step, creaking audibly as he stood. I walked with him to the lobby doors.

"I knew Trixie was still here," he said, wrapping a scarf around his neck. "I think I've always known. Even when I told myself it was only my imagination, or wishful thinking." He glanced around the lobby, as if seeking her out. "Goodnight, Trixie," he called. Then he gave me a rueful smile and left.

"Gabriela, do you need a ride?" Monica asked. "Or is Hector coming back for you?"

They'd come over to the doors. "I'm fine," Gabriela said. "Hector had that...thing, but I texted a friend a while ago. She should be here any minute."

"It was good to see you." Monica bent to give Gabriela a hug, then went back to gather her things from the stairs.

"That was some night," I said, suddenly tongue-tied with Hector's cousin.

"I've never really believed in...you know," Gabriela said. "But I felt something tonight. Someone." She shivered. "It was an intense cold, targeted, as if someone was holding an ice pack just an inch away from me." Her brows were bunched in concentration, remembering the feeling, then shook her head. "It was *so* weird. I'm just wondering..."

"What?" I asked.

She shook her head. "Never mind. Just an idea. I'll tell you about it later, if I can figure it out." She cleared her throat. "I'm also trying to figure out why Hector didn't even come in to say hi to you, after he suddenly had some bogus thing to do tonight. Any ideas?" She looked at me shrewdly.

I swallowed the urge to launch into a full-on rant about her cousin and how he'd disappeared after that amazing kiss. I might have confided in her if we were alone, but the others were still chatting and milling around, so I just shrugged.

"Something's going on with you two," Gabriela said. "You don't have to tell me what it is, but I'll tell you this: He's worth fighting for." She squeezed my hand. "And so are you."

We heard a car's horn from out in the street and I opened the door for Gabriela to go.

"Sooo," Callie spoke from behind me as I was watching Gabriela greet her friend at the sidewalk under the pail glow of the streetlights.

I turned around. "So."

Callie had loaded all her camera equipment onto a cart, ready to leave as soon as Lillian finished saying her good-byes. Earlier we'd all taken a look at the video the cameras had captured and had seen no sign of Trixie. Not even when she'd waved.

"That was literally..." Callie's voice trailed off.

"It was," I agreed.

"I mean..."

"Yup."

She looked at me. "What are we going to tell Marty?"

We were already keeping one secret from the world's grumpiest projectionist. A few months ago, Callie had figured out that I was the movie blogger Sally Lee. So far she'd not told Marty, who adored Sally. Finding out I was his blogger idol would have made his head explode, so I'd asked her not to let him know. What was one more secret?

"I think the least complicated thing to tell him is that we had the séance," I said. "And that some candles blew out."

She looked at me closely and nodded. "I mean, they did blow out, right?"

I thought about it. "Check the film again," I advised her. "The camera doesn't lie."

Which was nonsense. Cameras lied all the time. You just had to look at the tabloids to know that.

Monica and Abby were the last to leave. They offered me a ride, but I wanted to walk home. After they left I made the rounds of the theater, making sure doors were locked, lights were off, alarms were set, and ghosts were all gone.

"You did great tonight," I called to Trixie. "I'm so proud of you."

I never knew if she could hear me when she went away, but I figured it couldn't hurt to talk to her anyway.

Once again it was after midnight when I locked the lobby door behind me. I turned and looked down the walkway. There was no shadowy figure lurking near the ticket booth. No Hector.

I'd just gotten to the sidewalk when my phone pinged with a text. I pulled it out of my pocket, assuming someone had left something behind in the theater. When I saw the name on the message I cursed.

Lillian might not have conjured any new ghosts that night, but maybe her powers had conjured an old one.

The text was from Ted.

CHAPTER 22

Babe. I know you're angry. And I know I can't buy you. But I also know you're the only person in the world who can help me. Please say you will. I just need you to take a meeting. One meeting. Please help me out. Please.

Great. As much as I enjoyed the novel experience of my not-yet-ex-husband groveling, I really didn't want to deal with him in the wee small hours of the morning after a séance. I pocketed the phone and walked home without answering.

The morning brought a slew of emails from lawyers. Mornings often did that, but on this morning they were emails I actually wanted.

The most interesting was from Marc Picco, who had been Tommy's personal attorney. He'd replied to my request for information about who would inherit Tommy's quarter of the Palace with a request of his own.

"He wants a meeting with all the remaining owners," I told Robbie over the phone as I walked to the theater on that bright, brisk Tuesday morning. She was driving to a location shoot in Malibu, and I enjoyed picturing her in a red convertible with enormous sunglasses and an Hermès scarf tied around her hair, tooling up the sundrenched PCH. In reality she was probably in the back seat of a production car, surrounded with work and not even glancing out the windows, but I liked my version better.

"A meeting? Like, to read the will?" she asked doubtfully.

"The lawyer didn't mention a will," I said. "He just said he thinks it would be easier to update you all on the ownership status in person, so he could answer any questions that come up."

"I bet that means questions will come up," Robbie said.

"Well, we're talking about Tommy, so there's bound to be something weird and controlling about it." I waited to cross the street and saw a group of teenagers huddled together over their phones in front of the yarn shop. Probably looking for a cartoon gold coin when they should be in school. And with that thought, I officially became a cranky old lady.

"Does this meeting need to be in person?" Robbie was asking.

"No, Picco said he'd set up a video call." I crossed the street. "For tomorrow morning at nine, if you can all make it. I already talked to Monica, and she's in."

"Oh, good. You two can video in together," Robbie said.

"I'm not an owner," I reminded her.

"That's just a technicality. You should join the call. I'll ping Mitch and let him know. Hey, is everyone up there playing Tommy's game? All of LA seems to have gone nuts."

"They're nuts here too," I told her, passing the clump of truant gamers. They didn't even look up from their screens as they moved as one into the street. For the past few days I'd been paranoid that everyone involved in the game would recognize me as the woman the conspiracy theorists accused of murdering S and Tommy, but I needn't have worried. They'd have to look away from their screens for that.

"Remember what you said about inventing an app?" Robbie asked. "You should do it. Just think of something original and brilliant that will capture the imagination of the entire world. How hard could that be?"

"I'll get right on it," I promised. "Just as soon as I de-gunk the popcorn maker."

Another email I'd gotten that morning had been from my lawyers.

For once, they'd been able to respond to a question with an actual answer. Probably because the question had been about Tommy and S, and not my divorce from Ted.

They'd looked into it and were able to inform me that neither S's death nor Tommy's death made a bit of difference in terms of who got the profits from the game. It was a corporation-to-corporation agreement that bound them, never mind that both corporations had been headed by high-profile, now-deceased CEOs.

There were some excruciatingly boring details, but the takeaway was pretty simple: Tommy had not stood to gain from S's murder. So that eliminated his most compelling possible motive. I'd been briefly diverted by Kristy's theory of Tommy as killer-turned-remorseful-suicide, but this news sent me back to the much more likely theory that the same killer had poisoned both S and Tommy. Although I couldn't exactly count that as progress, since I still had no idea who that killer might be.

It crossed my mind that Kristy's insistence on Tommy as killer might be because she was hiding something. Was that crazy? I'd been thinking her value was as a potential witness, but maybe I should start thinking of her as a potential killer. She was at the scene of the first death, presumably with access to the bottle S drank from. On the other hand, I had no idea why she might want to kill her soulmate. But if I could figure that out, her motive for killing Tommy would be clear—to draw suspicion away from herself.

I had to talk to Kristy again. If she was just a witness, maybe I could get her past her conviction that Tommy had killed S and just tell me clearly everything she'd actually seen at the launch that day. She might have seen something important. And if she was a suspect, there were all kinds of questions I wanted her to answer.

It was too early for the Potent Flower to be open, so I sent at text to Monica asking when Kristy would be at work.

As I got closer to the Palace I saw that Marty was up on the ancient wooden ladder, changing the marquee to the new lineup. Technology Week had finally ended.

"Happy Mid-Month Musicals," I greeted him.

Mid-Month Musicals marked my latest attempt to increase ticket sales. People loved musicals. They were the gateway drug of classic films. So I'd decided to sprinkle them liberally throughout our offerings. Each month, in the middle of the month, we'd feature a musical lineup. That week we were showing Fred Astaire, with *Swing Time* (1936, a young Astaire and Ginger Rogers in a nightclub act that really made me wish nightclubs were still a thing) and *Silk Stockings* (1957, an older Astaire and Cyd Charisse as dancing opposites who very much attracted).

Marty scowled down at me. "Thanks for cleaning up the stage and putting the screen back down after all your folderol last night."

"We have hours and hours until the first show," I said. "I'll take care of it now."

"Except I was here hours and hours ago and already took care of it." He started down the ladder. "You're welcome."

"You didn't have to, but thank you," I told him.

"I did have to if I wanted somewhere to sit in the break room." He began folding the ladder. "Dare I ask if you made contact with the undead last night?"

"Technically, the undead would be vampires, or possibly zombies," I informed him. "We were looking for spirits."

He snorted. "I think I'd know if I'd been working side-by-side with a Vaudeville showgirl or a wisecracking thirties usherette for the entire time I've been here."

"Yeah, you'd think," I agreed.

The wisecracking thirties usherette was nowhere to be seen inside, so I busied myself with the details of keeping the Palace running. I'd hoped to skip out and go talk to Kristy at some point, but Monica had responded to my text with frustrating news.

Kristy called in sick. So did two others and I bet they're all out playing that stupid game. If it's important, here's her number. One thing you can be sure of, she'll have her phone with her.

A link to a phone number followed. I clicked it, and after a few rings got Kristy's voicemail. I hung up, knowing enough about millennials to know a text was more likely to get a response.

Kristy, I'd really like to talk to you again about everything that happened at the launch event. It's important. It won't take long, and I can come to you. Just let me know where you are.

I'd just pressed Send when I heard a clatter from the hall and my office door burst open.

"Did you hear?" Brandon panted. "They found the second coin!"

It was a full week since the game had launched. A full week since S's murder. So the coin that had been found in a Tokyo alley was worth eight million dollars.

"Is the game still profitable at this point?" I asked Brandon.

We were on the game's website, watching live video feeds of people reacting to the news of the latest coin.

He looked away from the screen long enough to send me a withering look. "Only by about a billion dollars or so."

"Wait, what?" I shut the laptop, causing him to squeak in protest, or possibly withdrawal. "I thought you said it was going to lose more ground as the payout got bigger."

"Sure, but that was before the first coin was found. Since then the whole world started playing. And everyone's buying clues and equipment and maps and shortcuts." He'd been standing next to me at the desk, looking over my shoulder. Now he went over to look out the window. "It kind of sucks. I can't compete with people who are spending thousands of dollars a day to—"

"*Thousands*?" I yelped.

"Especially in hot zones," he said. "Now that one coin has been found in Europe, and one in Asia, people are saying that the other three are bound to be in North America, South America, and Africa." He looked out the window again. "One of them is here. I just know it."

Possibly, but North America was pretty big, last I checked.

"I've got to go," Brandon said, turning from the window.

"To school, I hope." It was still only late morning.

"Sure. *To school*," he grinned. "Um, but about later, can I have the day off?"

"Go," I waved my hand, giving up. "Find a coin. Buy a yacht and take me sailing."

He left, and I thought over what he'd said. It looked like Tommy had been wrong. S really had been a genius. Had they lived, they both would have made a fortune with the game. And their companies still would. Maybe even more than they would have if the two high-profile CEOs hadn't been murdered.

I wondered again about whether the murders could be some sort of sick publicity stunt. I opened the laptop again. *Follow the money* was a tried-and-true adage for a reason. Where did that much money lead?

I knew a lot about classic movies, and I knew a lot about how to work a Hollywood party. What I knew nothing about, I realized after scouring press releases and corporate profiles for over an hour, was how giant tech corporations were structured. My most up-to-date reference on the subject was *How to Succeed in Business Without Really Trying* (1967, Robert Morse and Michele Lee) and that was so dated it featured a steno pool.

I couldn't figure out who was now in charge of either S's company or Tommy's. But I thought I knew someone who might. Gabriela worked at a giant tech corporation. She might be able to help me understand the hierarchy among all the corporate job titles that started with Chief.

I sent her a text and was happy when she responded right

away with the news that she was already planning to come to the theater.

I'll be there later tonight. I want to show you something. You have to tell me if I've lost my mind.

I wasn't sure I was in any position to judge that, but I told her I was willing to try.

By the time Gabriela got to the theater it was almost nine and *Swing Time* was heading toward the big finish.

"I came straight from work," she said. "I usually don't like to drive my van in the city, but I had this crazy idea and I just had to show it to you."

"I'm so glad," I told her. "I wanted to ask you something, too."

She shrugged off her jacket and looked up at me, startled. "Me?"

Usually incredibly fashionable, today Gabriela had pulled her hair into a ponytail and wore jeans and a long-sleeved tee displaying the logo of the Silicon Valley company where she worked. But even dressed more or less like me, she still looked great.

"You're the only person I know who understands the tech industry," I told her.

"No one understands the tech industry," she said. "But I'll do my best. What do you need to know?"

We'd gravitated toward the concessions stand. I took her jacket from her and put it on the counter. "I'm trying to figure out who's in charge at Tommy and S's companies now," I explained. "I want to know who stands to gain with them both gone. But I have no idea what any of the job titles actually mean. I get what a Chief Financial Officer is, and a Chief Marketing Officer, but would a Chief Operating Officer outrank a Chief Knowledge Officer? And what the heck is a Chief Engagement Officer?"

"Probably not what you're thinking," she said.

"Probably not. But is it obvious to anyone with a clue who the next in line is? I mean, I was looking for something like a Vice President, but—"

Gabriela shook her head. "VPs are small potatoes," she told me. "And every company's different, really. S and Tommy were both such larger-than-life chief executives, I'm not even sure there would be a cut-and-dried successor for either of them. Both of the companies have boards of directors, and the boards will probably end up appointing someone from inside, at least for the short term, but ultimately they may do a headhunt and bring in someone from outside the companies."

I sank onto a stool behind the counter. "Nobody obviously stood to gain."

"Sorry," she said.

I tried another angle. "Am I at least right in thinking that the Chief Marketing person would be the one to stage anything like a publicity stunt?"

Her eyebrows went up. "You think two massively powerful CEOs were murdered for the *publicity*?"

"Well, not when you put it like that," I admitted. I groaned. "I think I'm back to square one, and not for the first time today."

"Sorry," she said again.

I waved a hand. "Don't be. That's not even why you're here." Then I remembered why she'd come to the theater. "You said you had something to show me?"

Gabriela grinned. "I couldn't sleep last night," she said. "I had this crazy idea, and I had to figure it out. Then I went into the lab and worked on it all day."

She reached for a large backpack that was hanging off the back of her chair. "I've got an incredibly rough prototype. Where can we set up?"

Which is when it hit me that I couldn't say "my office" and dash up the stairs with her. There were no elevators at the Palace. There was one a small gender-neutral restroom off the lobby for moviegoers with disabilities, and spaces for wheelchairs in the back rows of the auditorium, but that was it in terms of accessibility.

Gabriela saw the look on my face and understood what I'd just realized. It must happen to her all the time.

"Never mind," she said. "Everyone's in watching the movie. Let's just set up out here."

"Perfect," I agreed. "I should stay down here anyway. Albert's gone home for the night and every teenager who works for me called in mysteriously sick today. Either there's a pandemic or they're all off searching for coins somewhere, so I'm on my own." Callie was out in the ticket booth and Marty was upstairs in his projection domain, but I was the sole minder of the lobby and candy counter.

Luckily, nobody had gotten around to taking the old metal desk back down to the basement after the *Desk Set* party. Gabriela and I went over to it and she began unpacking something from the backpack while I brought a stool around from behind the counter.

I had no idea what she meant by a prototype. When I joined her at the desk she laid out what looked like a computer keyboard with small semi-sheer mesh panels on each of the keys, connected to a tablet propped up in a holder.

"What is it?" I asked.

She pushed away from the desk to face me and took a deep breath.

"Last night during the séance I felt something," she began. "Intense cold. I felt it near my shoulder, and then it spread all across my back, as if I'd been draped in a chilled blanket."

She'd been draped in a chilled Trixie. "That's the same sensation Lillian gets."

Gabriela nodded vigorously. "And it got me thinking. You know that I work with adaptive technology for people with disabilities, right?"

"Right. Robot artificial limbs and things."

She grimaced. "Close enough. After last night, I started wondering what I could do to link that sensation of cold with technology."

"You mean to record the temperature? To prove the ghost is real?"

She pushed her glasses up. "No. I mean to create a highly temperature-sensitive input device."

I blinked.

"A keyboard," she said. "For a ghost to type on."

CHAPTER 23

"Oh. My. God." I stared from Gabriela to the keyboard and back again.

Trixie was going to absolutely love this.

If it worked.

"I know it's crazy," Gabriela said. "I don't even know if we can summon the ghost again, or if we need Lillian, or what, but—" She shrugged. "I just had to do it."

"Does it work?" I gingerly touched one of the semi-transparent pads on the keys. Every tiny pad had a tiny wire, all those tiny wires meeting up in a bundle connected to a larger wire that was attached to a circuit board and from there to the tablet.

"I don't think we'll know until we can contact the ghost again," Gabriela admitted.

My tap on a random key had done nothing.

"I tested it with a rubber glove filled with crushed ice," Gabriela said. "Just hovering the cold glove over the sensor without touching works. But that's as far as I got today."

I stared at her. "Oh, that's all? Just inventing a device that will get the entire spirit world on Twitter? What did you do with the rest of your day?"

She laughed. "Like I said, contacting the ghost will be the hard part."

Which is exactly when I would have loved to hear Trixie's voice saying something like "Gee, that's not hard at all. Here I am!"

Sadly, the lobby remained silent.

"Should we have another séance?" Gabriela asked.

I didn't know if I could take another séance. Or if Trixie could.

"Let's ask Lillian," I hedged.

Gabriela nodded. "I'll start working on a more refined version." She began gathering her things. "Meanwhile, I'll leave this one with you. We should put it out somewhere the ghost can find it, if she comes back."

"I know just the place," I told her. "There's a cold spot in my office." That wasn't technically true. But there was a spot on the arm of the couch where Trixie liked to perch. "I'll set it up there. Do I need to plug it in?"

"Just the tablet," she said, digging in her backpack for the charger. "That'll keep everything powered up." She handed it to me, stifling a yawn.

"Are you driving all the way back down to Menlo Park?" I asked. I knew she lived down the Peninsula, close to her work.

She shook her head. "I'm too tired after being up all last night. I'll just crash at Hector's and get an early start in the morning."

Hector. We'd managed to spend all this time without even mentioning him.

"Shall I tell him you say hi?" she asked.

I was spared an answer when the auditorium doors opened and people began straggling out of *Swing Time*, just as Marty began playing "A Fine Romance," one of the best numbers from the film, over the theater's sound system.

Say what you will about Marty, his timing was perfect.

I had to work the concessions stand between the shows, so I didn't walk Gabriella out to her van. I did take a minute to put an empty M&Ms carton over the keyboard, just to avoid curious stares from the patrons who were showing up for the nine-fifteen.

"Let me know what Lillian thinks," Gabriela said before she left. "I'll try to have something more refined by next week, just in case."

I hugged her. "You're a genius, you know that, right?"

She waved a hand. "Or a lunatic. Just don't tell my boss what

I've been up to. I'd rather not have them send the men in the white coats after me."

I knew exactly how she felt.

Callie closed out the ticket booth and came in after *Silk Stockings* had gotten underway.

"How's your mom?" I asked her.

"Impossible." She slid the cashbox across the glass countertop of the concessions stand and dropped onto one of the stools with an epic sigh. "And exhausted. She slept all day and still doesn't feel a hundred percent." She polished a spot on the counter with her sleeve. "I mean, she's always said she has this 'gift.' Don't even ask me about what happened at my middle-school fundraiser." She shuddered. "But those candles last night—" She shook her head. "It was, like, an order of magnitude more than she's ever experienced. She wants to try again as soon as she can."

"So does Gabriela," I said, pouring her a cup of coffee.

"Okay, but Gabriela isn't an old lady with high blood pressure getting herself all worked up."

"Your mother is not an old lady," I told her. Lillian was only a dozen years older than me. "But I didn't know about the high blood pressure." That was concerning. And it was clear that Callie, however much she claimed to be embarrassed by her mother's eccentricities, was truly worried about her.

"What about you?" she asked. "Do you want to try again?"

I turned to find Callie scrutinizing me. I'd been about to say something flip and noncommittal, but instead I handed her the coffee and told her the truth. "I don't think it's a good idea."

I didn't tell her why. Because telling her why would mean telling her I was afraid that it had all taken too much out of Trixie, as well as Lillian. It was close to twenty-four hours since Trixie had disappeared, and I didn't like that she hadn't come back. I wasn't officially worried yet, but I would be soon.

"My dad's been talking about taking a vacation," Callie said carefully. "Like, taking my mom to Paris or Venice or somewhere." She looked at me. "I could, I mean, maybe suggest that they don't need to wait until June?"

"Paris is very nice in April," I offered. "They write songs about it."

"And, like, it's *almost* April."

"It is," I agreed.

She held up the coffee in a toast. "To Paris."

There was the sound of clomping on the balcony stairs and we turned to find Marty coming down. "What about Paris?"

I poured another cup of coffee and handed it to him when he got to the counter.

"Thanks. Are we doing Paris musicals next month? *April in Paris*? *Funny Face*?"

I exchanged a look with Callie. "Well, we are now."

Once again I waited until everyone left and then did a sweep of the Palace, talking to Trixie whether she could hear me or not. I cleared off a small table in the office to set up Gabriela's paranormal keyboard, plugging in the charger and leaving it all on, just in case.

When I finally came down the balcony stairs, to a lobby lit only by the glow of the exit lights, I saw a figure silhouetted outside the glass lobby doors. I froze. The figure took something from a pocket. I reached into my bag for my phone as I moved carefully down the rest of the stairs, dialing 9-1, ready to hit the last digit if necessary. I wasn't taking any chances. There was still a murderer running around.

Then the figure spoke.

"Nora, it's me. I was just about to text you. I didn't want to frighten you again."

Hector.

I experienced roughly fifteen thousand different emotions in the time it took to cross the lobby and open the door. The minute he stepped into the dim lobby I settled on one: indignant fury.

"What the hell, Hector?"

This was apparently not the greeting he was expecting. I could tell by the way he backed up, his eyes widening.

"Three days? We finally both admit there's something between us and you stay away for *three days*? You *wave* at me from the sidewalk? You don't even send a damn *text*? Nothing? For three days? You give me arguably the best kiss of my life and then *vanish*? With not one word? What in the actual *hell* do you—"

"The best kiss?" he interrupted. He'd stared at me with something akin to panic as I'd blasted him, but now his mood shifted. He looked suspiciously as if he might smile.

"*That's* all you just heard? The part about the kiss?"

"The *best* kiss," he corrected.

I stared at him, stone-faced. "Arguably," I reiterated.

He moved a step closer. "It was arguably the best kiss I've ever had as well."

I looked up at him. "Then I repeat...What the *hell*?" But this time it didn't come out as furious. It came out frustrated and hurt and fifteen thousand other things.

"Nora, *mi amor.*" Now he was very close. "Please let me explain."

He'd never called me *mi amor* before. It had the oddest effect of turning my spine into something squishy and gelatinous. I was in danger of melting into the well-worn carpet of the lobby floor.

I took a deep breath.

"This better be good."

"My father was an adulterer," Hector began.

For the second time in as many days I was seated on the balcony stairs. But this time it was with just one other person, and he had a lot of explaining to do.

"Your father was also a criminal kingpin and a drug lord," I said. "I fail to see what he has to do with anything."

"He was all of those things, and worse," Hector said, his voice low. "But the only thing about him that matters tonight is that he was a lifelong, dedicated, enthusiastic adulterer. He broke my mother's heart. Many times."

I still didn't know where he was going with this, but he had my attention.

"I have done many things in my life that I am rightly ashamed of," Hector went on. "But there is one thing I promised my mother I would never do."

He was seated on the step below me, something he'd probably planned, because it allowed him to look up at me with those damn eyes of his. He took my hand in both of his. "On her deathbed, I vowed to her that I will never become an adulterer."

For a moment I was so focused on the warmth of his hands and the heat in his eyes that I didn't take in what he'd just said. Then it caught up to me.

"You're *married*?" I snatched my hand away and jumped to my feet. "How could you—? What do you—? *Who*?"

"No!" he yelled, standing.

"Don't you dare!" I took a step away, my back against the stairway railing.

"Nora! I'm not married! You are!"

I stared at him. "*What*?"

He ran a hand through his hair. "In the eyes of the church, having relations with a married woman is committing adultery," he said. "And if I had stayed with you for one more minute the other night..." He gave me a meaningful look.

I mustered my dignity. "That's *awfully* presumptuous of you."

He just looked at me. Smoldering

I cleared my throat. "Although possibly accurate," I allowed.

"Can you understand?" Hector asked. "Do you see that as long as you remain married to that...that..."

"Lying, cheating, lying rat," I supplied.

"Yes, him." He blew out a breath. "I know your marriage is over. I know this is an absurd technicality. But I have tried to change my life in the years since my mother died. I have tried to become a better man. A man deserving of a woman like you. That man cannot break a promise made to his dying mother."

I stared at him. Then I did the only thing I could think of. I took my phone out of my pocket, dialed a number with no regard for the fact that it was after one in the morning, and left a voicemail when nobody picked up.

"Ted. I was wrong. You can buy me. I'll handle that meeting if you finalize the divorce."

CHAPTER 24

I had three reasons to go to the Potent Flower the next morning. I was going to join the call with Tommy's lawyer to learn the fate of his share of the Palace, I was going to corner Kristy and figure out what exactly she'd seen and possibly done before S was poisoned on that stage, and I was going to spill my guts to Monica about Hector.

Since I got there half an hour before the meeting and well before Kristy was due in, we started with the last item.

"Wow," Monica said when my guts were sufficiently spilled. "I wouldn't have guessed Hector was a stickler for the rules."

"Only some rules, I suspect."

We were in her soothing saffron-colored office, drinking coffee that I'd stopped for on my way to Monica's shop.

She took a sip. "You're not seriously going to bail on getting Ted to cough up what's rightfully yours, are you?"

"I got a little overly dramatic in the moment," I admitted.

"It sounds like it was quite a moment," she grinned. "So where are you now? With Hector, I mean."

"We've agreed to keep seeing each other, and to 'exercise restraint.'"

She laughed. "I'm guessing those were his words."

"They were." I sat back in my chair. "And, honestly, it's for the best. I'm still all tangled up with Ted and I'm not looking for anything serious. I need to get my head straight before I'll be in any condition—"

"Yeah, sure," Monica interrupted, still grinning. "There's only one thing wrong with that."

I looked at her.

"Um," she said, as if she were about to state the obvious. "It's *Hector*."

I exhaled. "It's Hector," I agreed. I finished my coffee. "Meanwhile, Ted hasn't called back, *of course*, but I emailed my lawyers this morning telling them there's an increased urgency to finding where he hid the money so we can finalize the settlement."

"*Increased urgency*. Is that what you kids are calling it these days?" Monica was enjoying this way too much.

"I also sent a text to Ted this morning," I continued, ignoring her obvious delight. "Telling him I misspoke in the voicemail. What I meant was that I'll handle that meeting he wants me to if he sends the paperwork authenticating those gowns," I told her. "Which was what he was after all along, so I'm not happy about it, but I can't afford to care about that anymore. Once I have the authentication I can sell them, or exhibit them, or whatever makes the most sense."

"Oh, I forgot about the gowns." Monica sat up. "I wanted to see them the other night, but with the séance and everything..."

"There was a lot going on," I agreed. "And you may have missed your chance, at least for a while. The storage people are picking them up this afternoon."

"Do I even want to know how much that's going to cost?"

"You don't," I said. "You really don't."

The video call started on the dot of nine. Monica and I used the big screen in her shop lounge, Robbie and Mitch were each at their desks in LA, and Marc Picco, Tommy's lawyer, was in an expensive-looking conference room, presumably at his law firm. I was surprised to see he was alone. In my experience, you never talked to one lawyer when six would do.

"Thank you all for joining on such short notice," Picco began, once introductions were out of the way. He was probably in his comfortable fifties, with thinning gray hair and a tailored gray suit. "Let me begin by offering my condolences on the loss of your partner and friend."

"Thanks," Mitch said. "Can we cut to the chase? I'm due on set and all I really want to know is who inherits Tommy's share of the Palace. I'm assuming it isn't one of us."

Mitch was a successful sitcom director not generally noted for his diplomacy off the set.

Picco cleared his throat and opened a leather portfolio on the highly polished table in front of him. "Yes, of course." He donned a pair of reading glasses only so he could take them off when looking back at the video camera. "I will begin by enquiring if any of you were aware that Thomas May sold his one-quarter share of the Palace Theater three days before his death?"

Digital cameras captured four jaws dropping simultaneously.

"He *what*?" Robbie was the first to speak. "He *sold*?"

"Could he even do that?" Monica asked. "Without telling us?"

"He could and he did," the lawyer informed us.

"That was the day after S was killed," I said, working backward on a mental calendar from the day of Tommy's murder.

"Was this something he'd planned?" I asked Picco.

"Just that week he was making all kinds of threats to close the Palace if we didn't turn it around," Robbie protested. "Why would he have called that whole special meeting if he knew he was going to sell?"

"This is crazy," Monica said.

"And just like Tommy," Mitch fumed. "Giving us one more rattle to the cage before he buggered off. That conniving snake!" He realized we were all staring at him. "May he rest in peace."

"Mr. Picco," I spoke above the new round of protests that broke out. "Who did he sell to?"

The protests abruptly came to a halt. We all looked at the lawyer.

Another use of the glasses to consult the paperwork that I was pretty sure he knew by heart. Another removal of the glasses to face us.

"The reason I felt it was best to meet like this was to inform you that the purchaser wishes to remain anonymous."

The owners were silent for one stunned moment, then they all started shouting at once. I sat back in my chair, a cold feeling of dread settling in my stomach. Eventually Picco got tired of everyone yelling at him and held up his hands.

"Please! Please!" he shouted. "The wishes of the purchaser are very clear and quite legal, if unorthodox." He straightened his jacket, having gotten everyone to simmer down, at least for the moment. "All business relating to the Palace Theater will be handled through me, for the time being," he informed us. "I will personally attend any board meetings, and you should consider me the owner's proxy in all matters."

"Now, wait just one minute!" Mitch yelled. Robbie and Monica were also demanding answers, but Mitch's voice drowned them out.

I let them have at it. I was thinking. And I had two thoughts about who might have bought Tommy out on the condition of anonymity.

Because I knew two people that I'd expressly forbidden to do any such thing.

Hector. Tell me the truth. Did you buy Tommy's share of the Palace? Be honest. I promise I won't be angry.

I'd be livid.

I sent Hector the text from Monica's office after the meeting concluded. There had been many more demands, protests, and accusations, but Picco had held firm. No further information was forthcoming.

Hector's response was prompt. Whether it was truthful, only time would tell.

Buy his share? Of course not. You were quite clear in your feelings on that subject.

Damn right I was. Hector texted again.

Are you saying someone bought his share? Who?

Well, that was the question. If it wasn't Hector, odds were it was the other person who'd recently offered unwanted financial help. Otis Hampton, no doubt scheming to get me further in his debt so he could continue to entangle me in his plot against Ted. I was about to send a fiery email in his direction when Monica opened the door. She'd gone out front to open the shop after the video call, leaving me to stew and text in private.

She came in with a worried look on her face. Worried enough that I put the phone down. "What's wrong?"

"Maybe nothing," she said.

"What's wrong?" I repeated.

"Kristy." She sat at her desk and opened her laptop. "You know how I told you she called in sick yesterday? I figured she was just off with the rest of them, playing the game." She glanced from the screen to me. "But the others are here today, and they say she wasn't with them yesterday."

For the second time that morning I got a very bad feeling. "Have you heard from her today?"

She shook her head, consulting the laptop and dialing a number on her phone. "It's ringing." She waited, and apparently got Kristy's voicemail, as I had the day before. "Kristy, call me when you get this. We're all worried about you. Hope you're okay."

Monica and I exchanged a look when she hung up.

"Kristy was there the day S was killed," I said. "If she saw something..."

Monica nodded.

"Do you have her address?"

She looked relieved. "You think we should check on her?"

I stood. "Let's go."

Kristy's address was only a few blocks away, the top flat in a tall converted Victorian on Pine. We hurried up the steep flight of stairs from the sidewalk to the locked front door. There was no answer when we buzzed Kristy's flat. We tried another apartment number, and the lock on the door clicked in response.

Once inside, we were starting up the stairs when a tall thin guy with bed head opened a door on the first floor.

"Aren't you UPS?" he asked. "I'm expecting a package."

"Sorry," I called as we took the stairs up.

We reached the attic flat and knocked. There was no answer. We knocked again, louder.

"Should we call the police?" Monica asked. "Detective Jackson?"

"Just a second," I said. There was a deadbolt above the doorknob, but I couldn't tell if it was locked. "If the deadbolt isn't locked, maybe..."

I reached for the doorknob, wondering if I could use a credit card or something on that lock. I'd seen it done in the movies and it didn't look too hard. But when I gave it a test jiggle, the knob turned.

"It's unlocked."

Monica and I exchanged looks as I opened the door.

"Kristy?" She called.

Nothing.

"Kristy, we're coming in," I announced.

The apartment was small, with the pitched roof and odd angles of a Victorian attic. Everything seemed neat in the tiny living room and kitchen. There was evidence of tea having been made on the countertop.

"Kristy?" Monica moved toward the bedroom, barely big enough for the double-sized bed. Again, nothing seemed to be disturbed.

"Maybe she just went out of town," Monica said doubtfully.

I smelled something. Something floral.

"Bubble bath?" I said, crossing the bedroom to the bathroom.

It was a tiny room painted white, almost all the space taken up by an old-fashioned claw-foot tub beneath a round window.

In the tub, pale and waxen, her lavender hair floating around her like Ophelia, was Kristy.

CHAPTER 25

I rushed to the tub. The water was cool, the bubbles long gone. Kristy's skin was puckered, her lips tinged with purple. I heard Monica repeating "No, no, no, no, no" as I put two fingers on Kristy's neck.

"There's a pulse!"

Hours later Monica and I were in a hospital waiting room. We knew only that Kristy was unconscious but hanging on. We'd made the mistake of telling the truth when the admittance nurse asked if we were relatives, and we'd gotten no more updates since.

There had been a flurry of making calls and sending texts, but once that was over we'd settled into a numb sort of shock, staring at the muted TV screen because it was easier than making conversation with any of the other groups of worried people speaking in halting, hushed tones while waiting for their news.

Eventually the hushed tones were interrupted by a deep authoritative voice coming from the nurse's station. I stood and motioned for Monica to come with me. We saw a large familiar figure talking to a nurse.

"Detective Jackson."

He turned as the nurse moved busily away. "Ladies. They told me you were here. I'm going to need you to answer some questions."

"Arsenic." I stared at the detective.

"Not as much as Tommy May had in his system," he said, "but enough to put her into a coma."

We'd moved to a small consulting room, and Jackson had asked us for every last detail of what had happened before confirming that Kristy had been poisoned.

"Will she be all right?" Monica asked.

"They tell me it's too soon to say," he said heavily. "But she's lucky she didn't drown."

"What can we do?" I asked.

"Tell me anything you think might be relevant."

"Do you think something was tampered with?" Monica asked. "That she ate or drank something?"

"There was tea on the counter in her kitchen," I said, remembering. "Will they..."

The look on Jackson's face said "duh" pretty clearly. Of course the police would test the beverage Kristy had presumably drunk just before falling into an arsenic-induced coma.

"You know Kristy was at the game launch in Palo Alto when S was killed," I said to Jackson.

He nodded. "We questioned her at length."

"She thought Tommy did it," I told him. "Did she tell you that? She thought Tommy killed S in a fit of rage and then committed suicide."

"So she said," Jackson agreed.

"She was wrong," I said. And I was wrong for thinking, however briefly, that she might have been the killer. "The same person who killed them poisoned her."

The two-thirty was well under way by the time I got back to the Palace. Callie and Albert were huddled together over the candy counter, Callie showing him something on the tiny screen of a video camera.

Albert came around the counter as soon as he saw me. "Nora, how are you? How is the young lady? Any update?" I'd texted them with the news once it became clear I wouldn't be around to open the theater that morning.

"I'm fine," I said. "And she's holding steady. That's all we know for now."

"I mean, it's a good thing you and Monica are the worrying kind," Callie said.

I rubbed my eyes. "For once that paid off," I agreed. "Kristy's parents got in from Fresno before I left. Monica's staying with them at the hospital for a while. Is everything okay here?"

"We're a well-oiled machine," I heard Marty say from behind me. He was coming downstairs from his lair. "What could go wrong?"

"Please don't say that," I said. "There's enough going on without tempting fate."

"People who believe in fate have given up," he told me, crossing to the concessions stand to get himself a soda. "What happened at the owners' meeting?"

I slumped onto one of the stools at the counter. Had the meeting with Tommy's lawyer only been that morning? "That feels like a hundred years ago."

"Who did Tommy leave his share of this place to?" Marty asked. "Or are we going to be in probate hell for the rest of our lives? He probably didn't even leave a will. Guys like that think they're immortal."

"He didn't leave it to anyone," I said before he could get up a good head of steam. "He sold it. The day after S died."

They all stared at me.

"The buyer is anonymous."

The employees of the Palace freaked out in much the same way the owners of the Palace had freaked out that morning. I let them get it all out of their systems. Once I explained exactly what the lawyer had told us, there were several more minutes of "I can't believe he—" and "How could he have—" before Albert cleared his throat and asked a coherent question.

"Who do you think bought it?"

I took a breath. "My first thought was Hector, in some misguided attempt to make my life easier," I said.

"I mean...yeah," Callie agreed. "That tracks."

"Right, but I'd already told him I didn't want him to, and he says he didn't."

"So who?" Marty demanded. "And why?"

"The only other person I can think of is Otis Hampton," I told them. "And the *why* is that he somehow thinks it could be a bargaining chip in his war with Ted, or he thinks he can use it to control me, because I'm another pawn in his whole twisted..." I gave up. "I know I'm mixing metaphors, but you get what I'm saying. He's secretive and manipulative and always has an agenda, so it could be him."

Albert had poured a large cup of coffee while I'd been babbling. He slid it across the counter to me. "What did Mr. Hampton say when you asked him?"

My eyes flew open. "I didn't!" I grabbed for my phone. "I was just about to text him when Monica told me Kristy was missing."

I quickly finished the text I'd been writing to Otis that morning.

Someone has anonymously bought Tommy May's one-quarter share of the Palace. Was it you? Tell me the truth or I'm done.

Callie was putting her camera away. "I mean, *why* would Tommy have sold?" she asked.

"The *why* isn't so hard to figure," I said. "He wasn't happy with the Palace profits being down, so under normal circumstances it wouldn't be weird for him to sell. But the *when* is definitely weird. Why would you yell at all your partners—not to mention your hardworking manager—on a Sunday if you're planning to sell your share the next Tuesday? Why even call the Sunday meeting?"

"Perhaps he thought he'd get his way in the Sunday meeting," Albert suggested. "And when he didn't, he decided to wash his hands of it all."

"Maybe," I said doubtfully. "But S was killed the day between the meeting and the sale. I can't imagine Tommy would have been thinking of anything but the murder and what it meant for the game at that point. He had a lot more at stake with that investment than with the Palace."

"Maybe he *was* thinking of the murder," Marty said. "He probably knew he'd be arrested. He knew he'd need quick money for expensive lawyers."

"How would he know he'd be arrested?" Callie asked.

"Because he killed S," Marty said authoritatively.

The lobby erupted in objections.

"Hang on," I finally said. "If Tommy killed S, then who killed Tommy? And tried to kill Kristy?"

"You haven't seen nearly enough movies," he said, inaccurately. "*Kristy* killed Tommy *because* he killed S. Then she took just enough poison herself to throw the police off the track. It's classic noir stuff."

I stared at him. "Please tell me you've shared that ridiculous theory with your boyfriend the homicide detective."

"I mean, is it ridiculous?" Callie asked. "The second two poisonings were different from the first. Bee pollen, arsenic, and arsenic, right?"

"May I remind you that Kristy is in a *coma*?" I pointed out. Even if I had suspected her myself, I couldn't imagine anyone being crazy enough to poison themselves as an alibi. I mean, outside of a movie.

"I never said she was a good poisoner," Marty sniffed.

"All right," Albert gave him a firm look. "That's one theory. Who has another?"

"Could the buyer be the killer?" Callie suggested. "Whoever bought Tommy's share of the Palace?"

"Because someone wanted a fourth of a broken-down classic movie theater enough to kill for it?" Marty scoffed. Then he looked up in the general direction of the lobby chandelier. "No offense."

"The buyer," I ignored Marty and responded to Callie's suggestion, "would have had no reason to kill Tommy. They'd already done the deal." I thought about it. "This is a crazy thought, but what if Picco, the lawyer, who is now acting as this anonymous buyer's proxy, is actually the buyer? Or what if there really is no buyer? What if when Tommy died Picco saw his chance to take control? And he made up the whole story about the mysterious buyer so nobody would suspect?" I frowned. "But would he have killed Tommy to get control? And not just Tommy, but—"

"I've often accused you of suffering from a failure of imagination," Marty cut me off. "I take it back."

I wasn't offended. It was a crazy theory. It would have been shot down much more mercilessly in any Hollywood writer's room.

"One thing's for sure," I told them. "Tommy was totally manipulating me when he asked me to help him clear his name. He made all sorts of promises about what he wanted to do with the Palace, telling me he didn't want to close it, and talking about turning it into a non-profit, when didn't even own it anymore."

"To Tommy." Marty raised his soda in a toast. "A duplicitous rat to the end."

Speaking of duplicitous rats, I checked my phone. There was no response from Otis. Or from Ted.

After a while I left the gang in the lobby and went upstairs to the office. I no longer cared what the police might find in my browser history. I wanted to learn everything I could about arsenic.

When I opened the door I saw just about the only thing that could have distracted me from a mad poisoner. Trixie was perched on the arm of the couch, looking intently at Gabriela's invention.

"Hiya Nora," she beamed. "What's this thingamajig?"

CHAPTER 26

"Trixie!" I quickly closed the door behind me, relieved that everyone was downstairs out of earshot. "I'm so glad to see you. I was getting so worried."

"Gee, that's sweet of you, but I'm just grand." She kicked her legs as she hopped off the arm of the couch. "What did everyone say about me after I left the other night? It was just the other night, wasn't it? I checked the marquee..." A little frown appeared. She often got confused about the passage of time when she was gone and did her best to orient herself by looking out the window to see what was on the marquee. She could check that against the three-month calendar of lineups I kept on a large blackboard in the office.

"Just the other night," I assured her. "Today's only Wednesday."

"Oh, good." The frown disappeared, replaced with her previous excitement. "What did everyone say? Did they know it was me? Do they all believe in me now?"

"Most of them believed in you before," I told her. "But you made quite an impression."

She dimpled. "I did, didn't I? It was so clever of you to point me to the candles."

"I knew you could do it," I told her.

She perched on the arm of the couch again, chewing a red lacquered fingernail. "I wish they'd been able to see me, though. Do you think we could try again?"

"I heard something about Lillian going out of town," I hedged. "But Trixie, there's something else. Something amazing." I went to Gabriela's keyboard. "This is for you."

"Is it?" She stared at the apparatus. "Gee, it's...something, isn't it?" She looked at me, confusion mixed with delight. "What is it?"

"You know how you've always said you wished you could use one of those phones or computers?"

"Why, sure," she nodded, curls bouncing.

"Well, this," I touched the tablet. "Is like the screen of a phone or computer. And this," I swept my hand over the keyboard. "Is how you can use it. At least Gabriela thinks you can. And I think you can. Do you want to see if you can?"

I was more excited than Trixie at that point.

Her face had clouded over. "Oh, but..." she passed her hand through the tablet. "I can't..."

"Not like that," I said. "Try just touching one of the keys. Gabriela fixed it so it should be able to sense you, by temperature. Try 'T' for Trixie."

She blinked, looked at the keyboard, then looked at me again. "Really?"

"Really," I nodded. "Try."

She pointed at the 'T' key, hesitated, and then pressed her finger through it.

"I don't quite..." she began.

Then we both screamed. Because the screen lit up and the letter 'T' appeared. It was quickly followed by the letters 'R,' 'G,' and 'Y,' but never mind. She had done it.

She jumped off the couch, backing away from the keyboard, pointing at it. "Did you see? I did it!"

"You did!" I yelled, forgetting that there were other people in the building who might wonder why I was shouting with excitement when I was supposedly alone in my office.

"Trixie, you did it," I said more quietly.

She stepped back to the device, peering at the screen. "Why did the rest of the letters show up?"

"It must be super sensitive," I said. "Try again, and maybe don't put your finger all the way through the key."

This time she hovered her finger right over the 'T,' but didn't pass through it. Sure enough, it appeared on the screen after about a second. This time alone.

"Nora!" Trixie threw herself at me. I know she intended it as a hug, but she was a little too enthusiastic and rushed right through me.

"Trixie!" The cold sensation of being charged by a ghost was one I'd never get used to, but this time I hardly noticed it. "I'm so happy for you!"

There was a loud staccato knock at the door, followed by Marty opening it.

"What are you happy about? Who are you talking to?" He looked suspiciously around the room. "Never mind. If you're losing it I don't even want to know."

Trixie moved away from me and I tried to look like I hadn't just been celebrating something earthshattering with a card-carrying member of the spirit world.

"There's a guy downstairs," Marty informed me. "He says he's here about some gowns?"

I left Trixie to experiment with her new technology and hustled down to the lobby. The guy from the garment storage facility looked to be in his seventies and spoke with a soft Russian accent. He was rightly horrified when I took him to the basement and showed him where I'd been keeping the famous gowns.

"Are these originals?" he asked, looking more than a little dazzled. He was the right demographic for recognizing an iconic Marilyn Monroe dress or two.

"I believe so," I told him. "I'm waiting on the authentication, but let's treat them like they are."

He treated them like they were priceless, and I wrote him an account-draining check. After he packed each gown reverently in its own sturdy travel container, I suggested he pull his truck around to the alley and leave by the back door. I didn't want to think about what rumors might get going if he were to tote what looked like six modest coffins through the lobby. We had rumors enough.

As I was locking the alley door behind him I felt my phone vibrate. I was surprised to see it was a call, not a text, from Otis.

"Otis, you got my message." I went back to the prop room, knowing the signal would be stronger there.

"I was glad to hear from you, Nora. After our last exchange I thought you might be cooling on our project."

Our project? I wouldn't let myself get sidetracked by whatever his latest scheme might be. "Otis, tell me the truth," I said, sitting on a table in the prop room. The gowns were gone, but the rest of my possessions were still scattered all over the place. "Did you buy Tommy May's quarter-share of the Palace?"

"Why? Do you want me to? No problem." He sounded busy and distracted, which wasn't unusual for Otis. A normal afternoon for him involved half a dozen underlings vying for his attention while he simultaneously tore some poor writer's screenplay apart and devoured a ham sandwich.

"Otis, you're not listening," I said, trying for patience. "I'm asking if you already have. Bought it."

"No, but I can. Just have him call me," he said, apparently forgetting that Tommy was in no position to call anyone. "Listen," he went on without a pause. "I've got an update on the Venice plan. I've arranged for Glen Hendricks to go with us. The press will eat it up. The story will be that you two met when he signed on as the lead in—"

I abandoned patience and cut him off mid-scheme. "Otis, what are you talking about? What do you mean *us*? And what's Glen Hendricks got to do with anything?" Hendricks, I knew, was the red-hot action star of a recent CGI-fueled video game masquerading as a movie.

"Glen Hendricks," Otis explained gleefully, "is seven years younger than your husband and about a hundred times hotter. Ted's only hope of landing any major franchise is if Hendricks passes on it first. You showing up at the Venice Film Festival with him is going to kill Ted."

"What are you talking about?" I wailed. I often ended up wailing when trying to talk with Otis. "I'm not showing up anywhere with Glen Hendricks. I've never even met him."

"You'll meet him, don't worry," he cackled.

"That's not my point. I'm not—"

"You're going to Venice with Glen Hendricks," Otis insisted, his voice hardening. "The press will go nuts and *nobody* will pay attention to Ted or Priya or their super-secret-but-carefully-leaked wedding plans."

I took a deep breath. "Otis, I'm doing no such thing."

He didn't hear a word. "Priya's going to see that Ted may be big now, but he's not going to be big forever. There will always be some new guy gunning for him, and sooner or later one of them will take him down. But I'm *always* going to be on top. I'm the one with the power to—"

"*Otis!*"

Miraculously, he paused.

"Otis, this has gone too far. I'm not going to traipse around Venice pretending to be with Glen Hendricks. I'm not going to do any of this anymore."

"Sure you are," he said. The man had an uncanny ability to hear only what he wanted to. "Think about it, Nora. This is how we'll get them."

"Listen to me very carefully, Otis. I don't care about getting them. I only care about getting the money that's rightfully mine, and to be honest, I'm caring about that less every day." As I said that, I realized it was true.

"Sure you care," he breezed. "Why else did you call me?"

I did my very best not to scream in frustration. "I didn't call you. I sent you a text. Asking if you bought Tommy's share of the Palace before he was killed. I take it your answer is no?"

"Oh, shit," he said. "No, I didn't. Was I supposed to?"

"Goodbye, Otis."

He was still talking when I hung up.

CHAPTER 27

My phone pinged with an incoming text almost as soon as I hung up from Otis. It was from Gabriela.

Hi Nora. I'm working on the next gen tablet for our friend, but it's going to take a few days. Any word from Lillian? Are we having another séance?

I saw the three gray dots that told me she was still typing.

I see you've been experimenting with the keyboard. Did you use ice?

She saw? I typed quickly.

How did you see? What did you see?

I watched the three gray dots impatiently.

I set it up so the input from the keyboard automatically gets sent to me as a text. I nearly died when I saw you type Hello Trixie *this afternoon, after what looked like a couple false starts. Are you trying to get her attention?*

I put the phone over my racing heart. Gabriela could see what Trixie was doing on the keyboard. I *really* wished I'd known that before. I wrote back.

Yep. Hey, do you mind fixing it so that the keyboard sends me a text as well? Since I'm usually at the theater it might make sense.

She answered immediately.

Great idea. Meanwhile, I'll keep working on this. Hope we're on for another séance!

I'll check on that. See you soon!

I ran all the way up to the office.

"Trixie!"

She wasn't there. I went to the keyboard and saw that the screen displayed her experimental Ts, then a few more random letters, then the word HELLO, more gibberish, and finally TRIXIE.

I sank onto the couch, my knees suddenly weak. What if she'd written something else? Something Gabriela wouldn't have assumed was me?

All the potential consequences of helping Trixie prove she was real descended on me in that instant.

If there was proof Trixie was real—genuine proof—would it mean that I could start letting people know I could see her? Without the fear of a quick trip to a chic little sanatorium nestled in the redwoods?

Maybe.

But.

It was a lot to ask anyone to go from believing that a disembodied spirit could manifest during a séance to believing that I regularly palled around with a very lively usherette who died in 1937. An invisible presence putting out candles was one thing, but would anyone believe Trixie and I spent rainy afternoons discussing whether Clark Gable or Cary Grant was better boyfriend material? (My answer: neither of them. Save your time and go with

Jimmy Stewart.)

No. The way I saw the situation, people still might—quite understandably—think I was crazy if the whole truth came out. And if people thought I was crazy, especially people who cared about me, people like Robbie, they'd want to get me away from the source of the craziness. For my own good.

I could see how it would play out. Robbie would, with all the patience in the world, tell me I'd been pushing myself too hard since Ted left. She'd tell me that taking over the Palace had been too much for me. She'd insist I get away and relax somewhere. Web links to meditation retreats and holistic spas would follow, and before I knew it she'd orchestrate getting me out of the Palace as smoothly as she'd orchestrated getting me into it.

And once I was out of the Palace, who would look out for Trixie?

"Trixie?" I called out again.

When she didn't answer I wrote a note on a yellow index card. I propped it up against the tablet screen.

Please don't use this again until after we talk.

Because there could be all kinds of consequences.

I was heading down to work the concessions stand before the seven-thirty show when I finally got a text from Ted. Or rather, a series of texts, pinging in one after the other. I stopped midway down the lobby stairs to read them.

"Nora?" Albert was restocking the licorice supply. "Everything all right?"

I looked at him numbly, then back to the texts.

Babe, you're the best. I knew you'd come through for me.
I have all the paperwork on the gowns. I knew you'd love them. I really want you to have them. Like I said, the only favor I need is for you to take a meeting with a producer.
I'm totally supposed to have the lead in that Scandinavian

franchise. You know, from those books you liked? With the reporter who's ex-CIA? And the fjords?

But now I'm hearing that there's a new producer on the deal, and he's not my biggest fan. He's talking to some other actor, Glen Hendricks. Like that dude could ever get a part where he keeps his shirt on.

Listen, you have to nail down this producer for me. Work your magic. I know if anyone can bring him around, it's you.

His name is Otis Hampton. Thanks!

Albert was still peering up at me from behind his little round glasses.

"You know those gowns?" I asked him.

He nodded.

"I'm never going to get them authenticated."

Albert went home once the seven-thirty started, and Callie left early as well, taking advantage of the fact that Brandon unexpectedly showed up during the nine-fifteen.

"I take it you haven't found a coin yet?" I asked him.

He looked like he hadn't slept since I'd seen him the day before. "It's impossible," he said, coming around the counter to get himself a soda. The machine made an alarming clanking sound, which I chose to ignore. "Have you heard what they're saying?"

"By 'they,' do you mean the crazies on the game forums?"

"Them," he agreed. He gulped down half the drink before continuing. "The latest thing going around is that there never were any coins, and the two that were supposedly found were just planted to keep everyone playing."

"So the people who found them..."

"Fakes," he said authoritatively. "Bots, maybe. Or plants who worked for S."

I wondered if that could be true. Which is exactly how conspiracy theories caught on, I told myself.

"Looking for the bright side," I said to Brandon, "does this mean 'they' have stopped talking about me being a homicidal maniac?"

"Oh, yeah," he said, as if he'd just noticed. "I told you they'd move on."

Thank goodness for short attention spans. At least in this case.

"Um, Nora?" Brandon said. "Could I maybe get some more hours for the next couple of weeks? I need to make some money to pay for all the stuff I bought in the game, and I need it before my mom gets her credit card bill."

"I'll see what I can do," I told him. "Meanwhile, how about heading downstairs with a mop?"

Which is how I found myself alone in the lobby when Detective Jackson stopped by.

"I'm only here to pick Marty up," Jackson said when he came in through the lobby doors and saw me behind the counter. He held up both hands. "Not to talk about the case."

"Of course," I said smoothly. "But before you go upstairs, have a free cookie. I've still got three left and I'd hate to have to throw them away."

He paused on his way to the stairs. I brought the tray of Lisa's cookies out from the glass case and held it temptingly.

"Maybe just one," he caved.

"Take the rest to go," I offered. "How's Kristy? Is there any news?"

He gave me a look as he reached for the tray. "So these cookies aren't free."

I shrugged. "Monica's been texting me. She's still with Kristy's parents at the hospital. She says there's no change yet, but they're still running tests. Have you heard anything more?"

He shook his head, munching. "That's as much as I know."

"What about the investigation? Have you found anything? Was there arsenic in Kristy's tea?" I poured him a cup of coffee and was happy when he accepted it and took a seat on the stool opposite me.

"I hate to tell you this, but you were right," he said. "We found a concentration of arsenic in the tea still in her cup, and an empty bottle containing traces of arsenic in her kitchen trash can."

I shivered. "Thank God she didn't drink the whole cup of tea."

He nodded. "That's probably why she's in the hospital, and not in the morgue."

"Hang on," I said. "Why was the bottle in her trash? Did the killer leave it behind? Isn't that a little cavalier? Were there fingerprints on it?"

"You're assuming the killer was there," he said, picking up the coffee.

I stared at him. "You're not saying you think it was suicide?"

"I'm not ruling anything out, but there's another possibility." He seemed to be enjoying this. I'd have to remember to bribe him with sugar more often.

"You're saying the killer tampered with something in her kitchen some other time," I guessed. "Something he knew Kristy would eventually eat, or drink. Like a bottle of milk or something. Almond milk! Isn't arsenic supposed to taste like almonds?"

"You're assuming that the killer is a man," he said reprovingly. "And you're assuming that the killer had access to her flat."

"Access to her flat was a cinch," I told him. "At least it was for Monica and me. I told you, the guy downstairs let us into the building and her apartment door was unlocked. I thought the killer must have left it unlocked when they left, but maybe Kristy was just careless about that."

He nodded, finishing the cookie. "Or..."

"Or..." I repeated, not getting where he was going. Normally he drove me crazy by not telling me anything. Now he was driving me crazy by telling me next to nothing. And he *was* enjoying it.

"It's not so easy, is it?" he said. "When you don't have the luxury of assumptions."

"I never claimed it was easy," I protested. "I respect the hell out of you, you know that."

"Really?" He looked genuinely surprised. "No, I didn't know that."

"Of course I do."

"Well, thanks," he said. "I appreciate that." He paused. "Listen, I really didn't intend to talk to you about this, but you were there when Kristy and Tommy and S all met for the first time, right? At the Potent Flower, the day before the big product launch where S was killed."

I blinked. "I hadn't thought about it like that—the three of them meeting that day. But yes, I was there."

"We've gone over the surveillance footage from the shop," Jackson said. "But there's no audio. Was there anything, even something that you can't imagine being important, *anything* that you noticed when those three were together? Did anybody say anything, or react oddly to anything?"

I grimaced. "I hate to tell you, but I didn't actually see those three together. I met Tommy, but he was talking to Monica and Abby when I got there. And then I met S, but just for a minute. Then Monica and Tommy and I went into our meeting and S stayed with Abby in the shop. She told us later that she introduced S to Kristy when he had more questions than she could answer. So I never actually saw the two of them together, with or without Tommy. Have you talked to Abby?"

He nodded. "She said all she noticed was an obvious, immediate attraction between Kristy and S."

"They were soulmates," I told him. "At least that's what Kristy said."

And now Kristy was in a coma, and her soulmate was dead.

CHAPTER 28

I got in early the next morning, stopping only to pick up the cookie order and a triple latte from Café Madeline before crossing the street to the Palace. It may not have been considered early by people with real jobs, but it was early enough that I didn't expect to find Albert and Callie in the break room.

"Hey, you two," I greeted them from the doorway. "What's all this?"

The battered round table in front of them was covered with photographs.

"Good morning, Nora," Albert said. "I'm afraid all this is a large portion of my childhood." The expression on his face as he looked down at all the photos was part bemusement, part dismay. "I haven't thought of some of these people in years. I'm sorry to say I have no idea who many of them are."

I joined them at the table. The photos, dozens and dozens of them, were all jumbled together, overlapping and in piles. They were almost all black-and-white, a few in faded color, mostly of people posing for the camera.

"It's, like, the most amazing source material," Callie said. "Albert's niece sent them for our documentary. His sister kept them all these years. Look." She pointed to a group of four photos. "It's the Palace!"

The pictures were from different eras, but all showed people out on the street with the Palace marquee in the background.

"They're incredible," I said.

Albert picked one up, passing it to me. "That's my mother in the middle," he pointed. "And this is my grandmother. I don't know who the blonde woman is."

"*Double Indemnity* was playing," I said, squinting at the marquee behind them. "This must have been late summer or early fall of 1944. Your mother was beautiful." She had dark hair and a generous smile. All three women wore hats and gloves and carried the kind of structured purse that I always thought of as a pocketbook.

Albert nodded. "Just so. I enlisted that fall, when I turned eighteen. Ah!" He saw something in another photo and picked it up. "Good heavens, I remember this. I must have been about ten or twelve here."

He passed me the picture. It featured three boys grinning widely, their arms around each other's shoulders, clothes rumpled and faces grimy, clearly glorying in some sort of athletic victory.

"Albert, I'd have known you anywhere." He was the boy on the left, stick thin and wearing little round glasses even then.

"I remember that day," he said. "Although I probably haven't thought of it in seventy years or more. Our school had a track-and-field meet, and we won the relay race." He smiled, looking half embarrassed at the naked joy on his younger self's face. "That's Jimmy Shoop." He pointed to the middle boy. "And that's Harry Shapiro on the end. He could run like the wind, Harry."

"What ever happened to them?" Callie reached for the photo.

Albert's face clouded. "Jimmy died at Iwo Jima," he said. "His father signed the forms so he could enlist at seventeen." He cleared his throat. "And Harry died not long after this photo was taken. He was riding a bicycle on the street and was hit by a delivery truck."

"Oh, Albert." I put my hand on his.

He placed his other hand on top of mine. "It was a long time ago."

"Still," Callie said, looking shaken, "I'm so sorry."

"My dear ladies," he said, withdrawing his hands and waving them dismissively. "If you ever get to be my age—and I sincerely hope you do—you'll find that every year you'll look around and realize more of your old friends are gone. Harry was the first friend

I lost, but with the war, and time—" He shrugged. "—he was far from the last."

"Gee, that's sad," I heard a voice say. Trixie appeared in the doorway, then came into the room to stand behind Albert, her hands hovering on his shoulders, looking at the sea of photos. "All my friends are gone, too. But then, I suppose I was the first to go."

"Well, you have new friends now." I was talking to both of them.

"Indeed I do," Albert said fondly. "I'm a very lucky fellow." He shivered. "Is anyone else cold?"

"Sorry!" Trixie stepped back from him.

"Let me get you another cup of tea." I stood and took Albert's mug over to the sink, giving Trixie a reassuring nod.

"I'm going to Ken Burns the hell out of these pictures," Callie said, gathering the images into stacks. "We're going to make a great documentary."

"I have full faith in you, my dear."

"Oh!" Trixie sounded startled. I turned from the hot water tap to see her peering at the photo of Albert's mother and grandmother with the unknown blonde woman in front of the Palace. "Oh, Nora, come quick. That's my mama!"

"Are you sure?"

Trixie and I had left the others in the break room and gone to the office, where I sat at the desk and Trixie shimmered excitedly around the room.

"Of course I'm sure, silly," she said. "Don't you think I know my own mama?"

"Of course you do," I agreed. "Was she friends with Albert's mother?"

Her face clouded. "I don't know. I think I remember her— Albert's mother, I mean. She seems familiar in that picture, but that might only be from working here. Everyone from the neighborhood came to the Palace. Gee, do you think you could get a copy of that photo for me? I'd love to have a picture of my mama."

"I'm sure Albert wouldn't mind," I said. "We can hang it here in the office."

"Oh, I'd like that." She settled in her usual perch on the arm of the couch, looking pleased. "Say, what's this?"

She'd noticed the index card I'd left on her keyboard.

"Oh!" I went over to her. "Trixie, we have to be careful with that keyboard."

"Did you see what I did?" She looked up at me eagerly. "I typed two whole words."

"I saw, and you're brilliant," I told her.

She wafted a hand. "Aw, it was nothing." Then she looked at the note again. "Why do we have to talk?"

"Right," I said, sitting on the couch. "You know how I told you Gabriela made this for you?"

Trixie nodded. "That was awfully nice of her."

"Yes," I agreed. "The thing is, she set it up so that whatever gets typed on that keyboard gets sent to her phone."

Trixie's eyes widened. "How?"

Actually, I didn't really understand myself how bits flew through the air and rearranged themselves on screens, so I was the last person who could explain the technology of it to Trixie.

"She uses science," I said instead. "She's very smart."

Trixie nodded. "I can tell," she said. "From her glasses. I bet she wears one of those white lab coats at her work. Oh! I bet she even works in a lab."

"Actually, I think she does, sort of," I said, although I was sure it was different from any lab Trixie was imagining. "Anyway, she said she was going to fix it so the words you type show up on my phone, too," I told her. "Shall we try it?"

"Sure. What do you want me to type?"

"How about the word 'test'?" I suggested. That should be innocuous enough for Gabriela to assume I was still experimenting.

Trixie turned to the keyboard, concentrating hard and holding her finger over each key until the letters appeared on the screen.

TEST.

A few seconds later my phone pinged. I checked the screen and held it so she should see it.

"Nora! It's magic! Why, it's just like sending you a telegram." She was excited, but she was also sort of flickering, in the way she did when she was depleted.

"It kind of is," I agreed. "Does it tire you out to use it?"

She shrugged. "A little. I never really liked typing, you know. Three of my sisters went to secretarial school, but I only ever wanted to work at the Palace."

I thought about it. "Okay, since it tires you out, we probably shouldn't use it again until we understand it better. Gabriela said she was working on a better version of it, and maybe that will be easier for you."

Also, maybe by then I'd be able to figure out how much it was safe for Gabriela to know.

"Sure," Trixie agreed. "That's fine by me."

She was flickering more.

"It's been such an exciting morning," she said. "First my mother's picture and then sending you a telegram on your thingamajig."

"A very exciting morning," I agreed.

"I think I'll just take a little rest," she said. Then she promptly disappeared.

Trixie was right. It had been quite a morning. I sat back at the desk and sipped my now-cold latte, thinking it all over.

I supposed it shouldn't have surprised me that Albert's mother and Trixie's mother had known each other—they were women of a similar age living in the same neighborhood at the same time. But it still seemed amazing to me. They might have come to the movies together, right here in the Palace

The Palace had a long history. If I had anything to say about it, it would have a long future, too.

CHAPTER 29

Hi Monica. How are you holding up? Any update on Kristy?

I'd waited until ten to send the text. I assumed Monica had had a late night at the hospital and I didn't want to disturb her until she was likely to be awake. Her reply came almost immediately.

Still no change. I got her folks a hotel room and they're taking shifts so they can get some rest. I'm at the shop now, but I'll go back to visit at lunchtime. Want to come along?

I wrote back.

Absolutely. But you didn't answer my question. How are you?

There was a pause.

Too busy to think right now. I'll collapse later.

That sounded like her.

Let me know when. I'll bring you wine and Doris Day movies.

Since I knew Abby was usually in the shop on Tuesdays and Thursdays, I planned to get there a little before I was due to meet Monica. I wanted to follow up with Abby about Detective Jackson's questions. Had she seen anything odd when Kristy and S met that day? Something she might have thought too trivial to tell him? I couldn't recall noticing anything myself, but maybe if Abby and I put our heads together...

My thoughts were interrupted by a knock on my open office door.

"Dare I ask what's going on in that fascinating mind of yours?"

A jolt of energy—or something—shot through me. "Hector, what are you doing here?"

He'd already come in, and now sat comfortably in one of the guest chairs. I'd half risen, not sure if we were kissing hello these days, but then I sat again, because apparently we weren't.

"Delightful to see you, too," he said. "I was hoping you'd be free for lunch later."

"Oh. I was until about five minutes ago." I held up my phone. "Monica and I are going to see Kristy at the hospital. But I'm extremely free for dinner."

"I'm extremely glad to hear it," he said. "How is Kristy?"

"No change," I said. "Do you know anything about comas?"

"Only what I've seen in the movies. Is that what you're so worried about?"

"What, me worried?" I smiled. "No, I was thinking about something Detective Jackson said, about how I was there the day S and Tommy and Kristy all met."

Hector's eyes narrowed. "Does he think that puts you in danger?"

Of course that's where his mind went. I was one of the world's great catastrophizers, but Hector was right up there in the top rankings with me. Which, given his criminal past, might be one of the reasons he was still alive.

"He didn't say so," I answered. "And if I'm in danger then so is Monica, and Abby, and everyone who was in the shop that day. No, he was just hoping I'd noticed something—anything—about when the three of them met."

"You mean when the two men met Kristy," he corrected.

"Tommy and S already knew each other."

"Right," I said. "And partly because Tommy and S were so connected, I've been assuming that Kristy was only poisoned because she saw something when S was killed, something she didn't realize was important because she was so convinced that Tommy was the killer."

"It seems to make sense that Tommy and S were the intended targets, and Kristy was just a loose end that needed to be taken care of," Hector said.

"Right," I agreed. "According to that theory, S was killed by some unknown person for some unknown reason—money or revenge or jealousy."

"The classics," Hector nodded. "Tried and true motivations. And Tommy?"

I grimaced. "For the same reasons? If it's money, that might make sense since he and S were in business together."

"If it's jealousy or revenge, the killer could be some other game developer," Hector said thoughtfully.

I sat up. "That was one of the wild theories on the online forums, when S was first killed." I tried to remember. "Some guy claimed he'd invented S's game." I blinked. "I wonder if the police are looking into that." I'd have to ask Detective Jackson.

"If it was something like that," Hector said, "it fits that Kristy was attacked because of something she saw that day. Or something the killer thought she saw."

"Something like a mysterious game developer stirring bee pollen into S's drink backstage?" I said

Hector cocked an eyebrow. "I would imagine she'd have mentioned that."

"I would imagine so," I agreed. "But here's what I was just wondering: What if that whole line of thinking is wrong? What if Kristy wasn't just a loose end? What if she was the catalyst for the whole thing? What if the reason those three were all poisoned started that day at the Potent Flower?"

"And that reason is?" Hector asked.

I slumped back in my chair. "When I figure it out, you'll be the first to know."

Abby was at the Potent Flower when I got there just before noon. She was deep in conversation with a customer at the same tall display table in the back corner where I'd met her the first time.

Abby was too involved with her customer to notice me, so I went over, out of her eyeline but hovering close enough to hear her conversation.

"Ragweed," she was saying. "That's very common. Do you know you should avoid chamomile tea if you're allergic to ragweed?"

The customer, a middle-aged woman who seemed a little overwhelmed by the whole Potent Flower experience, shook her head.

"They're in the same family," Abby told her. "Stay away from it when you're choosing your herbal teas. Here, I think this will be perfect for you." She plucked a tiny bottle topped with an eyedropper from the displayed assortment on the table and handed it to the woman.

I winced. I'd totally forgotten about the similar tiny bottle Abby had given me on the night of the séance. It was probably still in my jeans pocket, at home in my laundry basket.

The customer thanked her and moved away, and Abby looked around the shop for someone else to help.

"Abby? Hi!" I tapped her on the shoulder, and she jumped when she saw it was me.

"Nora!" she put a hand to her chest. "I didn't see you there. How are you?"

"Fine," I said. "Just fine. Your tincture worked marvels." I hadn't tried her tincture, but it seemed like the polite thing to say, especially when she was trying to sell more.

"Did it?" she blinked. "Good. I'm so glad. I knew it would. Are you here for Monica?"

I nodded. "We're going to visit Kristy at the hospital. But I wanted to talk to you. Have you got a minute?"

A short heavyset man in his forties joined us at the table. "Excuse me," he said. "They told me you do custom blends of some sort?"

Abby gave me an apologetic look. "Can we talk when you get back?"

Just then the door to the lounge opened and Monica emerged. "That sounds perfect," I said to Abby. "See you then."

Once we were out on the sidewalk, Monica gave me an appraising look. "Why do you need to talk to Abby? I've never known you to be interested in cannabis."

"Really?" I said innocently.

"What I have known you to be interested in is murder investigations. What do you think Abby knows?"

"Maybe nothing," I said. "Or maybe something that she thinks is nothing."

"Does Detective Jackson know you're asking questions?"

"We've come to an understanding," I said breezily. "Forged in cookies."

"Uh huh," Monica said. "Just be careful. I don't want to have to visit you in the hospital next."

"It's fine," I told her. "I'm just going to talk to her about the other day to see if it jogs either of our memories."

But I didn't, because when we got back to the Potent Flower after visiting Kristy, Abby had packed up her things and gone.

"How's the kid?" Marty asked when I got back to the theater. I knew by "the kid" he meant Kristy.

"Still no change," I told him. "But the doctors say that could be a good sign. Why are you down here?"

Marty hardly ever ventured out of his lair once customers started showing up at the Palace. He might actually have to talk to them or something. But now not only was he in the lobby, he was behind the candy counter, as if he might actually wait on someone.

"Albert was feeling tired, so he left. I don't know what you and Callie did to wear him out so much this morning. You two need to remember he's frailer than he looks."

"Marty, you're very sweet to look out for him, but I promise Callie and I didn't take advantage. Did you see all the photos?"

He harrumphed, turning away from me and fiddling with the soda machine. He hated it when I called him sweet, which is why I did so at the slightest provocation. "Of course I saw the photos," he said. "I think I might have spotted Mel Blanc in one of them."

"Mel Blanc? As in Bugs Bunny Mel Blanc?" The actor had voiced practically all of Warner Brothers' most famous cartoon characters.

"He grew up in San Francisco." Marty's tone said any fool would know that.

"Huh. I wonder if he ever came to the movies here? That could be another thing we could do with an app." I came around the counter to see what he was doing with the soda machine. It was making a disturbing and not unfamiliar clanking sound, and I now saw Marty had an array of wrenches and screwdrivers lined up next to it. "Famous visitors to the Palace, returning as AR holograms."

"The *app*," he repeated derisively. "Are you still on that?" He took up a wrench.

"I'm still on anything that might make us money. What's wrong with—" But before I could finish asking, the soda machine belched and a spray of syrup spewed all over. Marty leapt away, catching only a little of it, but I was immediately drenched in sticky brown liquid.

I turned to him, dripping, and was about to launch into an indignant tirade when he stopped me cold.

"I suppose this isn't the best time to mention it," he said. "But Otis Hampton is waiting for you in your office."

CHAPTER 30

I stared at Marty. "*What?*"

"Otis Hampton," he said, wiping the soda into his flannel shirt. "The producer. He got here about half an hour ago. I told him I didn't know when you'd be back, but he said he'd wait."

"And you didn't think maybe you should send me a *text*? Or at the very least *tell me* as soon as I got here?"

He sniffed. "I assumed you had an appointment. I don't know what you get up to with those big fancy Hollywood types."

"*Marty!*" I looked down at myself. My sweatshirt and jeans were ruined, not that they'd been great to begin with. "Do I look like I was expecting a big fancy Hollywood type today?"

"Do I pay attention to how you dress?" he countered. "Why don't you keep a spare shirt or something here?"

"Why? I...I..." I was sputtering incoherently. Luckily, someone else was capable of rational thought.

"I mean, you have all those clothes downstairs."

I whirled around to see that Callie had come in from the ticket booth. So had several people who were presumably customers for the two-thirty show. They were all staring at me.

I took a breath. Then I turned on Marty. "*You*, go upstairs and tell Otis to wait. And get him out of my office. I don't want him snooping around. *You—*" I pointed to Callie. "Get these lovely people anything they want besides soda and meet me downstairs the minute Brandon shows up to take over up here."

I sprinted for the stairs to the basement.

*   *   *

"I mean, wow."

This was Callie's reaction when she joined me in the prop room fifteen minutes later.

"Have you seen Otis?" I asked her. "Where is he?"

"Marty put him in the balcony," she said. "He's watching *Silk Stockings*. You look amazing. Is that Chanel?"

She meant my jacket. "It is," I said. "I figured if I was going to put on my battle gear I might as well put on the best."

I'd chosen a pair of black jeans that did magical things to my butt, a white silk shirt that had cost more than it would take to get the soda machine repaired, and a black-and-white speckled Chanel jacket that took the whole thing to the next level.

"I mean, you have to wear these booties," Callie said, pulling a black stiletto Louboutin from a pile.

"They hurt like a—"

"*Otis Hampton*," Callie stopped me. "He's one of the biggest guys in the business and you're a former screenwriter who ran away from Hollywood. The least you should do is be taller than him."

I blinked. "You're right. See if you can find a lipstick somewhere."

"I'm on it," she said. "And then, like it or not, I'm going to give you a messy bun. What do you think he wants?"

"Something insane to do with Ted, no doubt," I told her. "I'm just trying to figure out how to leverage that into getting Ted the part he wants in that movie."

I turned to find her staring at me, boots in one hand and a makeup bag in the other. "You're helping Ted? The Ted who left you? The Ted who stole all your money? You're—"

I took the makeup from her. "I'm only helping Ted because he's holding the paperwork on those gowns hostage. And if this goes the way I think it will, I'm really not doing him any favors."

"He's using you," Callie said.

"Yup." I rummaged around in the bag for a lipstick or mascara or something. "He's using me to manage Otis, and Otis is no doubt here to use me against Ted. I just have to figure out how I can use them both to get what I want."

"What do you want?" Callie asked.

"Both of them out of my life."

"Otis." I came around from my desk. "I had no idea you were in town. Why didn't you let me know?"

I'd taken the back stairs to my office, asking Callie to bring Otis to me. When he arrived I specifically didn't apologize for keeping him waiting.

"Nora." He air kissed me on both cheeks and then stepped back to give me the kind of appraising head-to-toe sweep that I was sure many lawyers had told him never to subject a woman to again. Ugh.

Otis himself was nothing special to look at. Not as tall as he thought he was, or as fit. He was well into his fifties and tended to go a little overboard with the Botox. He wore the muted tones of casual Hollywood. His teeth were blindingly white.

"You look amazing," he said. "I heard you were letting yourself go. I'll have to defend your honor the next time anyone says anything."

Ah ha. That's why he was here. He was afraid his plot to make it look like Glen Hendricks and I were dating would fall flat if I hadn't kept up my hair color or if, God forbid, I'd gained six pounds.

"San Francisco agrees with me," I told him. "Have a seat. What brings you here?"

I'd maneuvered him to one of the guest chairs. I took a seat behind the desk. Any little edge I could have would help.

"Can't a friend just stop by to say hello?" he asked, the picture of innocence.

"Sure," I said. "But that usually doesn't involve getting on a plane."

He grinned. "Okay, you caught me. I was on my way to my ranch in Montana and I had a craving for dim sum," he said. "I told them to re-route through San Francisco."

Sure. That sounded plausible. Even whimsical, in a billionaire-with-a-private-jet sort of way. "We do have good dim sum," I allowed.

"The best!" he enthused. "I'm just sorry I didn't think to ask you to join me. But when we were leaving the restaurant and I realized how close we were to this place...well." He smiled one of those Hollywood smiles that I really didn't miss.

"Well," I agreed and leaned forward, my tone becoming chummy, "as a matter of fact, Otis, I'm glad you're here."

"Really?" He gave me a sharp look. "Because when we last spoke I got the impression you were cooling on our plan." He paused for effect. "That's not something you want to do."

I bit back a comment about there being no such thing as "our" plan, and overlooked his implied threat. I didn't have time for either.

"The truth is, I'm concerned," I said instead. "After all, the Venice Film Festival is months away. I want to finalize my divorce, and that means finalizing the settlement, and that means finding the money Ted stole. I don't want to wait months for that."

"Sure," Otis agreed. His phone buzzed and he took it from his pocket, reading a text while he talked to me. "Don't worry about that. I've got my guys working on the money angle."

Now that he was confident in my cooperation again he'd clearly lost interest. He read another text, frowning.

"Otis, I have a better idea."

"Yeah? Great. Listen, why don't you email it to me? I've got a plane to catch..." Still looking at his phone, he moved to stand.

"Your plane will wait," I said.

Something about my tone got his attention.

"We need to do something about Ted sooner rather than later," I told him. "Put down your phone and listen. I've got a plan."

I fixed him with the kind of look I hadn't had much use for

since coming to the Palace. But apparently I still had it, because he pocketed the phone, his faintly amused look telling me he was intrigued enough to humor me for a minute—but just a minute.

"You've bought in as a producer on that new Scandinavian franchise," I said quickly. "And Ted wants the lead."

"I've bought in as a producer on every deal in town that Ted could possibly want," Otis said smugly, a glint of something dangerous in his eye. "Just to make sure he doesn't get it. We'll just see how much Priya wants to be with a has-been. Once he's been black-balled—"

"Sure," I cut him off. "But I want you to give it to him. The Scandinavian thing."

He sat back, a look of distrust crossing his face. "Nora, if you're going soft on me—"

"If you give him that part, you own him." I said impatiently. "You're his boss. You control where the location shoots are, and how long he has to be off on some frozen fjord. You control his schedule, which means you control his life. *And* you control his career. Make sure the franchise tanks and he won't be nearly so attractive to Priya."

I waited a moment for that to sink in. When he blinked I knew I had him.

"Give Ted what he thinks he wants," I said. "And then make his life hell."

He leaned forward. "I'm not the only producer on the project. They won't just let me tank the whole—"

"Buy them out," I said. "You've got the money. Spend it on what you really want. And that isn't another ranch in Montana."

He hesitated. "What's in it for you?"

This was a rare show business negotiation in which honesty was the best policy. "Short term, I've done him a favor by getting you to see he's right for the part," I said. "Which means he'll give me something in return. But long term..."

Otis was all attention.

"If I know you at all, you're going to make him miserable on that shoot," I said. "Maybe so miserable that after a few weeks he'll come to you, offering to do whatever it takes to get out of his contract. You'll tell him what it will take."

"He has to leave Priya," Otis said.

"No. That's not what you want."

He looked startled.

"You want Priya to leave him."

Otis blinked. His face became grim. "Yes," he said roughly. "Yes, I do."

"Then this is your play," I told him. "Your price for letting Ted out of his contract will be him miraculously recovering the money he stole from me and agreeing to a settlement."

"Leaving him broke," Otis said.

"Leaving him a multimillionaire movie star," I said dryly. "But closer to broke than he was. Then you recast Ted's part and make that movie the biggest grossing blockbuster of the summer. Without him."

"He'll look like a fool." An ugly smile spread across Otis's face. "And that's when Priya will leave him."

I felt a moment's sympathy for Priya. Then I stood, looking at my watch. "Now, you said something about a plane to catch?"

All About Eve
1950

Let's talk about a scheming woman. Let's talk about a woman who manipulates, and plots, and plays a long game of using whoever she can to get what she wants. Let's talk about Eve Harrington. And while we're at it, let's talk about Margo Channing.

Bette Davis plays Margo, and some would argue that the brilliant, insecure, ageing stage actress is the role of her career. Margo is a firestorm of willfulness, passion, and ego. In short, she's glorious.

The story begins at a theatrical awards banquet, and we're immediately in the excellent hands of our narrator Addison DeWitt. He's a theater critic, played by George Saunders at his most unctuous, which is saying something. He delivers every line like an aristocratic cat who just finished a particularly delicious bowl of cream.

At the banquet, DeWitt introduces us to the playwright Lloyd Richards (Hugh Marlowe), his wife Karen (Celeste Holm), and ultimately, Margot Channing. The camera moves to Bette Davis, lighting her own cigarette, pouring her own drink, and very clearly bored with the proceedings. She is, DeWitt informs us, "A great star, a true star. She never was or will be anything else or anything less." Damn right.

But Margo isn't getting the award. No, that's going to another actress. A younger, fresher actress—Eve Harrington (Anne Baxter.) And the rest of the movie is going to tell us all about Eve.

Flashback! Karen the playwright's wife has noticed a mousy young woman standing outside the stage door every night as Margo stars in her husband's hit play. One night she invites the poor waif inside to meet her idol Margo. The great actress is covered in cold cream and being attended to by her dresser Birdie (Thelma Ritter! Oh, how I love the skeptical, practical joy that is Thelma Ritter.)

Eve immediately ingratiates herself to Margo, spinning a heartbreaking tale that leaves not a dry eye in the dressing room. (Except Birdie's, of course.) The mood is broken when they're joined by Margo's director and beau Bill Simpson. (Gary Merrill, who divorced his wife to marry Bette Davis soon after they made this movie. She's that good.)

Bill is about to leave Broadway to go to Hollywood, a betrayal of the theater of the highest order, and something that makes Margo nakedly insecure. She's of a certain age, and he's going to the land of starlets. "Am I going to lose you, Bill?" It doesn't look that way to me, but then there's the Eve factor.

Eve moves into Margo's guestroom that very night and immediately makes herself indispensable to the star. Margo didn't know how much she needed someone until Eve became her "sister, lawyer, mother, friend, psychiatrist, and cop." Too much, you think? You're right.

The honeymoon doesn't last long. Eve is just a little too eager to step in and help. Especially when it comes to boyfriend Bill. Boundaries, Eve. Seriously.

Thelma Ritter as Birdie seems to be the only one who sees what's going on. Trust me, whether you're planning a banquet or caught in a bar fight, she is the woman you want at your side.

It all comes to a head the night of Bill's welcome back party. Margo finds him chatting and laughing with Eve downstairs when she was waiting for him to come to her room. She immediately starts hurling accusations, but Bill's had it with her "age obsession." She has no cause to worry, he insists. Eve isn't a threat. She's just "an idealistic dreamy-eyed kid." Note to all men: This is not how to reassure your aging girlfriend that you're not interested in a younger woman.

This is when the party gets going. And *this* is the Bette Davis drag queens worship. Her every word is tinged in witty poison and uttered between drags off cigarettes and slugs of dry martinis. The minute Karen arrives she can sense a fight is in the air. "Is it over or is it just beginning?" Margo pauses, drinks, steps onto the stairs and turns. Then she delivers The Line For All Time: "Fasten your seatbelts, it's going to be a bumpy night." Yes!

Margo gets gloriously drunk, and wallows in the self-pity of an aging beauty. Lloyd's new play has a lead written for a younger woman, but he still wants Margo to play it. He sees her as ageless. She's in no mood to hear it. "Lloyd I'm not twentyish, I'm not thirtyish, three months ago I was forty. *Forty. Four-O.*" The number sounds like a death knell, and she realizes she's never said it out loud before. "I suddenly feel as if I've taken all my clothes off."

It isn't that she cares about being older. She cares about being older than Bill. He's thirty-two and he looks it. He'll probably always look thirty-two, because men are just lucky that way. "I hate men." Sing it, sister.

Meanwhile, upstairs, Eve is being heartfelt and earnest with Karen. She implores Karen to arrange it for her to be Margo's understudy. Karen, dear sweet idiotic Karen, doesn't see what harm it could do to give the kid a break.

You see where this is going. So does Margo.

I won't say more, because you absolutely have to experience this movie for yourself. I don't say this often, but this one is mandatory. There are schemes and plots and double-crosses and twists, and it's all just so, so smart. Yes, it's all overblown and overly dramatic, because these are overblown and overly dramatic people, Margo chief among them. Addison DeWitt describes her best. "You're maudlin and full of self-pity. You're magnificent!"

So many perfect lines

Joseph L. Mankiewicz rightly won the Oscar for Best Screenplay for this one. Anything else would have been a crime. There are so many brilliant exchanges, and so many iconic lines. It's a screenwriter's treasure trove.

Bill to Birdie, as he's headed to Hollywood: "What do you want me to tell Tyrone Power?
Birdie: "Just give him my phone number. I'll tell him myself."

Margo: "I'll admit I may have seen better days, but I'm

still not to be had for the price of a cocktail, like a salted peanut."

Margo, upon being accused of playing a silly game of cat and mouse: "Not mouse, never mouse. If anything, rat."

Eve, storming to a door and pulling it open: "Get out!" Addison, unfazed: "You're too short for that gesture."

Marilyn!
Addison DeWitt brings Marilyn Monroe to the party, playing the dumb-but-savvy-starlet role she'd perfect throughout her career. DeWitt points her toward a producer and tells her to do herself some good. She sighs. "Why do they always look like unhappy rabbits?" Then she doffs her fur, squares her shoulders, and sparkles to sex goddess life. A star is born.

Movies My Friends Should Watch
Sally Lee

CHAPTER 31

I walked Otis down to his waiting car and sent a text to Ted the minute he drove off.

I got you the part. You'll get the offer from Otis as soon as I get the paperwork on the gowns.

That part was non-negotiable. He wasn't going to weasel out of giving me those receipts, even if Otis somehow weaseled out of giving him the part.

Ted's response was immediate and effusive. I'd never seen the word "awesome" used so many times in so few lines. I stayed out on the sidewalk in front of the Palace, thinking long and hard before I sent him the next message.

If you're smart you'll turn down the part.

I'd warned him. My conscience was clear. Or clear enough.

But Ted had never been smart.

When I came down to the lobby before the seven-thirty show I found Callie and Brandon buried in their phones behind the concessions stand. When they heard me on the balcony stairs and looked up I could tell something was wrong.

"What happened?" I asked. "Is it Kristy?" I rushed down the remaining stairs.

Callie shook her head. She held up her phone, but I couldn't see what was on it until I got closer. "It's awful," she said. "Two kids were killed while they were playing the game."

She handed me her phone, but I didn't need to read. Brandon supplied the details.

"They were with a group following a clue, but they got it wrong," he said. "They followed some train tracks into a tunnel, and when a train came they couldn't all get out of the way."

"They were eleven years old," Callie said.

I sank onto a stool at the counter. "How horrible." I shuddered. "Where was it?"

"Someplace outside Philadelphia."

"Are they stopping the game?" I asked. "They have to now, don't they?"

"That's what everyone's saying." Brandon shrugged, just as his phone buzzed. He checked it. "Wait. Tommy and S's companies just released a joint statement."

The two of them went face-down into their screens. I pulled mine out of my bag, but Brandon was already muttering as he read the statement.

"It says their thoughts and prayers are with the families—"

Callie snorted derisively.

"Wait, listen to this," Brandon said. "'As truly heartbreaking as this incident was, the fact is that the app is rated twelve and up.'" He read a moment longer before looking up. "They're saying the kids shouldn't have been playing."

"They're, like, blaming the parents," Callie agreed.

"You can't be serious."

"Not, like, outright," she said, still reading. "But it's implied."

"That's disgusting. They can't get away with this. They have to stop that game."

"Um, I don't think they will," Brandon said. He held it up his phone for me to see why.

"A team in Argentina found the third coin. It's worth ten million dollars."

*   *   *

"It's despicable," I said, sinking into the soft leather of Hector's front seat. It was half an hour later and Hector had picked me up for dinner.

"It's been all over the news," he said, pulling away from the curb. "They reported another half a million people have downloaded the app since the third coin was found."

"I wonder how many parents have deleted it from their kid's phones."

"According to the news, the companies are recommending that parents play the game with their children," he said. "To provide a level of supervision."

"Do those companies seriously just get to dust off their hands and walk away?" I asked. "I can't imagine what those parents are going through."

"Hell, I would think," Hector said.

My phone pinged with a message. It was from Abby.

Nora, I'm so sorry I had to run off today. But I'd like to talk. Can you meet me for coffee in the morning? How about that place across from the Palace? Around eight?

"It looks like I'm having coffee with Abby in the morning," I told Hector, sending her a reply.

"I thought you saw her this afternoon." He took a right on Divisadero.

"I did, just for a minute, but when Monica and I got back from visiting Kristy at the hospital Abby was gone. She told one of the guys at the shop that there was some emergency on her farm."

"She has a farm?"

"According to Monica, it's a little family place up near Petaluma where Abby grows all the organic herbs and botanicals she mixes in with her concoctions. Hey, where are we going?"

"I don't know yet," he said, gliding into a parking place across the street and down the block from the Potent Flower. "It depends on where that car goes." He nodded toward a light blue Toyota across the street.

I looked from the car to him. "Whose car is that?"

"Earlier today you said something about how if you were in danger, so was everyone who had been in the shop that day. That got me thinking. Who else had been in the shop that day? Who was working? Who were the other customers?"

"Excellent questions. So whose car is that?"

Hector grinned. "His name is Adam Bennett, and he's been working at the shop for a little under two months. He was working the day you, Abby, and Kristy met S and Tommy," he said. "In fact, he rang up S's sale, and based on the video footage from the store, he spent more than a little time with S in the shop."

"Do I want to know how you saw the video footage?"

"Why? Do you think I stole it from the police evidence locker?"

"*Did* you?"

"I might have. Or I might have asked our friend Monica if I could have a look."

"Oh." I was irrationally disappointed that he'd done something so tame.

"In any case," Hector continued. "I haven't had the time to look into everyone who was there, but I began with Adam Bennett. Would you like to know why we're waiting to follow him tonight?"

"I'm very curious," I said.

He gave me a look that reminded me strongly of Cary Grant, in one of his I-know-something-nobody-else-knows-and-I'm-enjoying-it-immensely moods. Which was interesting, because I've always thought Hector leaned a little more toward Clark Gable than Cary Grant.

He revealed his secret. "Adam Bennett has made three substantial cash deposits to his savings account in the past ten days."

"Three deposits?" I stared at him. "Deposits like payments for three poisonings?"

"It's an interesting coincidence, isn't it?" Hector nodded toward the shop. "There he is, right on time."

The guy who had given me Abby's message earlier in the day was just leaving the Potent Flower. He was one of Monica's salesclerks, in his early twenties with close-cropped blond hair and a wide-ranging assortment of tattoos. He nodded at the security guard and went down the street toward the blue car. Hector started his engine.

"What are we doing?" I asked. "Are we following him?"

"We are," Hector said. "I've got sandwiches, snacks, and a thermos of coffee in the back seat. I know I offered to take you for dinner, but..."

"We're on a stakeout," I realized.

"Technically, we're on a tail." Hector checked for oncoming traffic before pulling out and making a swift U-turn, winding up a few cars behind Adam. "Once he gets wherever he's going we'll be on a stakeout." He shot me a look. "This is our first official date. I wanted it to be special."

"So we're dating."

Hector plucked the bag of potato chips from my hand. "I certainly hope so. I don't share my mesquite barbeque chips with just anyone."

"I feel very special," I told him. "I hope you don't regret it when you see all the crumbs I've gotten in your car. Just out of curiosity, if we're dating now, what have we been doing for the past six months?"

"I don't know about you," he said, "but I've been practicing admirable self-restraint."

I laughed.

We were parked in front of a ramshackle Victorian in the lower Height. We'd been there for about twenty minutes, so if Adam was at all consistent we could expect him to emerge soon.

"There he is," I said.

Hector handed the chips to me and started the car. We followed the blue Toyota for about five minutes, until he parked in front of another house, this one on Grove in Hayes Valley.

"I don't get it," I admitted, watching the young man lope up the stairs. "I don't know what I expected from a possible poisoner. Maybe that he'd lead us to his secret arsenic lab somewhere?"

"That would be great," Hector said. "Although the odds were probably against it."

"Understood. But this is the fourth place he's stopped at tonight. I thought at the very least he'd meet up with a group of friends to play the game or something. But he doesn't even have his phone out. What's he up to?"

Hector turned to me. "Seriously?"

"What? You're saying you know?"

He sighed, rubbing his eyes. "I have a pretty good idea."

"What are you seeing that I'm not? Is he our poisoner?"

"It's seeming less and less likely," Hector said. "I'm pretty sure he's a pot dealer."

"Sure. That's his job. Although Monica frowns at the word 'dealer.'"

"Right, but I think he's delivering it."

"No," I told him. "Monica's shop doesn't—Oh!" I grabbed Hector's arm when I got it. "He's stealing pot from the shop and selling it."

"That's what it looks like."

"Oh," I said again, deflating. "So the three cash deposits may not have been in payment for poisonings."

"Possibly not."

I let go of Hector's arm, somewhat reluctantly. "At least we can let Monica know what he's up to."

"True." He put his hand on his arm where I'd touched it.

"And, to be fair," I said, "this may be a bust as a stakeout, it's still an exceptional first date. I mean, you did give me my choice of sandwiches."

"I am nothing if not a gentleman," he said, a glint of something that made me shiver in his eye.

"You certainly are," I agreed. "Chivalrous, even." I looked out the window, humming a tune.

"Thank you," Hector said. "Although I'm feeling something less than gentlemanly at the moment." He shifted to face me. "Have I told you how good you look tonight?"

In point of fact, he hadn't. I'd kind of thought the heels and the clothes and the lipstick that I'd worn for the Otis meeting might have registered with Hector, but he hadn't said a thing when he'd picked me up. I stopped humming long enough to answer.

"I thought you didn't notice."

"I notice everything."

The car was suddenly very warm. I started humming again.

"What's that tune?" he asked.

"I think it's our song," I told him. "It's from *Swing Time*."

"Our song is something I don't know from a movie I haven't seen?"

"If you haven't seen it you have no one to blame but yourself. It's been playing since Tuesday."

He grinned. "I've been busy. Why is it our song?"

I started singing, very softly. "A fine romance, with no kisses. A fine romance, my friend, this is..."

"I think there's been a misunderstanding," Hector said.

"Oh?"

"Nobody said anything about no kisses."

I have no idea when Adam Bennett left the building.

CHAPTER 32

"Morning, Marty."

I stood on the sidewalk outside the theater, squinting up at him in the bright morning sun. Marty was changing the marquee for the weekend's lineup. We were sticking with Fred Astaire, featuring the out-of-season holiday movies *Easter Parade* (1948, Astaire and Judy Garland) and *Holiday Inn* (1942, Astaire and Bing Crosby).

"I'm not sure we have enough 'a's for *The Band Wagon*," Marty called down to me. He was rummaging around in the cardboard box of letters that was probably older than either of us.

"Do your best," I said. *The Band Wagon* (Astaire, Cyd Charisse, and a short red flapper dress that was soon to be my authenticated property) was our midnight movie.

"Name one time when I didn't," he challenged.

"That's why I know you'll prevail," I told him. Then I spotted Abby coming around the corner opposite, walking briskly toward the café. I waved at her.

"I'm going to go grab a coffee," I called to Marty, heading across the street. "I'll pick up the cookie order and be back in a bit."

"Yes, I'd love a triple mocha," he yelled after me. "Thanks for asking."

"Is this all right?" Abby asked when we met in front of the café. "You're not too busy?" She glanced nervously in Marty's direction.

I waved a hand. "Don't mind him," I said. "I'll bring him a mocha and a brownie and he'll be mine for the day. I hope you can come to *The Band Wagon* tonight."

"I'll try to," she said. "I had such a good time last week with

Desk Set."

We chatted about the plans for that night's event as we stood in line, placed our orders, and found a table. My usual, by the window, was just about to be nabbed by a couple of guys in suits when Chip, the server, waved them off.

"This one's reserved," he told them, motioning for Abby and me to come over.

"You didn't have to do that," I said when I got to the table.

"But you're a regular, and I know how much you tip," he said with a wink.

"I'd be a regular, too, if I worked right across the street," Abby said. She'd gotten an almond croissant and broke off a piece as soon as we sat but didn't eat it.

"Lisa, the owner, is a friend," I said. "That's her in the back."

Lisa was in the rear of the shop, supervising something being done with a pastry bag. "She was at *Desk Set*, too, selling deserts from that big metal desk."

"Oh, of course," Abby said. "I thought she looked familiar."

"I've been thinking about the day we all met, in Monica's shop," I said. "You, me, Monica, Kristy, Tommy, and S. I just realized that everyone except S was there the night of the *Desk Set* party, too."

Abby blinked rapidly. "Kristy and I were with Monica, but I didn't see Tommy."

"Oh, but—" I stopped. I was sure Tommy had told me that night that he'd seen Monica and the women from her shop. He'd been angry that they hadn't told me he was there. I shook my head. "That's right. He didn't show up until after everyone was gone."

I wasn't entirely sure why I didn't choose to press her on the issue. Maybe because she was so clearly agitated already.

"Oh, good." She tapped a finger to her head. "I'd hate to think I was slipping." She glanced out the window. "It was right here, wasn't it, where he died?"

"Yes." It hadn't even been a week. I looked outside, remembering Tommy as he'd staggered, stopped, and fallen.

I shook my head. Across the street, Marty had found all the "a"s he needed to complete the marquee and was headed down the ladder. Then a movement at the office window above the marquee caught my eye. When I looked closer I saw it was Trixie, waving at me. I held up one hand, discretely. She waved back, grinning.

"Here you go, ladies." We both turned as Chip set our coffee orders on the table in front of us, along with the warmed slice of quiche I'd ordered. "Enjoy."

"Thanks," I said as he left. I reached for my coffee like the addict I was. It had been a late night on my stakeout with Hector, and I still hadn't managed to buy a bag of beans for my own kitchen.

"Oh!" Abby yelped. She'd knocked over her latte, and it was spilling all over the table and into her lap.

"I've got it." I put down my mug, threw my napkin down onto the spill and stood, already moving toward the counter to get more napkins. I grabbed some and got back to the table just as Chip also arrived, dry towel in hand.

"I'm so sorry," Abby said. "I don't know why I'm so nervous."

"No worries," Chip said smoothly. "It happens all the time. I'll be right back with a new latte. Decaf, right?"

She nodded, and he took her empty mug and hustled away. I resolved to leave an even more generous tip than usual.

My phone pinged with a text as I sat down, but I ignored it. "Are you okay?" I asked Abby.

"I'm fine," she said. But she didn't look fine. She looked like a nervous wreck.

"Abby, what's wrong?" I asked.

She looked at me, and I saw something wild in her eyes. "Nothing. I'm just...tired."

My phone pinged again. I reached into my bag for it and flipped the ringer off before setting it face-down on the table. Something was going on with Abby and I didn't know if it was related to the murders.

"Every woman I know who runs a business is tired," I said.

"They told me you had an emergency at your farm yesterday. I hope it wasn't serious."

She waved a hand. "Oh, there's always an emergency at the farm." She pushed my coffee toward me. "Go ahead. Don't wait for me."

I reached for the coffee as the phone vibrated with another text.

"I'm so sorry," I said, picking it up. "Let me set it to—"

There were three messages visible on the screen.

COFFEE
DON'T DRINK!
SH PUT SOMTHG IN YR COFEE!!

I stared at the messages, then I looked up at the office window across the street. Trixie was jumping up and down and waving like a maniac. I held up the phone and nodded, and I could see her put her hand over her heart in relief. I'd gotten her warning.

I turned to Abby. "Sorry." A million thoughts raced through my mind.

"Do you have to go?" Abby asked worriedly, glancing at the phone. "At least have your coffee first."

Chip came back with her second latte. Had she spilled the first one on purpose? To get me away from the table? So she could slip something into my drink? Something like arsenic?

She took a sip of her drink as soon as the server left. "Oh, that's so good."

My instinct was to reach for mine as well. Which is apparently what she wanted. But why?

I couldn't let her know I knew. I scrambled for any innocuous conversation that would give me time to think. "What's it like to run a farm?" I asked her. "How long have you had it?"

She looked surprised, but started talking, which gave me a precious minute. Could Abby have killed S and Tommy? Could she have poisoned Kristy?

Owning a farm, she might have access to arsenic for pest control, and it's possible she might use bee pollen in some of her concoctions. But why? Why would she have killed anyone?

Something in her tone of voice changed. I tuned back into her. She wasn't looking at me. She was staring off into space, talking about her farm. About how it had been in her family for three generations. How she had planned to pass it on to her son.

Her son.

With those words it was as if a curtain went up in my mind. I saw it all, unspooling like a movie.

The urban legend was wrong. There was no vengeful father whose child had died while playing S's first game.

There was a vengeful mother.

Abby had stopped speaking. She was watching me, every muscle in her body tensed.

"I'm so sorry," I said. "I'm a million miles away. Do you mind if I just answer this one text?"

"Of course not." The words fell like ice shards from her lips.

I sent a very brief text, then I met her eyes.

"Abby," I said softly, "tell me about your son."

A tremor went through her body.

"He didn't die in a normal hit-and-run, did he?"

She froze, her eyes wide, staring at something beyond me.

"He was playing S's game," I said. "The old one, with the space monsters."

She made a sound that was sharp and filled with pain.

"And S didn't take any responsibility. Did his company even get charged with anything?"

She swallowed, her head twitching in one short negative shake.

"Then you saw that he was going to do it again. That he had a new game. And that more kids might die. Like those two in Pennsylvania, yesterday."

Her jaw flexed but she still didn't speak. She looked like one tiny nudge would shatter her into a million pieces.

"I noticed something," I said. "When you saw S in the shop that day. Everyone else was looking at him like he was some sort of god. I thought you were, too. I noticed it and I thought you were starstruck. But you weren't. You recognized him."

I wasn't sure if she would speak. I wasn't sure if she could. But finally, after an agonizing pause, she did.

Her eyes flickered, still looking into the distance. "I thought it was fate," she said. "Fate brought him to the store that day. Fate put him in front of me. Fate owed me, for putting my boy, my Lucas, in front of that car. Fate wanted me to make it right."

I nodded. "S told you about his allergies," I said softly. "You told me he gave you his medical history. You knew he was allergic to bees."

She nodded, her face a mask of pain.

"How did you get the pollen into his drink?" I asked.

She blinked. "I didn't. He put it in himself."

I got it. "You gave him samples that day."

"It was fate that I happened to have a CBD tincture to boost immune response," she said, her voice robotic. "It has a high concentration of bee pollen. It's very healthy, usually."

"You just handed it to him," I said, "knowing that whenever he decided to use it..."

She didn't move a muscle.

"But you couldn't have known he'd die so publicly. That the whole world would demand answers," I said.

"There were only two people who could have figured it out," she said. Then, for the first time since I'd brought up her son, she looked at me. "And I couldn't let them say anything." Her voice changed, becoming desperate. "Don't you see? Not when Fate wanted me to—"

"It wasn't fate that put arsenic in Tommy's juice," I said harshly. "You can't tell me you just happened to have a bottle in your pocket—"

"Oh, but I did," she said. "I told you there were only two people who could have figured out what I'd done. Monica and

Kristy. I had three vials of arsenic that night when I met them for the midnight movie. One was for Monica, one for Kristy, and one for myself."

My blood turned to ice at the thought of what she'd almost done.

"But then—" Abby swallowed. "Fate put Tommy in the theater with us."

"You did see him," I said.

She blinked. "That's when I understood," she said. "Fate was guiding them to me. And later, when Lillian hummed that tune at the séance, I knew I was right. I knew I was doing what Lucas wanted me to do."

"You gave Tommy the bottle of arsenic." I said. "The night of the midnight movie. What did you tell him it was?"

"An energy boost," she said. "I told him to take it in the morning."

And he had. He'd put it in his juice. The juice he'd drunk in front of the Palace while I'd watched him from the table where I now sat with his killer.

"Why?" I asked. "He didn't have anything to do with the game that killed your son."

"Other people have sons," she said, her voice catching. "He was putting more of those games into the world. He had to be stopped. And I was the instrument of Fate who could stop him."

"What about Kristy?" I demanded. "She was no threat to you, or to anyone. She was convinced Tommy killed S, and then killed himself."

"Maybe at first," Abby protested. "But then you started asking questions. You got her thinking."

"Is that when you decided to kill me, too?" I asked. "Did that bottle you gave me the night of the séance—"

But we were interrupted before I could get her to admit it. Detective Jackson had gotten my text, and three police cars were racing up the street, lights and sirens blaring.

Abby heard them and looked at me, blinking. "Thank you," she said. "I'm ready." She took a long shuddering breath. "I miss my Lucas so much."

Then she grabbed my coffee and drank it down.

CHAPTER 33

"Trixie, you saved my life. And Monica's."

It had been hours, but this was my first chance to speak with Trixie. She'd hovered anxiously at the top of the balcony stairs while Detective Jackson and the rest of the police had kept me in the lobby, asking me everything about what had happened.

"I'm just so glad for that contraption," Trixie said. She'd thrown herself at me—through me—the minute we'd been alone in my office.

"I would have drunk that coffee if it wasn't for your message," I said. "I had it in my hand." I shivered. "I don't know how Abby thought she'd get away after poisoning me, but she had two other bottles of arsenic on her, and she'd made plans to meet Monica at the shop."

I'd called Monica immediately when the police arrived, holding my breath until I heard her voice, then babbling that she shouldn't eat or drink anything Abby had been near.

"Abby seemed so nice," Trixie said. "How could a nice person be so horrible?"

I collapsed on the couch. "She was grieving," I said. "That can do horrible things to a person. I think her plan was always to drink the last bottle herself."

"You were so clever to get her to confess," Trixie said. She'd heard me tell everything to Jackson. "And so clever to use your phone thingie."

I'd opened a voice memo app and pressed Record after sending Jackson the text, leaving the phone in my lap under the table. Which meant the police now had Abby's full confession. They also had my phone, as evidence, which was not the worst thing that could have happened to me that morning.

We heard heavy footsteps in the hallway and Marty appeared in the doorway. He was rubbing his eyes the way he usually did when he'd lost track of time in his booth, tinkering with ancient equipment.

"Where have you been?" he said blearily. "And where's my mocha?"

Which is when, after having nearly been killed and watching a woman kill herself in front of me, and much to Marty's horror, I did what I hadn't yet done. I burst into tears.

When Callie and Albert came in for their regular shifts they found me explaining everything to Marty in the break room. I started all over and caught everyone up, Trixie chiming in when she thought I might leave out some detail.

"I had no idea," I insisted, in response to a question from Albert. "I thought we'd just have coffee and try to figure out if we could remember anything odd happening at the shop that day. I honestly didn't realize she was the poisoner."

"I mean, she gave you a bottle of poison the night of the séance," Callie said.

"Well, I know that *now*," I replied. "At the time I thought it was just one of her tinctures. When Detective Jackson told me a bottle had been found at Kristy's place he didn't describe it. I thought he meant a milk bottle or a juice bottle or something. Something that had been tampered with. Although..."

"Although what?"

I grimaced. "Abby did seem startled at Monica's shop yesterday, when I lied and told her how well her tincture worked. Maybe I should have asked myself why."

"You think?" Marty said.

Trixie had been flitting in and out of the room while we talked. It killed me that I couldn't tell everyone how she'd sent me the text that had saved my life, but she didn't seem to mind.

"When did you realize Abby was the killer?" Albert asked. "What gave her away?"

I looked at Trixie. She waved a hand. "Aw, go on," she said. "It's fine."

I told them the same thing I'd told Jackson and the rest of the police. "It just came to me, because of the two kids who were killed yesterday, and you telling us about your friend who had been hit by a truck. I remembered Abby telling me her son had been killed." I shrugged.

Trixie winked at me, then seemed to hear something from outside. She went to the door and looked down the hall.

"Um, Nora?" she said, a tiny worry line between her plucked brows. "Hector's here. And he doesn't look happy."

"You didn't call? You didn't text? You didn't even think to tell me?"

Hector was very not happy. I'd told everyone else to set up for the twelve-fifteen and whisked him away to my office, closing the door firmly behind us. Now we stood and faced each other, having what might be considered our first fight.

"I couldn't call or text," I explained. "The police took my phone. It's evidence."

"There is still such a thing as a landline!" He pointed an accusing finger at the evidence of a such a phone on my desk. His sexy accent came out a little more when he was livid. Which probably wasn't what I should have been focusing on.

"I don't know your number," I told him. "It was programmed in my cell. And I knew you were going to come by for lunch, which you have, so—"

"I came by for lunch and saw the café was closed, with crime scene tape everywhere. And when I asked someone what happened they said a woman had been poisoned." He put a hand to his forehead, taking a step back from me. "Do you know what I thought?"

"I'm sorry." I closed the distance between us. "I should have found a way to contact you."

"She could have killed you."

"But she didn't."

He sank onto the couch, running a hand over his face. "When I turned my back on a career in crime I expected my life to be much calmer."

I refrained from pointing out that he had not been the one face-to-face with a multiple murderer that morning.

"It's fine," I soothed, sitting next to him. "I'm fine. It's all over now. And I promise I'll commit your number to memory."

"Do that." He took my hand. "Also, please stop getting involved with murderers."

"I'll leave them alone if they'll leave me alone."

The double features must go on. And *The Band Wagon* party wouldn't organize itself. Once I'd shooed Hector out of the theater I thought I'd be able to get to work, but it turned out quite a few people knew the number to the landline on my desk, including Robbie, who wanted to know everything, and Monica, who called with the news that Kristy had come out of her coma.

"Is she going to be okay?" I asked.

"They're running tests, but I was just there and she was talking to her parents."

"She's one lucky girl."

"We're three lucky girls," Monica said. "If you hadn't stopped Abby—"

"Let's not finish that thought," I told her. "I don't even want to think about it." I couldn't think about what would have happened if Trixie hadn't gotten me that message. And I couldn't stop seeing the look in Abby's eyes as she'd grabbed the coffee, drinking her lethal dose before I could wrestle the mug from her grasp.

I shook my head.

"Nora, you okay?" Monica asked. I'd probably been silent for a bit.

"I will be," I said.

"You know, everyone would understand if you cancelled the midnight movie. Or at least if you let Callie handle it and went home."

"I know," I said. "But I think being around people is better for me. And Fred Astaire might be just what I need."

Brandon came crashing through the lobby doors just as I was writing out a check to pay the soda machine repair guy. He was flushed with excitement and began shouting immediately.

"Nora! Did you hear? Where's Callie? Did you guys—"

"Calm down," I said. "They'll hear you over the movie." It was about mid-way through the two-thirty show and we had a surprisingly full house. Or, at least, full for us. By which I meant there were more than eight customers.

"Where's Callie?" Brandon asked again as the repair guy left.

"With Albert, down in the prop room. What's—"

He launched himself through the door to the back stairs. I looked around the empty lobby, figured it would okay to leave it unattended for just a few minutes, and ran after him.

I found them all in the prop room, where Callie and Albert had been rummaging around for decorations for the midnight movie.

"Did you find it?" Brandon was demanding of Callie. "Was it you?"

"Brandon, stop yelling," she said. "What are you talking about?"

"The coin!" he yelled. "They said a group of San Francisco State students found it, and I know you've been playing. Was it you?"

"I mean, do I look like I just won ten million dollars?"

He stared at her. "Eleven. It's eleven million today."

"I literally only played the game once," she said. "And I didn't find anything."

I perched on the edge of a table still covered in my things from

LA. "Where was it?" I asked.

"The doggy diner head," he said. Which made me think he might be having a stroke, until Albert explained.

"It's out by the zoo," he told me. "A large sculpture of a dachshund wearing a chef's hat that used to be on the roof of a diner. The diner's gone, but the doggy diner head is San Francisco history."

"The coin was in its mouth," Brandon said.

"You mean the cartoon of the coin—"

"The AR of the coin," he corrected me. "Yeah. But you could only see it if you'd already solved a gazillion puzzles." He slumped onto the table next to me.

"Well, it looks like you were right," I said. "There was a coin in San Francisco."

He didn't seem to take comfort from this thought.

"It's over." He looked a little dazed. "They found one in Cairo this morning. That's all five."

I was hugely relieved. I never wanted to hear about the game again. "Finally," I said, "the madness is over."

"I mean, until the next game," Callie said.

Brandon perked up. "Do you think there will be another one? Without S to make it?"

"It made a ton of money," Callie shrugged. "They'll figure it out without S."

I realized she was right. I also realized I'd left the lobby unattended for long enough. Telling Brandon to clock in and start working those extra hours he'd asked for, I left them and took the stairs back up to the lobby.

When I got there it wasn't empty. Gabriela was there.

"Hi," I said. "I didn't know you were—"

The way she was looking at me stopped the words on my lips. She held up her phone, and I saw the messages Trixie had sent on her screen. They'd been automatically sent to her as well as to me.

"Hi, Nora," she said calmly. "Anything you want to tell me about this?"

CHAPTER 34

"Is she here now?"

Gabriela looked at me. She knew. She knew Trixie was real.

She looked around the empty lobby. "Trixie? Are you here now?"

"She isn't," I said. My voice was so faint I was surprised she could hear me.

"But you'd know if she were," Gabriela said evenly.

I thrust a thousand images of psych wards out of my mind and nodded.

"And she talks to you?" For the first time Gabriela looked a little freaked out.

I couldn't speak. I nodded again.

"Okay." She looked away, and I could see that she was trying to process everything. When she looked back to me there was something else in her expression. Determination.

"Well, then. This changes everything."

The following Tuesday the lineup changed again, Kristy was released from the hospital, and I received a thick envelope containing all the paperwork necessary to authenticate six glamorous gowns, and prove they were now mine.

"Trixie, do you know what this means?"

"It's good, right?" She was standing behind me, watching anxiously as I hammered a small nail into the office wall.

"It's really good. We're going to have a film festival, and show the movies, and exhibit the gowns, and charge a bloody fortune for it." I tugged on the nail to make sure it was secure.

Trixie clapped. "Oh, Nora! What fun!"

I went over to the desk and unwrapped a photo that I'd had enlarged and framed at a shop near Union Square. I took it over to Trixie and hung it on the nail.

"Oh," Trixie said softly.

It was the photo of her mother with Albert's mother and grandmother, standing outside the Palace.

"Gee, Nora. This is wonderful." She reached out to hover her fingertips above the image of her mother's face. "I just can't thank you enough."

"Don't be ridiculous," I said.

"Who's being ridiculous?" Callie was standing in the doorway. Trixie gave a startled squeak and went *poof*.

"What?" I said to Callie. It was always a great comeback.

"Who—Never mind. Have you seen this?" She held up her phone.

"What is it?"

"They just announced who's got the lead in the new franchise based on those Scandinavian books."

"Right, with the fjords," I said, waving my hand. "I know."

"I don't think you do." She passed me her phone.

Priya Sharma to Helm New Franchise

In a gender-bending piece of casting that has us beyond excited, Hampton Productions announced that the damaged ex-CIA reporter at the center of the eagerly anticipated adaptation of the bestselling Scandinavian Quartet will be the kick-ass beauty Priya Sharma.

This should be interesting, as Sharma previously dated Otis Hampton, head of Hampton Productions, before leaving him for her current beau, Ted Bishop, who was reportedly a contender for the part himself. All the action may be behind the scenes on this one!

It was a while before I could stop laughing long enough to explain to Callie what was so funny.

"But Otis totally screwed you," she protested. "You had a plan."

"I had a partner with the attention span of a goldfish," I said. "We're talking about Otis Hampton. The odds were never great that he'd have had the patience to stick to a plan for more than a day or two. Why do you think I insisted that Ted send the dress receipts before he got the offer?"

"You knew this would happen?"

"Not this," I admitted. "This is twisted on too many levels for me. But I knew that if Otis saw a chance to screw Ted sooner, he'd conveniently forget anything we'd ever planned. And wow, does this screw Ted. I can just imagine what this is doing to him."

Callie grinned. "I mean, it must be killing him that Priya got the part."

"But he can't say a damn thing about it without looking like a jerk," I said.

"Which he is."

"Which he very much is. But he can't afford to look like one when he's standing next to her on red carpets."

"How long do you think they'll last?" she asked.

"That's Otis's concern, not mine. I just have to figure out what leverage I have now to get Ted to give me that damn divorce and get out of my life forever."

As if I needed more incentive to get that damn divorce, Hector picked me up after the last show that night.

"Hey, have you heard from Gabriela?" he asked as we went around the theater turning off lights and checking the locks.

"Um, why?" I'd heard from Gabriela about fifteen times a day since telling her about Trixie. She was working like a madwoman on a new ghost-accessible prototype. One that could change Trixie's

MURDER ON THE SILVER SCREEN

whole world.

"She hasn't been answering her texts," he said.

"I'm sure she's just busy," I told him as we got to the lobby. "She told me she's coming to Friday's midnight movie." Coming with a present for Trixie, I hoped.

I flicked off the last of the lights and opened the panel by the lobby doors to set the alarm.

"Hey," Hector said, "have I ever told you how good you look in the light from the emergency exit sign?"

"You're a true romantic," I told him.

"Yes I am." He was about to prove it when my phone pinged with a text.

"Maybe that's Gabriela now," I said, slipping from his grasp.

The text was not from Gabriela. It was from Otis Hampton.

I guess I should apologize for switching the plan about Ted. I couldn't help myself. But I want to make it up to you, so I got you a gift. It's information. You know how you thought I bought Tommy's share of the theater? I found out who really did. You're not going to like it. The new owner of one-quarter of the Palace is Ted.

I stared at the phone.

"Nora?" Hector said. "Is everything ok?"

I looked up at him. "No."

Everything had just gotten a lot more complicated.

The Band Wagon
1953

There are some people who say *The Band Wagon* is the best musical MGM ever made. There are other people who will duel to the death for *Singin' in the Rain*. Personally, I don't think "best" is something even worth discussing. Just watch and enjoy.

And you will enjoy. Because what you'll find here is maximum Fred Astaire. Maybe he wasn't at his physical peak (he was fifty-four when he made it) but he is at his most self-aware. Director Vincent Minelli didn't try to gloss over Astaire's age. He leaned into it. There's a lot about a performer's insecurities in this one, and a lot about what it takes to earn your place on the stage. There's also a massive amount of show-biz fun.

To the plot! When we begin, Tony Hunter (Astaire) is edging into has-been territory. He's been out in Hollywood making musicals, but his top-hat-and-tails type of dancing isn't in fashion anymore. He knows the times are passing him by, and he's largely resigned to it.

Astaire's first number, "By Myself," sums up where he sees himself. There's no fuss for him when he arrives at the station. That's okay. He makes his way by himself, reflecting on his situation. But this is Fred Astaire, people! Just walking along the platform he's dancing. Picking up a random book, he's dancing. And all the while musing in a song. "No one knows better than I myself, I'm by myself, alone."

But, the thing is, he isn't. Because his two old friends, who happen to write Broadway musicals, are there to meet him after all. Lester and Lilly Marton, played by Oscar Levant and Nanette Fabray, have written their best play ever, and they've lined up the hottest director on Broadway, Jeffrey Cordova (Jack Buchanan). Cordova is currently producing, directing, and starring in a ponderous production of *Oedipus Rex*. Sure, he's never directed a musical, but what could go wrong? (Lots, as we'll find out later.)

Tony is in, but he's also shocked at the carnival atmosphere on his beloved 42nd street. (One wonders what he'd make of it now.) You know what he needs to perk himself up? A shoeshine. I defy anyone to watch the "Shine on My Shoes" number and not feel better. About anything you can name.

As much as I adore Astaire when he's all glammed up, I do love his solo novelty numbers like this one. Anyone up for the firecracker dance in *Holiday Inn*? That's right you are!

Moving right along, Cordova casts the highbrow ballet dancer Gabrielle Gerard (Cyd Charisse) as "the girl" in the show. She's got "fire, charm, and beauty," but is she right for the part? Before they meet, Tony confesses that he's wildly intimidated to dance with such a talented—and tall—classical dancer, and Gabby confesses that she's wildly intimidated to dance with a Broadway legend. I have to point out that in this scene, Gabrielle's black lace dress (with scattered sequins and a dark green underskirt) is reason enough to cast her in anything.

The two dancers meet, and it isn't good. "I used to see all your pictures when I was a little girl," Gabby tells him. Whoops. They're both about to walk out on the whole thing when Cordova swoops in and steamrolls them. This show is happening!

Rehearsal montage! Costumes! Dancing! Fred Astaire in a little red neckerchief! The only problem is that Tony and Gabby still aren't meshing. Tony's part keeps getting smaller and smaller, until he finally loses his temper and walks out. But when Gabby shows up later at his hotel, wearing a white dress with a micro-pleated skirt that was just made for dancing, you get a whiff of a reconciliation in the wings.

And it happens, in a gorgeous number set to "Dancing in the Dark" (the Schwartz & Dietz one, I hasten to note, not the Bruce Springsteen one) somewhere in Central Park. There are no vocals, because this isn't about words. The dancers are communicating across their two different styles. And it's lovely.

Suddenly it's opening night. New Haven! Here we go! It's going to be great! It's going to be...It's...It's...not good. Very not good. Disastrously not good. It's overblown and self-important, much like its director. In the lingo of the time, it lays an egg.

Which causes the cast to wonder...Hey, why didn't they do that fun, light, entertaining show they originally set out to do? Could they still turn this show into that show? Reworking it on the road? They can! And they will!

What follows are some of the best numbers in all of Hollywood musicals. One after another, as they reimagine the show, moving from town to town. Philadelphia, Boston, Pittsburgh, Baltimore...with new numbers in each of them.

Don't even get me started on the classic top hat and tails number "I Guess I'll Have to Change My Plan." It's just two guys on a simple set, putting over a simple song with the kind of elegance that may not exist in our sorry old world anymore. It's perfection, and a triumph of Astaire's style.

There's also a triplets novelty number that will sound stupid no matter how I describe it, so I won't even try. But trust me, it's stupid good.

Then we're back in New York. And we've got a finale! It's a lurid pulp mystery set to dance—a murder mystery in jazz. Tony is the hard-boiled gumshoe and Gabby is the innocent blonde in innocent blue as well as the femme fatale in red fringe and sparkles. This number is a technicolor dream that perfectly captures what was going on in dance in 1954. It's heaven. And even more heaven if you're lucky enough to see it on the big screen.

But will the revised show be a hit? More importantly, will Tony still be alone? Going his way by himself? Or has he built a community? Has he made a home for himself in this new world that didn't think it needed him anymore? For that answer you'll have to watch the movie. Watch the movie!

That's Entertainment!

I love a show about show business. I love the cheesy pep talks on the first day of rehearsals. ("We enter with nothing but a dream, but when we leave, we'll have a show!") I love the kids in the chorus hanging out by a piano in their hotel room. And I love the whole notion of watching egos and chaos become art. Which leaves me thinking...hey kids, why don't *we* put on a show?

Movies My Friends Should Watch
Sally Lee

Want More Sally?

If you enjoyed Sally Lee's movie blogs, check out the Movies My Friends Should Watch website for more.

Visit moviesmyfriendsshouldwatch.com.
And watch good movies!

MARGARET DUMAS

Margaret Dumas lives in the San Francisco Bay Area, where she reads and writes books when she isn't watching old movies.

**The Movie Palace Mystery Series
by Margaret Dumas**

MURDER AT THE PALACE (#1)
MURDER IN THE BALCONY (#2)
MURDER ON THE SILVER SCREEN (#3)

Henery Press Mystery Books

And finally, before you go...
Here are a few other mysteries
you might enjoy:

PILLOW STALK

Diane Vallere

A Madison Night Mystery (#1)

Interior Decorator Madison Night might look like a throwback to the sixties, but as business owner and landlord, she proves that independent women can have it all. But when a killer targets women dressed in her signature style—estate sale vintage to play up her resemblance to fave actress Doris Day—what makes her unique might make her dead.

The local detective connects the new crime to a twenty-year old cold case, and Madison's long-trusted contractor emerges as the leading suspect. As the body count piles up, Madison uncovers a Soviet spy, a campaign to destroy all Doris Day movies, and six minutes of film that will change her life forever.

Available at booksellers nationwide and online

Visit www.henerypress.com for details

PUMPKINS IN PARADISE
Kathi Daley

A Tj Jensen Mystery (#1)

Between volunteering for the annual pumpkin festival and coaching her girls to the state soccer finals, high school teacher Tj Jensen finds her good friend Zachary Collins dead in his favorite chair.

When the handsome new deputy closes the case without so much as a "why" or "how," Tj turns her attention from chili cook-offs and pumpkin carving to complex puzzles, prophetic riddles, and a decades-old secret she seems destined to unravel.

Available at booksellers nationwide and online

Visit www.henerypress.com for details

Made in the USA
San Bernardino, CA
22 June 2020